17-19

P9-DHT-002

HEART OF BARKNESS

A CHET & BERNIE MYSTERY

HEART OF BARKNESS

SPENCER QUINN

THORNDIKE PRESS
A part of Gale, a Cengage Company

Farmington Hills, Mich • San Francisco • New York • Waterville, Maine
Meriden, Conn • Mason, Ohio • Chicago

LIBRARY OF CONGRESS CIP DATA ON FILE.
CATALOGUING IN PUBLICATION FOR THIS BOOK
IS AVAILABLE FROM THE LIBRARY OF CONGRESS

ISBN-13: 978-1-4328-6879-6 (hardcover alk. paper)

Published in 2019 by arrangement with Macmillan Publishing Group, LLC/Tor/Forge

Printed in Mexico
1 2 3 4 5 6 7 23 22 21 20 19

This book is for Norah

This book is for Moran

ONE

"Red-letter day, Chet," said Sergeant Rick Torres, our buddy at the Valley PD Missing Persons Department. "In the car."

Red-letter day was a mystery to me, and maybe red is, too. Bernie says I can't be trusted when it comes to red, something I've never understood. I knew fire hydrants were red, for example, knew that as well as I know my own name. Which is Chet, in case you missed it, right up there off the jump. I also know "in the car," and never need to be asked twice. Or even once. Rick opened the passenger-side door of the black-and-white. I hopped in, sat up nice and tall, totally alert, ready for anything. Was my tongue hanging out? Possibly. I got most of it stuffed back in. We have standards, me and Bernie, just one of the reasons that the Little Detective Agency is so successful, except for the finances part. It's called the Little Detective Agency on account of Bernie's last name being Little, but we're equal partners, Bernie handling the gunplay and the so-therefores and me bringing other things to the table. Maybe we'll get to my teeth a little later.

Meanwhile Rick stepped on the gas and we sped away from his place, where I'd been staying for what seemed like a long time. That was a worrisome thought. I tend to stay away from worrisome thoughts, like to spend my time in the here and now. At the moment in the here and now we had the possibility of cat sightings, and also food trucks. We're pals with every food truck driver in the Valley, me and Bernie. He says it's the best human invention since music. My choice would have been Slim Jims, but if Bernie says music, then that's that. And the truth is we're music lovers, big-time. What's better than blasting across the desert in the Porsche, sound cranked up to the max? Roy Eldridge's trumpet on "If You Were Mine"? It does things to my ears you wouldn't believe, maybe on account of your own ears, which are mostly about decoration. No offense.

Rick glanced over at me. He has a thick and bushy mustache that sometimes catches a crumb or two. Once I made a sort of play for those crumbs, perhaps not my best idea.

No crumbs in evidence now, but I could always hope, and I always do.

"In a good mood, huh, big guy?" Rick's eyes made one of those tiny shifts that means a human just had an idea. "You sense what's happening somehow? Is that possible?"

What was this? Of course I sensed what was happening! We were going for a ride in Rick's squad car and would end up wherever we were headed. What could be more obvious? I gave him a careful look. Was he having problems at home? Not that I knew of. Surely that little incident with the steak tips couldn't still be on his mind.

I was thinking about steak tips, not that little incident — more or less an accident, and one of the happy kind — but steak tips in general, when we pulled up in front of Valley Hospital. No surprise. Rick and I came to visit Bernie just about every day. First he'd been in a special room where they put people who weren't doing so well. That whole problem was on account of what happened at the end of the stolen saguaro case, a few confusing moments that had included the bad guys getting what they had coming to them, and then suddenly from out of nowhere — when it was all over! — Bernie taking that horrible blow to the head. I tried not to think about how he'd fallen, so slowly — like he came oh-so-close to staying on his feet — except sometimes my mind would think about it anyway. But less and less, because after a while Bernie had shifted to another room, not as special, and started moving around with a walker. A walker that happened to get me too excited, a small issue I was still working on when Bernie didn't need it anymore. Lately we'd been taking little strolls up and down the halls of the hospital. Was that in the cards today? I sprang out of the cruiser the instant Rick opened my door.

And what was this? Bernie, not inside the hospital but standing on the curb, duffel bag at his feet? Had I ever seen anything so wonderful?

"Chet!" Rick said, or possibly shouted. "Come back here! Sit! Stay!"

But I just couldn't. I flew across the parking lot — yes, not touching the pavement, or hardly — and jumped into Bernie's arms, only remembering in midair that I'm a hundred-plus pounder, so that maybe this wasn't such a good . . . .

But it was! Because Bernie caught me, like he always did, or maybe not quite exactly, what with a slight stagger, and a loud grunt that someone who didn't know him better might have taken for a cry of pain.

"Oh, my god!" said Dr. Bethea, who I hadn't noticed standing there beside us, me sort of in Bernie's arms, giving his face a nice lick, and him laughing. What a lovely sound! "Are you all right?"

"Couldn't be better," Bernie said, which was just what I wanted to hear. I eased myself back down and stood close to him, close as close can be.

"Whew," the doc said. "But at least we know you're back to normal — if in fact you used to be able to catch Chet like that."

"Not every time," Bernie said.

Dr. Bethea laughed, a surprisingly big laugh for such a small woman. Her glossy hair, curly and black, shook a little, giving off a smell like fresh rain. Normally the doc had a nice treat for me, tucked away in one of the pockets of her white coat, but today she did not, as anyone — although probably not you — could tell from one tiny sniff. No worries. I still liked her just as much as before. No one's perfect — except Bernie, goes without mentioning.

Right now he was gazing down at her. "I don't know what to say," he told her. He put his hand over his heart, then held it out. "Thank you, Doc."

Dr. Bethea smiled. They shook hands.

"Now that you're discharged, you can call me Eliza."

"Eliza," Bernie said. Their eyes met, then unmet, then met again. What was that all about? You're asking the wrong dude.

Rick drove us home. Home is our place on Mesquite Road, the best street in the Valley. On either side live the nicest neighbors anyone could ask for, except for our neighbor on the fence side, Mr. Heydrich. He's not a fan of the nation within the nation — which is what Bernie calls me and my kind — and also collects Nazi memorabilia, whatever that may be. On the other side, the driveway side, live Mr. and Mrs. Parsons — an old couple maybe not doing too well — and Iggy. Iggy's my best pal. The fun we used to have, in the days before the electric fence salesman paid them a visit! That adventure with the FedEx truck and all those boxes of Christmas hams — flimsy boxes, as it had turned out! But the Parsons could never get the electric fence to work, so now Iggy didn't come out much. As Rick turned into our driveway, I looked for him in their floor-to-ceiling window by the door. No Iggy.

We got out. For a moment I thought Bernie and Rick were lining up for some sort of hug, but they ended up bumping fists.

"Do I owe you a cut?" Rick said.

"Of what?" said Bernie.

"There was an office pool on whether this day would ever happen. I won a hundred bucks."

"Ten percent," said Bernie, which I'm sure just shows you how shrewd he is when it comes to money. If only finances had something to do with money, we'd have been all set, our financing having been derailed by unsold Hawaiian pants, filling our self-storage in South Pedroia to the roof, and Bolivian tin futures, which I'd actually never seen, but no time to go into that now.

Rick paid Bernie whatever ten percent was — we were raking it in already! — and drove off. Bernie unlocked our door.

"Home," he said. "Home is the hunter."

Whoa. I stopped right there, one paw already in the doorway. So hunting was finally in the picture? I knew all about hunting from TV, those hunting shows so exciting that I sometimes had to take a time-out or two. We'd even been invited on hunting trips by our buddy Bobby "Bwana" Buonaconti, but Bernie always said no. Why? Bernie's a crack shot. You should see him shooting dimes out of the air! Bwana himself is not a crack shot, as he proved on that

13

confusing day we found out he wasn't actually a buddy but more of a perp, meaning I'd had to grab him by the pant leg, grabbing perps by the pant leg being a big part of my job at the Little Detective Agency.

"What's the holdup, big guy?" said Bernie, standing in the hall.

Wasn't it obvious? Hunting was an outdoor activity, so why go in the house?

"Don't you want to be home?"

I did! I did want to be home! But what about hunting? I started in on a quick back-and-forth thing in the doorway, not so easy in such a small space. Bernie reached out and laid his hand on the back of my neck, very gently.

"Been hard on you, huh?"

What was he talking about? I had no idea. All I knew was that his eyes were moist. Just a bit: Bernie was no crier. I pressed myself against his leg. Bernie's a strong dude, hardly lost his balance at all.

"You're a good boy," he said, and scratched between my ears as only he can do, just right. I rose up and looked him in the eye, my paws on his shoulders.

Bernie's eyes cleared up and he laughed. "Let's get back to normal life."

Sounded good to me! Was hunting part of

14

normal life? I was still wondering about that when Bernie closed the door. With us on the inside. Meaning hunting was not in the picture after all. So I had no more thoughts about it — I can shut down my thinking just like that! Sometimes it doesn't even wait for me and shuts down all by itself. Who has it better than me?

Meanwhile I was already busy sniffing my way around the house. You enter someplace you haven't been in a while and you sniff around. That's basic. I started in the hall, two rhythms happening at once, the sniff-sniff-sniff and the trot-trot. Mongo Santamaria, whoever he might be — possibly a perp, so I hope he looks good in orange, and the truth is I still haven't seen even a single human who does — has nothing on me, Bernie sometimes says. I ramped up my sniff-sniff-sniff trot-trot ba-boom ba-bing in the front hall and through the living room, topping out as I darted into Charlie's room, the mattress bare on account of Charlie living mostly with Leda, his mom, and her husband, Malcolm, with the long, skinny toes, and into our bedroom — at one time mine, Bernie's, and Leda's, then just Bernie and Leda's, and finally Bernie's and mine — and into the kitchen, where I smelled no food at all, an unusual and

15

bothersome development, and finally into the office, with its elephant-pattern rug. I'd dealt with a real elephant once, name of Peanut, perhaps a story for another day, but the crazy thing was that whenever I sniffed the elephant-pattern rug I got a whiff of her, even though Peanut had never been in the house, not even once. What was that all about? I had no idea, but was busy sniff-sniffing at the rug when Bernie came in, a glass of bourbon in hand. The bourbon and elephant scents mixed together in a very pleasant way, hard to describe.

"What's so interesting?" Bernie said. Then came something that had never happened before, kind of a shock. He set his glass on the desk, walked over, and . . . could it really be? Bernie got down on all fours and . . . whoa, stop right there! From out of nowhere I suddenly understood four, having never gone past two in my whole life. One, two, four! I'd cracked the code at last! And that wasn't even the most astonishing thing we had going on in the office, because there was Bernie, down on all fours and sniff-sniff-sniffing the rug, just like me! So much went zooming through my mind, all way too fast to catch hold of, but one thing stuck: we were going to be even better than before! Wow! I barely heard Bernie say, "Don't smell a thing." In fact, I might have imagined it.

Not long after that, we were outside. A beautiful day, nice and warm but not too hot, and the sky clear and bluer than it had ever been. Bernie stripped the tarp off our ride and we hopped in.

Our ride's an old Porsche, not the one that went off the cliff or the other one that got blown up, but our new one, which happened to be the oldest one of all, and the only one with the martini glasses pattern on the front fenders. A lovely touch, added by our buddy Nixon Panero at Nixon's Championship Autobody, all on his own as I recall but a total success in the end, except for how we maybe got pulled over out on the highway more than before.

What's better than riding shotgun in the Porsche? Nothing, baby! Although from out of nowhere came a memory of a case we'd worked in Mexico, and the sound of she-barking from behind a cantina on a full-moon night. Funny how the mind works. Right now it was caught up in the events of that night — possibly even getting kind of excited about them — but then Bernie turned the key, snapping me out of it. ROAR! And we were —

17

But no. The engine went whirr-whirr, whirr-whirr, puff. Bernie tried again. This time there was just the puff, accompanied by a ball of smoke, not really very big. Then out came the tools, and after a series of developments that led to Bernie using the kind of language he hardly ever does, he got on the phone, Nixon's wrecker soon rumbling into view. Not long after that, we were in the yard back of the office at Championship Autobody.

If you loved the smells of oil and gas and welding torches and hot metal and pipe grease and sweat and chewing tobacco — and I do! — then you loved the yard back of Nixon's office. Nixon himself came over right away, even before his boys had the Porsche on the lift.

"Well, well," he said, "look what the cat brought in."

Whoa! What was this? A cat was somehow involved? I was dumbfounded. There were no cats anywhere on the premises. I check out every premise I've ever been to for cats, first thing, don't even need to think about it. You can't miss their scent: it says I'm better than you, and in the clearest possible way. Please tell me you know that already. And of course no cat had been driving the wrecker, the driver being Nixon's sister

Mindy Jo, who had tattoos of all her boy-friends' faces going back to high school up and down her big strong arms.

Meanwhile Bernie and Nixon were shaking hands.

"Lookin' great, Bernie."

"I've been lucky."

Nixon shook his head. "You know what they say about luck — it's the residue of . . . something or other." He spat a gob of tobacco chew out the side of his mouth. Over by the lift, Mindy Jo did the same thing. Did that mean tobacco spit residue was lucky? Wow! I was on fire!

"Hey, Chet," Bernie said. "What are you doing?"

Me? I seemed to be standing over a small tobacco-y gob — Nixon's, not Mindy Jo's, which was considerably larger — and possibly giving it a little taste. No sense in not getting on the good side of luck when the chance comes along. My, my! How unusual! Had I ever experienced anything tangier? Not that I remembered. Plus there was a strong — what would you call it? Dirty quality? Even sewery? Something like that. In some ways it reminded me of fresh puke, but in others —

"Chet! Get over here!"

I trotted right over to Bernie, licking my

19

muzzle. I'm a team player, don't forget, and those two fascinating gobs weren't going anywhere. Meanwhile Nixon started in on a discussion of stripper pole decals he'd designed, and how one or two might look not bad on our bumper. I wandered over to the back door of the office where my old pal Spike was lying by his waterbowl. Spike was one big dude, a lot bigger than me, and a warrior you couldn't help but like. The bloody battles we'd fought! But now they were just memories on account of how old Spike had gotten, his face all white and one eye always closed. His other eye was following my every movement and sending a friendly message, like glad you dropped by, old buddy, and I'd kill you if I could. I was considering helping myself to some of his water, when a man spoke inside the office. The door was open and I could see him, sitting on a plastic chair in the waiting area. He was a lean dude, dressed in tight black jeans and a black shirt, snakeskin cowboy boots, and a black cowboy hat that hid his face in shadow.

"That depends," he said. "Depends on whether you treat me nice."

"How can you say that, Clint?" said a woman who had her back to me. She had a big head of silvery blond hair and wore lots

20

of perfume. I could almost feel it flowing through the doorway. "I always treat you nice."

"Don't start," Clint said.

"I'm not starting," she said. She reached out as though to touch him but didn't quite. Her hand was a bit of a surprise. Not the big jewels she wore; big jewels — lots of them unreal, according to Bernie — were a common sight in our line of work. The surprise was that her hand looked much older than her hair, if that made any sense. Also, it was trembling a bit. "I'm only —" she began, but then Mindy Jo came into the office and said, "All set."

Clint and the woman rose and followed Mindy Jo through the back door and into the yard. I got a good look at the woman's face, a soft face older than her hair but younger than her hand. She had light blue eyes and bright red lipstick. What else? Her neck was the same age as her hands. In short, she was kind of a puzzle. Mindy Jo led her and Clint to a big white convertible with pink seats and handed Clint a sheet of paper. Clint passed the sheet over to the woman, who opened a glittering purse, counted out some cash, and gave it to Mindy Jo. Clint got behind the wheel and the woman sat in the passenger seat, sort of leaning toward Clint. Clint sort of leaned away.

I headed over to Bernie, standing by the lift.

"Know who that is?" Nixon said, pointing his chin — one of my favorite human moves — at the white convertible.

Bernie looked that way. "No clue."

"Lotty Pilgrim."

"The country singer? I didn't even know she was still alive."

"Blast from the past," said Nixon. "And still on the road. She's at the Crowbar to-night."

"The Crowbar?" Bernie said. "It's a dump."

"The arc of showbiz," Nixon said.

Bernie nodded. "My parents danced to that song."

" 'How You Hung the Moon,' " Nixon said. "Went platinum. But underneath the paint job that Caddy of hers is a clunker." He and Bernie watched it drive out of the yard, onto the street, and away. Nixon took two tickets from his pocket. "The boyfriend or manager or whatever he is comped me. I got a meeting."

"With your PO?"

"Six more months," Nixon said, "till I'm free as a bird."

Nixon was a good buddy, but before that he'd been a perp. We were buddies with lots of perps we'd busted, just another perk at the Little Detective Agency.

Bernie took the tickets. Not long after that, the Porsche was good to go.

"Put a new battery in there for you, Bernie. Eight hundred and fifty cold cranking amps."

"Is that good?"

"Take you to the moon."

"Sounds pricey."

"No charge."

"Huh?"

"Fact is," Nixon said, looking down and toeing at the dirt, "I, um, won a nice chunk of change. They run a sports book over at the Buffalo Head Casino."

"Football?"

"Not exactly," Nixon said. "Sometimes they feature what you might call one-of-a-kind specials."

Bernie gazed at Nixon. Nixon kept looking down. "You bet on whether I'd live?"

"Hunnert to one against." Nixon shrugged. "Gotta like those odds on practically anything."

"What'd you stake?"

"Five Cs."

"Nice," Bernie said. "But if you really

believed, you could've been set for life."

"Tell me about it," said Nixon. "Been kickin' myself ever since."

TWO

"Should've bet on myself, Chet," Bernie said as we took our Porsche up into the hills on back roads that got more and more backroady until it was just us. "How come no one told me there was all this action?" We rounded a bend, and through the space between the branches of a fire-blackened tree saw the whole Valley spread out below us. Bernie slowed down to almost nothing. "Tell you a secret. There were times back in the hospital when I might have bet the other side."

We came to a stop, got out of the car, gazed at the view. Bernie took a deep breath, let it out slowly. I felt something from inside him, something peaceful combined with other things I didn't know. All I knew was that his secret, whatever it was, exactly, was safe with me. As for betting, we'd once slapped down ten grand we didn't have on a horse named Billie Holiday

25

even though the only reason we'd gone to the track was that Cus "Crybaby" Babitsky had told us that his horse Stomper was a stone-cold lock on account of something he planned to slip into the feed bags of all the other horses. "How can I bet against Billie Holiday?" Bernie had said, when we got to the track and he checked the Racing Form. The memory of Stomper ambling across the finish line with the rest of the field still on the back stretch and Billie Holiday dead last was one of the clearest I had. That was the day I learned that when you bet ten grand you don't have and lose, you end up not having much more than you didn't have before. Got that? I sure don't.

As we drove away from the lookout, I studied Bernie's face, hoping to see some sign that our betting days were over. All I saw was his beauty: Could that jaw have been any stronger? And how about those thick eyebrows with a language all their own? And the unforgettable nose — not quite straight as the result of some long-ago dust-up but all the lovelier because of that, life being hard to explain at times — plus other good things too many to mention. Especially his eyes. Was there a new line or two around them? All the better. My Bernie.

Back home a taxi sat in the driveway. "I wonder . . ." Bernie said, and then a woman stepped out of the back — a woman I didn't recognize at first, even though I knew her very well.

"Suzie," Bernie said quietly.

And yes, it was Suzie, although her hair was shorter and she seemed taller and also more . . . forceful, if that was how to put it. There was always a lot of force inside Suzie Sanchez, of course, except today it was showing on the outside, if that makes any sense. But was that enough to make me miss that it was her? I'd known Suzie for I didn't know how long. I actually never really do when it comes to that kind of thing, but that wasn't the point, the point being that Suzie was Bernie's girlfriend. At one time, she'd been a reporter for the *Valley Tribune.* Now she worked out of London for the *Washington Post,* and before that terrible saguaro case — did we even get paid? and if so by who? — she'd asked us to come live with her in London. Where London might be was a mystery. I knew London Flats, a fleabitten town down near the border with actual fleas that actually bit, but I was pretty sure Suzie meant something else, on account of the fact that she never scratched herself on any of her visits to the hospital, not even once.

We walked over to her, me more or less running. Let's call it more. Suzie gave me a pat. What a great patter she was! Bernie came up. Suzie put her hands together.

"Oh, this is wonderful," she said. "You look terrific."

"Um," Bernie said. "Pot." And then, "Er, kettle." Was he offering tea? They were both coffee drinkers. That was as far as I could take it before Bernie wrapped his arms around Suzie and held her close. Normally I don't let that sort of thing go on for very long before squeezing myself in between, but this time I just stayed where I was. Why? Because of the expression on Suzie's face? She was looking my way over Bernie's shoulder and yet I got the feeling she might not have been seeing me. Her eyes — always so deep and dark and shining like our countertops — weren't shining now, a first, in my experience. Instead they were cloudy, like there was bad weather on the way. Meanwhile she was holding on to Bernie so tight that her knuckles were the color of bone. I had a strange thought: maybe knuckles were in fact made of bone, so no problemo. But here's something I've come across in life: sometimes you can think your way to no problemo while you still keep feeling yes problemo. So there I was, going back and forth — not actually, but in my mind, although — Whoa! I turned out to be doing some back-and-forthing in the driveway after all — when Bernie said, "Come on inside. Wish you'd told me — there's nothing to eat."

Nothing to eat? Yes problemo, and for sure.

"It was a spur-of-the-moment decision," Suzie said. "I . . . I just had to."

They looked at each other. Then Bernie glanced at the taxi, which seemed to be taking a long time to hit the road. "Where's your stuff?"

Suzie shook her head.

"You came all the way from London with no luggage?"

For a moment Suzie's face started to lose its shape, like some sort of falling apart was going on, but she gave her head a quick shake — always a why-not move, in my opinion — and stood very straight. "It's a bad time for this, but there'll never be a good time," she said. "I'm so . . . beyond happy, beyond relieved, to see you back to you. It's like the world is just, after all."

"But?" Bernie said.

Suzie took a deep breath. "We have to decide, Bernie. I need to get on with my life. I can't think of a non-cliché that says it."

"You want to get married?"

"That's not it," Suzie said. "Well, yes, I do. But that's not the issue — which is I plan on being in London for at least the next three years, and whatever happens after that won't be happening here in the Valley."

"So for us to stay together I —" His eyes shifted to me. "— we have to move to London, no dodging around it?"

"Yes," said Suzie.

Bernie just stood there. His gaze rose up over Suzie's head, over the houses across the street, maybe all the way to the Comanche Mountains, where the sun went down every day.

"Oh, Bernie," Suzie said. "You can't help it. You're just not a modern man."

"What do you mean?"

"It's one of the best things about you. You have roots. The Valley, this desert, this street, the canyon out back. You'd never be happy in London."

"I could try."

Suzie shook her head. "It — your conscientious effort — would dominate our lives, even with the best intentions."

Bernie opened his mouth like he was going to say something, but no words came. Instead he looked over at the taxi driver, caught his eye, waved him away. The taxi drove off. Bernie took Suzie's hand. We went in the house.

First we were in the kitchen, where Bernie poured water for him and Suzie, and topped up my bowl. We all drank, me the noisiest, Suzie the quietest, Bernie in between. After that they went into the bedroom, meaning our bedroom, mine and Bernie's. I didn't follow. Through the closed door I heard talking, hard to understand. For example, Suzie said, "Sometimes I wish I was stupid — we wouldn't even be in this situation. Except then you wouldn't love me." "Sure I would," said Bernie. "We'd have more in common." That made Suzie laugh, but it turned out to be one of those laughs that ends in tears, which sometimes happens with women and never with men, in my experience. Puzzles on top of puzzles! I was much happier when they went silent. After that came sounds of movement, kind of rhythmic, reminding me of humans exercising at the gym, and then silence again. Maybe I nodded off for a while. I'm an excellent napper — world class, Bernie says.

Were there napping competitions? Heads up, world!

Some time later, the bedroom door opened and Suzie came out. Now her eyes were blurry, her face damp, everything about her miserable. I couldn't stand seeing her like that, so I pressed against her leg. She bent down and hugged me, then whispered, "I'm going to miss you every day." I felt her tears in my fur. Miss me every day? Why? What was going on?

I followed her to the front door. She opened it. Outside a car pulled into the driveway, one of those black cars that were like taxis but not. Was it some kind of racket? All I knew was that lots of our perp buddies were doing the driving.

Suzie wiped her face on the back of her sleeve. "Why is life so goddamn complicated?" she said.

Was it? Oh, no! I'd completely missed that.

Suzie bent again and kissed the top of my head. "Take good care of him, Chet." Of course! Went without saying.

She walked out and closed the door. I heard her footsteps moving from the stone path to the paved drive. A car door opened and closed. The car drove off. I listened to it until the sound faded down to nothing, which was quite a long time, maybe enough for me to sort out whatever had just gone down. My takeaway? It was all about her having no luggage. That meant she'd had to go buy some things — clothes, toothpaste, a comb — and would be back soon. An idea with lots of parts, way beyond my usual, so it had to be on the money. Wow! I'd thought my way right back to no problemo.

I stood outside the bedroom door and listened to Bernie breathe. Nice and even, the kind of Bernie breaths I like to hear. After a while there came a bit of muttering. Muttering is one of those strange human things. Why do they do it? No idea, but it never sounds happy.

Bernie and I had done a lot of work on doorknobs, although not lately. Doorknobs are a big deal in our line of work, and there are some I can handle easily now. The round kind gives me trouble. We'd been working on them before that terrible saguaro case. You had to stand up, like this and . . . what came next? *Gotta use both paws on the round ones, big guy.*

Both paws! That was it! So hard to remember, for some reason. *One goes here, just like this, and the other one here. Atta boy!* And Bernie would put a hand on each of my paws and kind of move them like I

33

was . . . was steering a steering wheel! What a thought! Brand new to me and as exciting as it gets! Because . . . because was it possible? Could I actually drive the car? What would my life — already perfect — be like then? More perfect than perfect? Chet the Jet scores again!

Meanwhile I seemed to be inside the bedroom, so I must have figured out the doorknob trick at last. I tried to remember the details, but none came. No matter. I deserved a treat, big-time.

I moved toward the bed. Bernie lay on his back, eyes closed, breathing quietly, fast asleep. Humans give off a sleepy smell when they're sleeping, maybe a new little fact for you. I knew two things for sure. One — he needed his sleep. Two — I needed a treat. Right there is why it's usually better to know just one thing. I raised a paw — actually it pretty much raised itself — and rested it on the covers, not touching Bernie at all. Or only very slightly.

His eyes opened. First they were blank. Then they went very dark and Bernie . . . flinched? Yes, like someone was about to hit him. Which could never happen, not with me around, amigo. I put my paw on his chest, let him feel a bit of my strength. His eyes shifted my way and brightened, at least a bit, and he smiled a small smile.

"What's up, big guy? Need to go out?"

No. Well, now that he'd raised the subject, I did sort of need to. Funny how just thinking about peeing can make you want to pee. Even pee desperately. Which was where I suddenly was.

Not long after that we were taking a nice walk in the canyon that runs back of our place. I peed in several locations — against a palo verde I knew very well; on a red rock marked by another member of the nation within, unknown to me, his presence now covered by mine, always a nice feeling; and beside a thorn bush where a javelina had lurked, and not long ago. Normally I'd have set out on a search for the critter, but Bernie was huffing and puffing a bit, so I headed for home.

"Really? That's it? I can keep going, you know."

Of course he could! But I had to take care of him, end of story.

It was getting dark when we entered the house. Bernie switched on the kitchen lights. On the table were the tickets Nixon had laid on us. Bernie picked them up.

" 'The legendary Lotty Pilgrim — her only Valley appearance. Fifteen dollar cover, two drink minimum.' " Bernie gave me a look. "What do you say?"

I couldn't. But if I could have, my answer would have been: "The same as you."

THREE

"A dump," Bernie said as we parked in front of the Crowbar. "But a dump with a history. Hank Williams, Buck Owens, Lefty Frizzell — they all played here, Chet."

Hank, Buck, and Lefty? I knew a Hank, a Buck, and several Lefties, all of them now breaking rocks in the hot sun up at Northern State Correctional. I sat up straight and tall, on high alert. A single dim light shone on the Crowbar's sign. What was this? A faded picture of a crow hoisting a drink at a bar? That made no sense to me. Plus I was no fan of birds, and crows were just about the worst. That caw-caw-caw! You can't imagine what it does to my ears. I got ready for anything.

We hopped out of the car — me actually hopping — and walked up to the swinging doors, a kind I knew well from a movie set case we'd once worked. An unusual case — the shot glasses in the movie saloon had been filled with tea, for one thing — where we'd made some Hollywood connections including a cat named Brando, who I sometimes had bad dreams about. Did we end up getting paid? I was trying to remember, when an enormous dude stepped out of the shadows. He had a mean, lumpy face and squashed-up tough-guy ears. He stared down at us and then smiled. And stopped looking mean at once! Amazing what the human smile can do. Is it . . . is it like tail wagging? What a thought! Not me at all. Was it someone else's thought? But in my head? Yikes! I was getting close to scaring myself.

"Well well," he said. "My buddies Bernie and the Chetster!"

What do you know? Shermie "Shoulders" Shouldice!

"Hey, Shermie," Bernie said. "What are you doing on the loose?"

Exactly! Hadn't we sent him up the river not so long ago? No water in that particular river, but not the point. Why wasn't he in an orange jumpsuit and doing whatever they do up at Northern State when the hot sun goes down and they have to stop with the rock breaking?

"Early parole," Shermie said. "On account of overcrowding. This is a civilized country, don't forget."

"It's hard sometimes," Bernie said.

Shermie laughed and slapped his knee. It sounded like a gunshot. "You can say that again."

Bernie did not. Instead he went with, "You're the bouncer here?"

"My mom's tight with the owner," said Shermie. His face pinkened a bit. Was Shermie blushing? I'd seen plenty of human blushing, but never on a face like that. Right away I knew it was one of those once-is-enough things.

"Everybody loves somebody sometime," Bernie said.

"Wow!" said Shermie. "That's so true!"

Bernie handed Shermie the tickets and we went inside.

Yes, a dump, but the kind of dump we liked, me and Bernie. Dirty? Sure, but old dirt, dirt going way back, worn deep into the old, uneven walls and floors. Plus we had a nice mix of greasy smells — greasy food, greasy hair, and some interesting greases I couldn't pin down right away. What else? A bar along one side, a small stage at the other end, a few tables. As for how many customers, don't ask me. But even though the Crowbar was a small place, we had plenty of room.

We sat at a table, not far from the stage, Bernie taking a chair, me at his feet. A waitress in a tank top and Daisy Dukes that she seemed to have grown out of, maybe not having the money for a new pair, poor thing, came right over.

"Hi, gorgeous," she said.

"Flattery will get you nowhere," said Bernie.

Wow! So quick! And whatever that meant, it was one of those lines that make a big impression: I could tell by the look on her face. If only those people — a surprising number actually — who said Bernie was clueless with women could see him now.

"Huh?" the waitress was saying. "Not you, fella — I was talking to this big guy right here. What's his name?"

"Oh," said Bernie, his grin fading fast. "Ah."

"He got a name or not?"

"Chet," said Bernie, crossing his arms over his chest. A human move you see sometimes, the meaning unclear to me, but they never look happy when they're doing it.

"Short and sweet," the waitress said. What was this? She thought I was short? That was strange, but before I had a chance to think about it, she scratched between my ears,

40

her nails nice and pointy, technique as good as it gets, and I forgot whatever it was. Then she spoke in that gurgly tone women use for babies and sometimes for me and my kind, a delightful tone in my opinion. "Who's the handsomest dude in the Valley?" she said.

Me! The Chetster! I was the handsomest dude in the Valley! Next to Bernie, of course, goes without mentioning.

"I'll have a beer," Bernie said.

"Get a load of that tail of his," the waitress said.

"When it's convenient," said Bernie.

"Could air-condition the whole goddamn place with it," she said, before turning and walking away.

"Do you think she heard me?" Bernie said.

A tough question. What humans hear and don't hear is a big subject. Meanwhile, the light, already pretty dim, dimmed some more. Then the bartender, a stubby guy with a toothpick hanging out the side of his mouth stepped onto the stage, went to the mic stand, stood on tiptoes, and said, "Welcome all you ladies and germs. Heh heh. To the one and only legendary Crowbar! Where we've got a special treat for you tonight — order any three tequila drinks and the fourth one is free!"

41

Over at the bar, an old man with runny eyes clapped his hands, just once. I myself was a bit confused. Tequila was the treat? What sense did that make? Chewies were treats. Slim Jims were treats. Maybe the bartender would soon realize his mistake. My ears went up, meaning they wanted to listen good and close. Here's a little something you may not know about me: I pretty much let my ears do what they want. So they went right ahead and listened good and close, which was how I knew for sure that the bartender said no more about treats.

"And now a blast from the past. Put your hands together for the Arizona cowgirl who wrote and sang" — he took a card from his pocket, gave it a quick glance — " 'How You Hung the Moon.' Let's hear it for the one, the only, Miss Lotty Pegram."

"For Christ sake," Bernie said, his voice low.

But maybe the bartender heard him, because he checked the card again and said, "Er, Pilgrim. Miss Lotty Pilgrim."

Then came some clapping, kind of quiet, on account of the size of the audience: a few people at the tables, a few at the bar, one baby-faced dude in a denim jacket with cut-off sleeves playing darts in the corner. I could hear the tiny whiz of the darts streaking through the air. Just putting that in so you'll know how quiet the clapping was.

Lotty Pilgrim stepped through curtains behind the stage and stood under the spotlight. The bartender made one of those all-yours gestures toward the mic stand. Lotty didn't look at him. She wore pink earrings, a creamy-colored western shirt with pink fringe, and black leather jeans, and had a guitar slung around her neck. Her eyes didn't seem so soft as before, maybe on account of all the black makeup around them, but I'm no expert on makeup, with only one real experience, way back in the Leda days, although I have a very clear memory of the taste of that particular tube, available only in Paris, wherever that might be. As for her hair, it was frizzier than at Nixon's yard, and looked less golden and more silvery. In a strange way Lotty looked both older and younger than before. She stepped up to the mic, played something zippy on the guitar, using just her thumb and two fingers, all her nails long and red, and then, looking at nobody, began to sing a real fast song that had trains in it and car wrecks and prison. A great song in my opinion, and I also liked her voice — happy until the car wrecks and then not so happy. And Lotty no longer looked both older and younger. Now it was just younger.

The runny-eyed guy at the bar clapped again, maybe not as loudly as he had for tequila. A few others joined in, sort of. The loudest clapper by far was Bernie. In the spotlight, Lotty Pilgrim made a slight nod, maybe in his direction, but it was hard to tell in all the dimness. "That was 'Birthday in Prison,' available in all the usual streams." And now she looked at Bernie, for sure. "Zero point zero zero zero three," she said. "Cents per download — the artist's share." Then, after a long pause: "But it adds up."

Bernie laughed. What was funny? I didn't waste any time figuring that out. Laughter is the best sound humans make, and Bernie's is the best of the best. He was still laughing when Lotty said, "This one's called 'Big Surprise,' " and started in on the next song, this one slower than the prison one.

Here's my new friend the locksmith,
'Case you hid away some key,
Gonna switch out this and that,
Keep your sweet distance from me.

And there was more like that, a fine story, in my opinion. It reminded me of a confusing case we'd worked — a case out in Dry

Wells involving a locksmith, his wife, his girlfriend, and the girlfriend's husband, also a locksmith — but at that moment I got distracted by the sight of Clint, Lotty's lean-bodied pal or manager or whatever he was, moving in the shadows and placing an empty glass jar on the edge of the stage, just beyond the spotlight beam. That would be a tip jar: you learn these things in our line of work.

The locksmith song ended. There was less clapping this time, mostly just Bernie. From one of the tables, a man called out, " 'How You Hung the Moon'!"

Lotty peered into the darkness. "Any other requests?"

" 'How You Hung the Moon'!" he called again, louder this time.

Bernie turned to look at the dude: a shiny-faced customer who'd had plenty to drink, the signs of that too many to go into now. He cupped his hands to his mouth, a human thing I've never liked. " 'How You Hung the Moon'!"

Bernie reached into his pocket. Were we packing the .38 Special? Good idea: shiny-faced guys like that had to be stopped before they ruined the evening. Bernie's hand emerged: no gun. Instead he had his wallet. He opened it, took out a bill, the

45

one with the picture of the old guy rocking the long-haired, bald-on-top look. Possibly a C-note, but don't count on me for info like that. Meanwhile Bernie was on his feet. He stepped into the shadows at the side of the stage and dropped that bill in the tip jar. I had to have been wrong about the C-note. That was my strong hope, and I'm a real strong hoper. Lotty's eyes shifted quickly to the tip jar, and then away. In a quiet voice, no louder than those darts, Bernie said, "Play whatever the hell you like." He came back to the table and sat down.

Had Lotty heard him? I didn't know. But she had the beginnings of a smile on her face when she leaned into the mic and said, "This one's called 'The Lousy Part of Jealousy.' "

"The Lousy Part of Jealousy" turned out to be a long song, hard to follow, that might have been about a man who kept running out the back door of some woman's place for reasons I didn't quite get. My mind wandered a bit, and when my mind wanders I tend to look around, checking out the action. And what was this? The baby-faced dart player — actually both baby-faced and fuzzy-faced — was on the move, kind of sneaking through the darkness just beyond the pool of stage light. Sneakiness is some-

thing that gets my attention, big-time —
just one of the reasons the Little Detective
Agency is so successful, if you leave out the
finances part.

There's a low rumbly bark I make when I
want Bernie's attention in a just-between-us
sort of way. I made the low rumbly bark.
Bernie didn't even look at me. Instead his
gaze went immediately to the dart player —
we're a real good team, me and Bernie,
something to keep in mind — just in time
to see the dart-player's hand . . . darting?
Wow! I came close to what felt like a big
understanding. Close but no cigar, which
was just as well. I'd once tasted a cigar butt.
Never again, amigo. Although there had
been another occasion. And one more after
that. And possibly —

But forget all that. The point was the dart-
player's hand darted into the tip jar, then
darted right back out, now with a good
strong hold on Bernie's tip. The dart player
vanished in the shadows.

FOUR

Something sneaky was going down. I knew that in a flash. You might be thinking, Wow, Chet, how fast your mind works! But you'd be wrong. My mind had nothing to do with it. My teeth were the smart ones. Sneakiness gives them this powerful urge, the urge to . . . to do something, let's leave it at that.

There are all kinds of sneaks in this world, human and not human. Take foxes, for example, almost always sneaky. You can tell by how their tails sneak around behind them. Elephants? Never sneaky, in my experience, although you still had to be careful when one was on the scene. Maybe we can get back to elephants later, specifically the time Peanut sat on a perp's car. How much fun was that? But right now Bernie and I were on the move, leaving the table, and following the dart player — a quick-stepping shadow sneaking toward the front door of the Crowbar. We were being very quiet about it, me and Bernie, almost . . . sneaky ourselves? A disturbing thought. I got my tail up nice and high and forgot whatever that disturbing thought had been at once.

The dart player slipped through the swinging doors, glancing back at the very last second. A passing car lit up his eyes, eyes that spotted us, no doubt about it. They widened, one of those perp looks I love. It meant *Whoa, is someone after me?* Got it in on the first guess, buddy boy! Right about now was when they either reached for a gun or took off. The dart player took off, which is usually our preference.

We took off, too, through the swinging doors and into the parking lot. Shermie, relaxing on a folding chair and smoking a little weed — the air over all parts of the Valley pretty much smelling of weed twenty-four seven nowadays — glanced up. "That bad, huh?" he said to us.

We kept running. And what a nice sight — Bernie was running as fast as I'd ever seen him. Which isn't at all fast, not even for a human, probably on account of his leg wound in the war, but it made me so happy to see him back to running not fast. As for me and my running, let's put it this way: I was delighted that the dart player turned out to be one of those humans who could really motor, especially after his flip-flops flew off. Why hadn't he gone into football or track instead of robbery? I wondered about that as I loped along behind him, trying not to catch up too soon and spoil the fun.

The dart player was headed for a yellow car parked in a far corner of the lot where the pavement stopped and the desert began. Halfway there, he glanced back once more, saw me, and ramped it up, really turning on the jets. I was starting to like this speedy dude, so I let him get all the way to the car and even wrench the driver's-side door open before I turned on my own jets — whee, baby! — gathered myself for a nice spring, way, way up there, and the next thing I knew I had him by the pant leg. My teeth stopped thinking at that exact same moment.

"Aiiee!" screamed the dart player, almost like he was in pain. Surely not possible: I could barely taste blood at all. But some humans are tougher than others, this dude being one of the others. "Here," he said as Bernie arrived, hardly huffing and puffing at all. The dart player tossed the C-note at Bernie. "Why does everything have to be so crazy?"

Bernie reached out but a gust of wind caught the C-note and wafted it up over his hand, out of the parking lot, and into the darkness. We'd dealt with situations like this before. Bernie's job was to go after the money, mine to keep doing what I was doing, namely holding the perp by the pant leg. Bernie switched on his pocket flash and moved toward a clump of bushes. I adjusted my grip on the pant leg. The dart player, half in and half out of the car, gazed at me. His eyes had a look you see in some humans, mostly men, a look that says, *Now comes something pretty clever.*

"Got a treat in my pocket," he said. "Just let me go and it's yours. T-R-E-A-T."

How strange! T-R-E-A-T was a way humans said treat when they didn't want you to know they were saying treat. But didn't he want me to know that a treat was coming my way if I cut him a break? Kind of weird. Maybe not worth thinking about, on account of the fact that Bernie and I had worked very hard on not accepting treats at moments like this, maybe the hardest thing I'd ever learned. And even if there were times I slipped a bit — who doesn't in this life? — now was not going to be one of them because I knew from one quick sniff he had no treat in his pockets. And in that same sniff, I picked up his scent, a rather pleasant combo of old sneakers and not showering very often.

"You don't like treats?" he said. "What kind of a dog are you?"

Tough question. Some sort of a mix, I'd heard Bernie say, and a hundred-plus pounder, as we discovered the time Bernie picked me up — the fun we had with that! — and stood on the scale. Also, my ears don't match, which people mentioned now and then. Was that good or bad? I went back and forth on that, and in fact was doing it again when the dart player wriggled around and . . . what was this? Squirmed right out of his jeans? And kept on squirming — across the front seat, and out the passenger door? Then he scrambled to his feet — one of those guys, it turned out, who didn't bother with underwear — and hurried across the road and into the scrub on the other side.

How could he think that was going to work? I zipped around the car to go after him — grabbing pantless perps by the pant leg is one of the highlights of this job — but just then Bernie came back, the C-note in hand, and said, "Forget it, big guy."

Forget it?

He smiled, his smile the brightest thing in

the night. "You did real good." He gave me a nice pat. "We can always track him down if we need to."

But, but, but. I was stuck on those buts when Shermie came over.

"What's goin' on?" he said.

Bernie was bending by the license plate of the dart player's car and writing on his hand with a pen, just one of the many cool things about him.

"Guy playing darts robbed the tip jar." Bernie held up the C-note.

"That's a first," Shermie said.

Bernie handed him our card, a card designed by Suzie, with flowers on it. Would we be ordering some new cards? An odd thought, which didn't make me happy. I hoped it wouldn't come around again.

Meanwhile Bernie was saying, "Let me know when he comes back for his ride."

"Sure," said Shermie, "but what if we're closed?"

"Interesting question," Bernie said. "Might make sense to temporarily disable it somehow or other."

Shermie leaned into the driver's side, grabbed the steering wheel, and jerked it right out of the yellow car. "Good enough?" he said.

"It's a start," said Bernie.

■ ■ ■ ■

After the rest of the show — which we watched from a table just inside the door, the kind of spot we'd choose if we were actually working the place, which we weren't unless I was missing something — we went up to the stage. Lotty Pilgrim was talking to her fans. Actually just one fan, a tall and stooping old man, leaning on his cane, and giving off that old man smell, the same kind you get from a stack of yellowed newspapers.

"Played it at my wife's funeral," the old man was saying.

"Uh-huh," said Lotty, unslinging her guitar. She winced and rubbed her shoulder with her free hand. The younger-looking part of her faded. I could see it happening.

" 'How You Hung the Moon,' " the old man went on. "Meant a lot to her."

Lotty nodded and glanced around, maybe expecting somebody. Like Clint, for instance, sitting at the bar and gazing at her over the rim of his glass. He stayed where he was.

"Have to admit," the old man said, "I was hopin' to hear it tonight."

Lotty gave him a smile. Humans can be

54

tricky with smiles and you have to watch carefully. This was the kind where the mouth did all the work and the eyes stayed the same.

"I don't sing that song," Lotty said.

"Uh, I see," said the old man. He opened his mouth like he was planning to say more, but Lotty spoke first.

"Thanks for coming."

The old man backed away, blinking once or twice. We stepped up, Bernie first and then me, on the move as soon as I knew stepping up was in the picture, and almost immediately in the lead.

"Great show," Bernie said. "Love how you pick — like a left-handed Mother Maybelle channeling Slim Harpo. If, uh, you don't mind my saying so."

"Well, that's a new one," said Lotty. "No, I don't mind. You play some yourself?"

"Just fool around on the ukulele. Not worth mentioning."

Not worth mentioning? You've never heard anything like Bernie on the ukulele, take it from me. Sometimes — like on "Death Don't Have No Mercy," one of our favorites — I join in with this little woo-woo thing I do. Once, practically the whole neighborhood came storming out of their houses for a listen. Most folks would now be telling Lotty all about that, but Bernie's not most folks.

He pointed to the tip jar, still sitting on the edge of the stage, now with a crumpled bill or two at the bottom. "You probably didn't notice the little problem with the tip jar."

"Problem?" said Lotty, glancing over at the tip jar. "I believe I saw you making a contribution. I thank you."

"Most welcome," said Bernie. "The problem was we had a thief in the house. A quick-handed type."

Lotty looked past us, scanned the club real quick.

"But we caught him, Chet and I," Bernie went on.

"Chet?" said Lotty.

"This is Chet."

Lotty looked at me. "Your dog?"

"That's one way to put it."

"Or the other way around?"

Bernie laughed. Then he reached out to give her the money and Lotty reached out to take it, but before she could Clint was suddenly with us, just in time to snatch the C-note away. A quick hand, with big rings on the soft, white fingers.

"I'll take care of that," he said. He and Lotty locked eyes for a moment. "Just so's we keep the books in order. Don't want any screwups, do we, Lotty?" He emptied out the tip jar.

After what seemed like a long pause, Lotty said, "Heaven forbid."

Clint gave her a great big smile and squeezed her hand. A little on the hard side, that squeeze: it left a red mark.

Clint turned to Bernie. "Much obliged, sir," he said. "I'm Clint Swann, Lotty's manager."

"Bernie Little," Bernie said. They shook hands. "And this is Chet."

"Yeah? Dogs are allowed in here?"

"Why not?"

Clint shrugged. "Good point. Ain't talkin' Carnegie Hall."

"Dogs are allowed at Carnegie Hall," Bernie said.

Lotty and Clint gave him a look, close looks but very different. They were both seeing Bernie in a new way, but not the same new way, if that makes sense. I liked Lotty's new way better. Clint seemed to be taking longer to appreciate Bernie's good side, which was the only side he had. A fun evening, all in all, if a bit confusing at the end.

"I wonder," Bernie said the next morning,

"why she doesn't sing 'How You Hung the Moon' anymore." Or something like that — hard to hear humans clearly when they're brushing their teeth. Janie the groomer does the brushing when it comes to my teeth. "Love those choppers of yours, Chet," she always says. I hadn't seen Janie in way too long. Was that why, not long after Bernie had finished brushing his teeth and laid the toothbrush beside the sink, I suddenly found myself in possession of it?

I trotted into the kitchen. Bernie was pouring coffee. "Hey, big guy, what have you got there?" He came over, grabbed one end of the toothbrush. Maybe not grabbed — it was gentler than that. I did this head-shaking-while-backing-away combo I like, and Bernie got a stronger grip on the toothbrush. Which was exactly what I wanted! If you're going to play in this life, then play! And is there anything more fun than playing a brand-new game? This one was called Who Gets the Toothbrush. A very promising game! I shook and backed, shook and backed — and don't forget my tail, wagging the whole time, so in fact I shook, backed, and wagged, shook, backed, and wagged, sort of dragging Bernie across the floor, meaning it was actually a case of shake, back, wag, and drag! Wow! The fun

58

we were having!

"For god's sake, Chet, give me the damn —"

The phone rang. Bernie picked it up. "Hello? When did —"

And a whole complicated conversation started up, possibly Shermie on the other end. I went over to the back door of the kitchen. No doorknob on the kitchen door: it had one of those lever things that humans thumb. No thumb necessary, by the way. In fact, this was the very first door I'd ever gotten the hang of. Now I opened it and strolled out to the patio, always a nice cool spot, especially if our swan fountain — left behind by Leda after the divorce — was turned on, which it was not. But I wasn't interested in the patio today. Instead I seemed to be drawn beyond it, to the lawn. Once it had been grassy, but we'd changed over to a desert-style lawn — all about ocotillo, spiny plants, stones, and dirt — on account of the aquifer, one of Bernie's biggest worries, and that made it mine, too. I'd actually laid eyes on the aquifer, a muddy puddle down at the bottom of a construction site. If that was it, we were in big trouble. But the truth was that most of the time I forgot to worry about it.

Like, now, out in the backyard: there I was

worry-free, feeling pretty close to tip-top. I went over to the fence that separates us from Iggy's side and got right to digging a nice little hole. And what was this? Iggy's yip yip yip? Had to be. No one else had a yip yip yip like that, so high-pitched and hard on the ears. That yip yip yip meant he heard me digging from inside his house, and wanted badly to do some digging, too. Tough luck for Iggy! This hole was mine. I put more energy into the dig, extra-noisy kind of energy. The yip yip yipping grew louder. There were so many pleasures in life! I ended up digging a much deeper hole than I'd had in mind, although what had I had in mind? I couldn't recall, and in fact almost asked myself why was I doing this? But not quite. Instead I dropped in the toothbrush, pawed all the dirt back in, and smoothed it over real nice, like a very good boy. Then I trotted over to the patio and licked up some scummy water from the bottom of the fountain. Fresh water's my preference but I don't mind mixing it up every now and then. Bernie's a bourbon drinker but I've seen him down a scotch or two. We're a lot alike in some ways, don't forget.

I was giving myself a good shake when Bernie appeared in the kitchen doorway. He gave me a look. I gave him a look back.

"What the hell's with Iggy?"

A tough one. Iggy was one of a kind. Maybe Bernie had forgotten that during all that hospital time. "Come on," he said. "Let's go."

I beat him to the car. Iggy's yip yip yipping followed us down the street.

Riding shotgun in the Porsche? Can't beat it. Were we headed someplace special or just out for a spin? They were both just as great! My tail tried to do some wagging but couldn't. After a while I realized I was sitting on it, and squeezed over, just being considerate. We swerved, not quite all the way across the road.

"Hey," Bernie said, "a little space, big guy."

Right. I knew that. Perhaps it had come up before. The problem was we didn't have quite enough room for me, a wagging tail, and Bernie. Did that mean one of us had to go? I tried to figure out how that would work.

"Chet?"

I squeezed over the other way, back to sitting my tail. No tail likes that but what could it do? I'm a hundred-plus pounder, as I may have mentioned before. But now came a strange thought: Did my tail weigh

61

something? If so, what? So, actually two thoughts. Beyond those two thoughts I sensed lots of others, stretching on and on like distant mountains. All at once I knew one thing for absolute sure: I did not want to visit those mountains.

Bernie glanced over. "Something on your mind?"

Nothing, nada, zip. Maybe not at that precise moment, but as soon as possible.

"Having some deep thoughts these days, aren't you?"

Absolutely not. What a suggestion!

We pulled into Nixon's Championship Autobody. That was a bit of a surprise. The car was driving perfectly. I can always tell from the sound it makes, a sort of deep purring, like a very big . . . oh, no. I'd come close to going somewhere I did not want to go. I loved the Porsche, but how could I go on loving it if it reminded me of . . . of something I won't mention. Maybe all this would go away and I'd be back to normal. I've always been a real good forgetter, probably one of the reasons for our success. If you forget about the finances. Which I always do.

I hopped out of the car — one of my very best hops, long and soaring — and felt totally free. Free of all bad things. Free as a bird. A freedom birds don't appreciate, by the way. Check out their angry little eyes next time you've got a moment.

FIVE

Nixon was watching one of his guys spray-paint a laughing woman on the side of a panel truck.

"Needs to be more buxom, Zoltan," he said.

Zoltan raised his visor. "Book-some, boss? Um, like in a book?"

"Book? What do I know about goddamn books? Tits, Zoltan. Ass. Tits and ass, not necessarily in that order. What makes the world go round."

Zoltan lowered his visor, raised the spray can. "Tits," he muttered to himself. "Ass."

"And don't be too . . . what's the word?"

"Subtle," Bernie said as we came up to them.

Nixon turned quickly to him, blinked, then nodded. "Yup," he said. "You do good work, Zoltan, but sometimes you get too subtle. You're in America now."

"Yes, boss," said Zoltan. "I love America."

64

And he began enlarging this and that.

"Ride okay?" Nixon said.

"Like new," Bernie said. "New used, is maybe how to put it."

"New used is what we do," Nixon said. "So what's up?"

"Just had a call from Shermie Shouldice," Bernie said. "He was watching a car for us out at the Crowbar in West Corona."

Nixon nodded. "We picked it up."

"So he said."

"Ten-year-old Civic," Nixon said. "Minus the steering wheel."

"That's the one," Bernie said.

Nixon shot him a quick look. "Shermie keeping his nose clean?"

Interesting question. Interesting dudes ask interesting questions, in my experience, and Nixon was an interesting dude. A perp, at one time, as I may have mentioned, sent up that waterless river by us, but now we were pals, plus he always carried the scents of two different women. That part's not so uncommon, now that I think of it. As for why he wanted to know about Shermie's nose, I had no clue. A human thing I always enjoy — well, more like a human male thing, since I can't recall seeing any females doing it — is the snot rocket, but I didn't

65

recall Shermie launching one. That was all I could bring to the table.

"Probably," Bernie said. "Within limits."

"Is he one of those guys who doesn't know his own strength?" Nixon said.

"Among other things."

"True you once knocked him out with one punch?"

"That's an exaggeration."

Exaggeration? Was that a way of saying absolutely true? That sweet uppercut of Bernie's — you could hear it in the air! And then Shermie's eyes had rolled up and his body had slumped down, already in dreamland. I wanted to see that uppercut again, like this very second. Any reason at the moment to use it on Nixon? He didn't seem to have done anything wrong but would he mind, seeing as how I wanted it so badly? I was wondering about that when Bernie said, "Where's the car?"

Nixon led us into one of the service bays. I kept my eyes on his chin the whole time, not sure why. He gestured toward the yellow car, same one from last night in the Crowbar lot. "Bent the whole damn column," he said.

"When's he coming to pick it up?" Bernie said.

"Who are you talking about?"

66

"The owner," Bernie said. "Young-looking guy, fuzzy-faced. Maybe not the owner, but he was driving it last night."

"First I heard of him," Nixon said.

Bernie's eyes shifted slightly. I knew that one: a sign that his mighty brain was firing up. I could feel his thoughts in the air. "Who called you?"

"To come get the car?"

"Exactly."

"You were out there last night?"

"Yup."

"How was the show?"

"Interesting. Who called you?"

Nixon was silent for a few moments. Now his thoughts, too, were in the air, much smaller and slower than Bernie's. "Can't see no harm in tellin' you. Confidentially, of course."

Bernie nodded. He has many nods. This one was one of my favorites, friendly but saying nothing. No one ever seemed to realize that.

"Lotty," Nixon said. "Lotty Pilgrim called it in."

Back in the car, Bernie picked up the phone like he was going to make a call, but it rang first.

"Bernie?" It was a woman, a woman I

knew, namely Dr. Bethea. Here's something you might not know about me: I'm good with voices. Once I hear a voice, I never forget it. Although . . . how could you . . . how could you be sure? For a moment I was almost . . . lost! Lost in my own head. Oh, how horrible would that be? How would you ever sniff your way out?

The moment passed. I've had a lot of good luck in this life, starting with the day I met Bernie. Would you believe it was the same day I flunked out of K-9 school? On the very last test, namely leaping? When leaping was my very best thing? How had it happened? My memory was dim on that. Perhaps a cat had been involved. But not the point of the story, which was all about meeting Bernie.

Right now, he was saying, "Oh, hi, Doc."

Was it a good time to give him a nice friendly lick? Had we been through something about nice friendly licks while the car was moving, maybe even recently? If so, were they good or bad?

"Please — not 'Doc,' " said the doc.

"Oh, um," Bernie said. "It's Eliza, right?"

"It is," said the doc. "How are you doing?"

"Medically?"

The doc laughed. She had a very nice

laugh, deeper than her speaking voice. "That, too, of course."

"Medically, good," Bernie said. "Nonmedically also good."

"Nice to hear."

"And you?" Bernie said.

"Same and same," said the doc. "A cousin of mine knows you."

"Yeah? Who's that?"

"Cleon Maxwell."

What was this? Cleon Maxwell? Our Cleon Maxwell, owner of Max's Memphis Ribs, best restaurant in the whole Valley, in my opinion. I noticed my paws seemed to be up on the dashboard, and got them back down on the seat, pronto. There are right ways and wrong ways when it comes to riding shotgun. I'm on the side of right.

". . . not actually blood cousins," the doc was saying. "His grammy and my grammy were best friends from childhood, back in Tennessee. But Cleon's just like family. He's a huge fan."

"Of you?"

"No, of you," the doc said. Then she laughed that lovely laugh again. "And an even huger fan of Chet."

Bernie laughed, too. For a few moments they were laughing together. That was nice, although don't ask me to explain why. I decided to think of the doc as Eliza instead of the doc. Don't ask me to explain that one either, but if you guessed it had something to do with Max's Secret Special Sauce you might be on the right track.

"So it was a small step from there to the idea of lunch, the three of us."

"Uh, the three of us?"

"You, Chet, me."

"At Max's Memphis Ribs?"

"The very place."

"Oh," Bernie said. He looked at me, as though for some sort of . . . advice? Could that have been it? Was he asking for my advice about lunch at Max's? Not possible. Who needed advice on something like that?

"But no pressure, Bernie," she said, her voice sounding as upbeat as before. "It was just an idea."

Bernie nodded. "Yeah," he said. "An idea. And . . . and a good one. When would be . . ."

"Tomorrow at noon?"

Bernie looked at me again, took a deep breath. "See you then." Of course we would. Why all the fuss? Best ribs in town versus anything else? This was what humans call a no-brainer. I've aced more than one no-brainer in my time. Just sayin'.

70

■ ■ ■

"Hey, Rick."

Rick Torres's voice came through the speakers. "You sound good. Feet up? Downing a cold one?"

"Actually sort of working on something. Can you run a plate?"

"Landed a gig already?"

"Uh-huh."

"Of the paying variety?"

"What other kind is there?"

Rick laughed. A slightly unpleasant laugh, possibly of the type called knowing. But knowing what? I thought of the C-note, first put in the tip jar by Bernie, then taken by the dart player, after that taken back by us and ending up in the hand of Clint Swann, Lotty's . . . manager, was it? I wasn't clear on that. Not important. The important thing was the gig. Paying or not? You tell me.

Meanwhile Bernie was squinting at the numbers on his hand, the ink somewhat blurry. "New Mexico plate, looks like three — no, more like two — seven four —"

"New Mexico I can't do in our system. Take me twenty minutes or so. Meet up at Donut Heaven?"

71

Donut Heaven? From time to time heaven comes up in conversation, always sounding like a nice place. But here in the Valley just about everyone knew that the very best heaven was Donut Heaven. We're blessed, whatever that might mean, exactly.

Ever bitten into a cruller?

"Yikes!" said Rick Torres, yanking away his hand. We were in the lot at Donut Heaven, Rick in his cruiser, us in the Porsche, parked cop-style, driver's-side door to driver's-side door, meaning I wasn't really that close to Rick when he said, "Got an extra cruller here. Any chance Chet might —"

What came next was kind of a blur, and when things got back to normal there I was in the shotgun seat, peacefully polishing off a cruller. That first bite is magic and all the others — one or possibly two if it's a real big cruller — are just as good.

Rick unfolded a sheet of paper. "Car's registered to a Rita Krebs, age nineteen, 929 Old Gila Road, Phantom Springs, New Mexico." He handed the sheet to Bernie.

"I owe you," Bernie said.

"No owing, brother," said Rick.

There was a little silence while the two of them didn't quite look at each other. Was it possible they were brothers? I was just finding that out now? Bernie had never once in all our time together mentioned a brother. How could —

"What's he barking about?" Rick said.

"No idea," said Bernie. "Chet — cool it."

Barking? Something about barking? I listened my hardest, heard barking, but very distant, surely not within human hearing range. She-barking, as a matter of fact. My mind wandered to other things.

Two-lane blacktop through desert hills and canyons: it doesn't get any better. To the metal, Bernie, to the metal! The big engine howled. I howled! Did Bernie howl, too? Hard to tell over all that howling. A sign flashed by and he eased off the pedal a bit.

"State line," he said. "New Mexico's a different kettle of fish — keep that in mind."

Fish? That got my attention. As a rule, I stay away from fish, having had a bad experience involving a trash bin in the kitchen of All Things Fishy, a restaurant where we'd gone with Suzie — Suzie! I missed her! — and I'd perhaps done some exploration by myself, ending up with a bone, tiny but nasty, wedged in my throat. I sniffed the air, picked up all kinds of scents, the lovely rainy smell of creosote bushes most of all, but not the slightest hint of fish. Fish meant water, of which I saw not a drop. But if Bernie said there were fish here in New Mexico then that was that. I sat up straight and kept watch on the fishless scenery gliding by, all the way to a little town backed against a mountain.

"Phantom Springs," Bernie said. "They took fifty million dollars' worth of silver out of that hill." We drove down the main drag, past a few solid-looking brick buildings, then turned up a street where all the buildings got less solid. "And used so much mercury doing it that the wells are still polluted, a century later."

All that sounded pretty complicated. Had they left any silver for us? Just enough to fill our trunk, not very big? That was my only thought.

We made a few more turns and started up the hill, passing a trailer park and a few shacks. The pavement ended, the way pavements often did out in the desert, and then we were on a dirt track, switchbacking up and up. A mailbox appeared. Sometimes you see bullet holes in mailboxes in these kinds of places, but not this time. I was a bit disappointed. We turned up a bumpy, rutted driveway, and parked in front of a small, low wooden house, maybe blue in

74

the past but now sandblasted by the desert wind. The windows of the house were all dusty, but I thought I saw movement behind one.

We hopped out of the car, Bernie not actually hopping. The air was still, the sun hot, but not as hot as back in the Valley. Way down below in the town, a glass shattered on someone's hard floor.

"Here's the question," Bernie said. "Why would Lotty Pilgrim make that call to Nixon when the driver of the car robbed her tip jar?"

Wow! Bernie had all that figured out? I understood the situation like no other situation I'd ever been in. But that was Bernie. Just when you think he's done amazing you, he amazes you again.

We walked up to the house, side by side. The front door opened and a young barefoot woman stepped onto the porch. She had big blue eyes, a long ponytail, and a shotgun in her hands. The muzzle wasn't exactly pointing at us, but neither was it not exactly pointing at us. I had an unsettling thought: no bullet holes in the mailbox but now this? Were we walking into a trap? That happened in our business, actually kind of often, now that I thought about it. So it had to be one of the things that made the Little Detective Agency what it was.

SIX

Bernie smiled a friendly smile. "Expecting someone dangerous?" he said.

The young woman's eyes hardened, like they'd become blue metal.

"That's not us," Bernie said.

The shotgun muzzle stayed where it was, close to pointing at my muzzle but not quite. I had a strange moment when my muzzle suddenly became very itchy, and even worse, like that other muzzle was making it happen. All I wanted to do was lie down and give my muzzle a nice good scratching with one of my back paws. Was this a good time? I thought not but what can you do when you're itchy? And then I got the idea of snatching that shotgun right out of the young woman's hands. I changed positions a little. The itching went away.

"Get off my property," the young woman said.

The smile stayed on Bernie's face, still

friendly. He's the friendly type. So am I! No way I was going to hurt the young woman. I was planning a very gentle encounter.

"My name's Bernie Little and this is Chet. Are you Rita Krebs?"

"Let's see a warrant," the young woman said.

"I'm not a cop."

"You look like one. Kinda."

"I'll take that as a compliment," Bernie said.

"Take it however you want. Just get the hell out of here."

Bernie nodded, like we were just about on our way. But we actually didn't move an inch, if I'm right in thinking that's not much. In fact, I kind of edged a little closer to the shotgun. At the same time, I noticed that she was one of those humans — there aren't many of them, no offense — with very nice feet. Giving them a quick lick? Was that in the cards? Maybe later.

"If you are Rita Krebs," Bernie said, "we've got news about your car."

Her eyes shifted, a real quick shift and then they were back on us. Bernie's good at making those quick shifts happen. What they're all about is a bit of a mystery, but they usually mean we're starting to roll.

"We've just come from Nixon Panero's shop in the Valley. Don't know how you found him, but you went to the best."

She looked Bernie in the eye. "You're not a cop?"

"I'm a music lover," Bernie said. "Country music in particular."

She opened her mouth, closed it, opened it again. "What's that supposed to mean?"

"I'm guessing you already know, Rita," Bernie said.

"Well, you're guessing wrong," Rita said, her voice rising. She had to be Rita or else she would have said . . . something or other. Bernie didn't make mistakes at times like this. He didn't make mistakes at all. Except for the Hawaiian pants and the Bolivian tin play. And . . . and . . . maybe somehow Suzie? What a bothersome thought! I wished it hadn't come at all. And it wasn't showing any signs of forgetting itself, if that makes any sense. There's really only one way to get rid of bothersome thoughts that won't forget themselves. You've got to move. I moved.

The next thing I knew I had the shotgun, holding it nice and tight at the wooden end. Bernie was on the move, too, catching Rita as she fell and setting her back on her feet. Had she fallen because of me? Oh, no! I went over to maybe give her a nuzzle, but that wasn't going to be easy with the shotgun in my mouth.

"Good job," Bernie said. "If, um, a little on the spontaneous side. How about sitting for a moment or two?" He took the shotgun, broke it open, pocketed the shells, and offered it to Rita. She didn't take it, backing away instead. "You've got no goddamn right to trespass in here and —"

A man's voice came from inside the house. "Rita? What's goin' on?"

Out on the porch, everything went still, even the air. I sniffed it and picked up the man's scent: a rather pleasant combo of old sneakers and not showering very often. Hey! A dude I knew. A friend? Not a friend? My mind came up empty on that question. But the door to this nice little faded and lopsided house was open so I trotted inside.

"What the hell?" said Rita. "Stop him!"

Bernie stepped past her and entered the house.

"What are you doing?"

"Can't stop him from out here," Bernie said, which was kind of strange since all he had to do was say, "Chet, come," or "Back outside, big guy," or even just "Che—et?" if he said it in a certain way. But before I could tackle this puzzle, Bernie was beside

80

me, the shotgun under his arm, and we were doing a little recon of the house, recons being one of our specialties. Rita followed us, hopping around a bit, maybe grabbing once or twice at the back of Bernie's shirt, and saying things I'm sure she didn't really mean.

Meanwhile Bernie was being a very nice guest. Very nice guests always said very nice things about the house. "Love these old shotgun houses," he told Rita.

Shotgun house? Because Rita had welcomed us with a shotgun in her hands? Did that make any house with a shotgun in it a shotgun house? If so, just about every house in some parts of the Valley was a shotgun house, including ours. Did that mean Bernie loved so many, many houses? Probably: there's lots of love in Bernie, even if most people don't see it right away, or ever.

We moved through a front room with a sagging couch and a big flat-screen, down a narrow corridor with a messy kitchen on one side and a messy bathroom on the other, and into a bedroom at the end. A dark bedroom, the curtains drawn. Humans are just about blind in the dark, but not me and my kind. The dresser, the bed, and the man lying on it were all visible to me, if a little on the dim side. I went over to the

81

bed, making what Bernie calls a mental note to circle back to that messy kitchen if I got the chance.

"Rita? Rita?" said the man on the bed, the sound of his voice actually more of a shriek.

"Sorry, Jordan," said Rita, somewhere behind us. "They just barged in. There was nothing I could —"

Bernie whipped open the curtains. Light came flowing in, bright desert light, extra-bright if it comes at you all at once.

"Aargh!" cried the man on the bed, covering his face with his arm. This, as I already knew, was my pal the fuzzy- and baby-faced dart player, but looking not as good as he had back at the Crowbar. His face was purplish and the one eye not hidden under his arm was swollen just about shut. We went through a time, me and Bernie — the first Christmas when Charlie was with Leda and Malcolm and not us — of watching old fight films on TV. The face of the man on the bed reminded me of Carmen Basilio after Sugar Ray Robinson was done with him.

Bernie sat on the bed.

"Aargh!" the man cried again.

"That bad, Jordan?" Bernie said. "What happened?"

Jordan moved his arm slightly, exposing

his other eye, also swollen, but very slightly open, just a narrow slit, somewhat oozy. That eye, what there was of it, shifted toward Bernie.

"Who are you?"

"Don't remember me? Maybe you'll recognize Chet here."

With a loud groan, Jordan raised his head a tiny bit off the pillow and turned it in my direction. Then he groaned again and laid his head back down. The narrow, damp eye slit stayed open. So — he recognized me or not? After we meet, just about everyone is happy to see me the next time. But not Jordan? Was there some way to make him like me a little better? Playing a fun game of tug-of-war with his sheets was my first and only idea.

Bernie turned to Rita. "Has a doctor seen him?"

"Huh? Like we have a doctor on call?" Rita said.

Jordan's mouth opened. There was dried blood on the inside of his lips. "Don't want no doctor."

"I know one who'll come out here," Bernie said.

He did? I waited to find out who.

"Yeah?" said Rita.

"Rita!" said Jordan. "For god's sake!"

83

"But you're hurt," Rita said.

"Bullshit!" Jordan yelled. Then he groaned again and his slit eye almost closed. The swollen lid quivered and he kept that eye on Bernie, its gaze dull and damp.

Bernie, still sitting on the bed, gave Jordan a very light shoulder pat. A wincey sort of look rose on Jordan's face and then vanished when he realized that it really was a very light shoulder pat, not hurting at all. Lots of perps — hey! maybe even most! — aren't tough guys. Jordan was in that group.

"Not hurt, maybe," Bernie said, "but a little nicked up."

Jordan thought about that. "Yeah, nicked up," he said.

"Who did the nicking?" said Bernie.

"Huh?"

"Who," said Bernie, making a little gesture toward Jordan's face, "did this to you?"

"I ran into, um, a telephone pole."

"Yeah? Where was this?"

"It was dark. I couldn't see."

"Where did you go after our little encounter in the parking lot?"

Even though Jordan's face was pretty beat up, it now got a look on it that reminded me of . . . of a fox! Yes! Jordan was the foxish type. The fox and human mix never turned out good. I ramped up to high alert. "It was

84

still dark," Jordan said. "So I still couldn't see."

Bernie laughed, a soft laugh he has when he's enjoying himself.

"What's funny?" Rita said.

Exactly my own thought! I took another look at her feet. I was starting to like Rita, had almost forgotten the not-so-friendly way she'd welcomed us.

"Nothing," Bernie said. "Well, maybe just life itself, and its little details."

"Huh?" said Jordan again.

"Little details like the fact that when last seen by us you were pantless. Pantless and a hundred miles from here. So what happened in between?"

Jordan and Rita exchanged a quick look, her two big blue eyes meeting his one open eye, moist and slitty. Rita turned to Bernie.

"If you're not a cop, what are you?"

"Just someone trying to understand," Bernie said.

Wow! Had I ever heard anything so important? I made another mental note: never forget what Bernie had just said, never ever, the thing about being someone who . . . who . . .

"Here's a recent problem, Rita," Bernie was saying. "First, Jordan makes off with one hundred dollars that doesn't belong to him. Second, the rightful owner of the money arranges the repair of Jordan's ride, damaged in the course of the theft. Third, someone beats the crap out of him." Bernie spread his hands. "What's the explanation?"

Jordan's and Rita's gazes met again. Neither spoke.

"A Christ-like level of forgiveness," Bernie said, "but I didn't spot *him* at the Crowbar."

Jordan and Rita remained silent, which was what perps were supposed to do but hardly ever did.

Bernie looked down at Jordan, then across the bed at Rita. "You two married?" he said.

No response from Jordan, but Rita shook her head, just a tiny movement.

"Me neither," said Bernie. "At the moment." He rose, went to the window, and stared out. For an instant or two I had the craziest feeling that his eyes were about to tear up. But they did not. That was Bernie, of course, not a crier — and besides, what was there to tear up about? We were back at work, kicking ass and taking names, except for the kicking ass part. I went over the names: Rita and Jordan. Did I have those names down pat or what? Chet the Jet! In the picture!

Bernie turned. "What's your last name, Jordan?"

"None of your goddamn business," Jordan said.

"Sure it is," said Bernie. "That was my C-note in the beginning."

Rita frowned. "You want it back? Is that what this is about?"

Bernie shook his head. "I already told you what it's about."

"That bullshit about understanding?" said Jordan.

"Not everything's understandable," Rita said.

Bernie's eyebrows rose. Have I mentioned his eyebrows already? The farthest thing from those thin and patchy eyebrows you see on lots of humans. And Bernie's had a language of their own. Right now they were telling Rita she had his full attention.

"Where'd you hear that?" he said.

"In a class."

"You're in college?"

"I was."

"Where?"

"Rita!" Jordan tried to shout. His voice broke and ended up soft and raspy, but still real angry. "Shut up!"

Rita closed her mouth.

"You may be right, Rita," Bernie said. "But in the end it makes no difference in how you've got to live. Did your professor mention that?"

Rita didn't speak, although I got the feeling she wanted to. Bernie glanced around the room. His gaze fell on a wallet sitting on the dresser. He went over and picked it up.

"Didn't I tell you it was bullshit?" Jordan said, his voice now even raspier. "It's always about the money."

Bernie opened the wallet, took out a driver's license, read out loud. "Jordan Wells, 299 Bluff Street, Phantom Springs." He replaced the license, put the wallet back down on the dresser, then approached the bed and looked down at Jordan. "Here's some free advice, Jordan — listen to Rita."

"Huh?" he said, his voice mostly rasps and escaping air. "About what?"

"Everything," Bernie said. He made a little click click in his mouth, meaning *hit the road.* I love that click click — what's better than hitting the road?

We were in the car and on the move before I remembered I hadn't given Rita's feet that quick lick I'd been looking forward to. Even after I'd made a mental note! That bothered me all the way down those switchbacks. And then it hit me that I'd also forgotten to circle back to the messy kitchen. Had this visit been a complete failure? Whoa! Don't tell me my mind wanted to go there of all places! Whose side was it on?

89

me my aunt wanted to go there at all places! Whose idea was it one

SEVEN

We drove down the mountain and into town. Phantom Springs? Was that it? First came one of those enormous holes you see sometimes in the desert, holes surrounded by orange and brown slag heaps which was all the stuff that had been dug out of the hole except for whatever the miners had been digging for, like gold or silver or copper. Or something like that. Bernie had explained all this to Charlie for a class project. Had Charlie wanted to do something else, perhaps the gunfight at the OK Corral? But Bernie had talked him into desert mines. Was C-minus-minus a good result? Had to be. Charlie was a top student — he'd just started all-day school and they already had him in the very first grade.

After the hole and the slag heaps came a brick school with school buses parked on one side and a baseball diamond on the other. Lots of days aren't school days and

90

this felt like one of them, no kids to be seen or heard, no one going in or coming out. Too bad. What's better than a bunch of kids running wild?

We slowed down, slowed down kind of slowly, like Bernie wasn't sure about slowing down. But then he pulled over and parked by the backstop. He reached under his seat, felt around, and pulled out a tennis ball. Not just any tennis ball, of course, but one of mine. All the tennis balls found in the Porsche, or at our place on Mesquite Road, inside or out, including all the other houses in all directions, are mine. As well as all other tennis balls I see first, plus ones I see second and possibly even later. In short, tennis balls are mine. But I'm always happy to share. Or at least I'll do it. Especially if a treat is involved. Maybe only if a treat's involved. And not for long. Got to be true to yourself — you hear that all the time.

"What do you say to a little fetch?" Bernie said.

Is there more than one answer to that? Fetch is a great human invention, probably their best. And fetch with Bernie doing the throwing is the best of the best. Have I mentioned that Bernie pitched at West Point, might have gone pro if he hadn't blown out his arm? But now even with a

91

blown-out arm he can throw tennis balls so far they turn into tiny yellow dots.

We stood by home plate — I know all the baseball lingo although the actual game is a complete mystery to me — and Bernie tossed the ball from one hand to another. He got a strange look on his face, almost like he was angry. Was there anything to be angry about? Not that I knew of. Were we getting this show on the road or not?

Bernie glanced down at me — well, not exactly down, since we seemed to be face-to-face, my paws somehow on his shoulders.

"You're right," he said.

About what? I was trying to figure that out when Bernie stepped away, reared back, and let fly. What an amazing throw — a frozen rope, as we say in baseball — right over the diamond, over the pretty-much-grassless outfield, the color of those slag heaps, and all the way to the fence without a single bounce. Wow! The ball hit the fence, bounced off, hit the ground, bounced again, and then I snagged it and zoomed back to Bernie, dropping it at his feet.

"Good grief, Chet. Are you getting faster?"

Sure! Why not?

After that we settled into a more normal game of fetch, although much longer than usual — what a fun day! — Bernie throwing grounders, flies, one hoppers, two hoppers, but not another one all the way to the fence. When it was over — Bernie always tosses the last one into the car — he rubbed his elbow and took a long breath.

"Married the wrong woman," he said quietly. "And then when the right one came along . . ."

I waited for more — and could feel more going on inside him, which was where it stayed. Bernie's face was all sweaty — a lot sweatier than normal after fetch — but he no longer looked angry. He started the car. I nosed the tennis ball under the seat for next time — soon, I hoped! — and sat up straight and tall.

We drove along the main street of Phantom Springs, past some stone buildings. Nice stone buildings, but with some cracked windows.

"Has there ever been a boomtown that made a comeback?" Bernie said. "What about a whole boom country?"

I searched my mind for an answer, a very rapid search since I had no clue what he was talking about. The stone buildings gave way to brick ones and finally wood. We turned onto a narrower street, sloping up into shabbier territory. Wind chimes chimed on just about every porch on this street and the cars had lots of bumper stickers.

"Two ninety-nine Bluff Street," Bernie said, pulling over in front of a yellow house with faded flowers painted on the door. "Still some original hippies living up here."

Hippies? We sometimes ran across hippies in our line of work, although not recently. I had no problem with hippies. They did a lot of yawning, gave off interesting smells, and were at their best when they got the munchies.

We walked up to the yellow house. Bernie raised his hand to knock on the door, but before he could it opened and a very big dude in a business suit came out, as wide as Shermie but taller. Also his face was very different, not mashed up or scarred, the skin smooth, like he took real good care of it. I had a strange thought: this is the kind of dude who does the mashing and the scarring.

He stopped dead, stared down at us. We stared up at him.

"Looking for someone?" he said.

"You live here?" said Bernie.

"You always answer a question with a question?" the big dude said.

"Why do you ask?" said Bernie.

The big dude smiled. "Sense of humor —
I like that." He looked past us, his gaze settling on the Porsche. Then he turned, closed
the door, made sure it was locked, all his
movements unhurried and relaxed. "Have a
nice day," he said, stepped carefully around
us — a much lighter-on-his-feet type of big
guy than Shermie — and started walking
up the street, trailing a hair-gel aroma, but
not nearly as strong as some you come
across, plus a faint scent of baby powder.
We stayed where we were. The dude disappeared around a curve at the top of the
hill. I heard a car door open and close, and
then an engine starting. Did Bernie hear
that, too?

"We'll catch the plate number as he comes
back down."

Meaning he did hear it! Good for Bernie!
I was proud of him, even though the engine
sound was now fading and fading, meaning
the big dude was driving off in another
direction.

"What's keeping him?" Bernie said after a
while. "Google shows Bluff Street dead-
ending at the top."

I tried to make sense of that, but not for
long. Finally Bernie turned to the door and
knocked. No answer from inside. He rattled
the handle.

"Smell anything in there, big guy? Something I should know about?"

Should he know about pizza? A toilet that needed flushing? A mouse issue? I wondered about all that as we started walking around the house. Bernie tried peering in windows, but all the shades were drawn. Around the back was a gully with one tiny puddle at the bottom, plus a busted-up fridge, a lawn chair or two, and lots of broken bottles. We went to the back door, much more flimsy than the front one, which was often the case. At the Little Detective Agency we have lots of ways of getting past flimsy doors. Bernie kicking them in is my favorite, but this time we got by with the credit card trick.

Bernie opened the door all the way, so that it pressed against the back wall, which we always do in case some perp inside is trying the hiding-behind-the-door-with-a-tire-iron trick. We know all the tricks, in case you're not clear on that yet. Also we're available for hire, especially if you don't have divorce work in mind.

We went inside with — after a moment of confusion in the doorway — me in the lead. When a place has been trashed you know it right away: overturned dressers, slashed mattresses, everything all over the place. We stepped carefully from room to room, ended up in the smaller of the two bedrooms.

"What was he looking for?" Bernie said. "And did he find it?"

I had no answers, didn't even know who "he" was. Bernie gazed at the walls. They were hung with posters, all of them showing a blond woman, usually dressed like a cowgirl, sometimes standing before a mic, sometimes playing a guitar. I came very close to recognizing her!

"Old Lotty Pilgrim concert posters," Bernie said.

Of course! And I'd practically gotten there by myself. My mind wasn't quite on fire, but almost. I was having a very good day.

Bernie bent down, picked a framed picture off the floor, set it on the desk. The glass cover was cracked, but I could make out the people in the photo. I knew two of them: Lotty and Jordan. They were standing side by side and smiling at the camera, Lotty with her guitar over her shoulder. There was another person in the picture, a woman in denim with a big head of curly black hair, not smiling.

"Jordan's a big fan," Bernie said. He tapped the face of the unsmiling woman in denim. "And who would she be?"

We went into the front hall. A sheet of paper was tacked to the door. Bernie read what was on it. "This was a courtesy call. Sorry I missed you."

What was a courtesy call? Who got missed? I waited to find out, but Bernie didn't say. Did he know? Was it important? I don't ask myself questions like that. And even if I did, it wouldn't be now, not with someone in squeaky sneakers — a man, actually, the walking-man sound being very different from the walking-woman sound, in case you've somehow missed that — coming up the path to the front door. I went still, on high alert. Bernie looked my way immediately, and went still himself.

The man halted outside the door. Then through the narrow slot came a wad of mail, plopping onto the floor. The footsteps went away. Bernie picked up the mail, riffled through it, dropped all but one letter onto a small table. "From the Arizona Department of Public Safety," he said. "Why would they be writing to Jordan?" He tapped the envelope against his hand a few times, gazed at it for a moment or two, held it up to the light, squinted at it — and finally tore the thing open.

Bernie took out the papers inside, unfolded them. "Application for a private investigator's license," he said. "What does Jordan want to investigate?" He refolded the papers, laid them on the table. "How about we ask him?"

What a great idea! I was so excited by Bernie's brilliance that I almost forgot about that pizza.

"Chet? Where you going?"

Nowhere. No place at all. Don't bother looking at me. I trotted into the kitchen — a trot very close to a run, but not quite, a run attracting too much attention at a time like this — and located the pizza box on the counter, snapping up the only remaining slice. Sausage and pepperoni, my favorite. I trotted back into the hall, all set for work, a total pro.

"What were you up to?" Bernie said.

Nothing. Zip. Nada. I gulped down the last of the pizza. We hit the road, although not for long, stopping at the top of the hill, where the pavement ended. But a sort of road kept going, narrow and rough, hardly even a track. It zigzagged down and down, finally meeting a highway in the distance.

"He didn't want us to see that plate, big guy," Bernie said.

Whoa! Did that mean somebody had put one over on us? I wondered who that might be.

Sometimes you don't know how hungry you

are until you happen to down a little snack, say a leftover pizza slice, of no interest to anyone. And then it hits you: you're starving! And there's no more pizza, no food of any kind, except for a single Slim Jim in the glove box, giving off the most powerful smell you've ever smelled.

"For god's sake, Chet! What's all the racket?"

Racket? I listened my hardest, heard nothing but the lovely rumble of the Porsche, and possibly a distant echo of something that might have been barking, but possibly not.

"Hungry? Is that it?"

Why, yes, yes indeed. On the same page at last! Bernie gave me a look. I gave him a look back. Then he popped open the glove box and the Slim Jim was mine. Well, it had always been mine, of course. It was just that now I . . . possessed it. Was that the expression? Possessing Slim Jims was one of those things that made life such a joy.

We drove back to the edge of town, then up those switchbacks on Old Gila Road to the faded blue house at the top. This time Rita didn't come out with a shotgun. She didn't come out at all. We went to the door. Bernie knocked. No answer. If anyone was home, they were making no sounds and giving off no smells. Did that mean the case was going well? Not well? Was this a case at all? Who was paying? Us? Had we some-how . . . paid ourselves with that C-note? Would that be a good business plan? What was our business plan, again? I had a faint memory of a discussion about that with our accountant, Ms. Pernick, but the details were gone.

EIGHT

We swung by the Crowbar on the way home. No cars in the lot. Shermie was outside, hosing down the front steps.

"Hey, guys," he said. "Don't open till four, but I can grab you a cold one outta the cooler."

"That's all right," Bernie said. He made one of those chin gestures — one of many human things I love to see, like snot rockets which I may have mentioned already, although not as surprising — at the hose.

"Washin' off the puke," Shermie said. "Comes with the territory."

"Speaking of the territory, it's only got the one aquifer," Bernie said.

"Huh?"

Bernie explained about the aquifer. I'd heard this many times, didn't really listen. Instead I watched Shermie's face. Was he getting the aquifer thing or not? I couldn't tell, but his lumpy, eyes-too-close-together sort of face was starting to grow on me, hard to explain why.

"But here's the thing," Shermie said when Bernie was done. "Nobody likes the smell of puke."

Was that true? Certain pukey smells aren't bad at all, in my opinion. Once we'd taken Charlie to the county fair and caught the end of the hot dog eating contest. Why they're called hot dogs when they're clearly sausage is a bothersome mystery, but forget about that. The point is the end of the hot dog eating contest, which was all about a bunch of dudes puking — not all at once, but sort of one after another, like . . . like it was a catchy idea. They did their puking offstage, in and around buckets. In some way I can't quite recall, I managed to . . . how would you put it? Corral, maybe? I'd managed to corral one of those buckets for an all-too-short period of time. I still remember the smell: complex and fascinating. Plus there were pretty much whole hot dogs in that bucket, hardly chewed on at all. That was when I realized I didn't understand hot dog eating contests. And wanted to see another one right away.

When I tuned back in, Bernie and Shermie had moved on from puke and aquifers.

"What time does Lotty get here?" Bernie

was saying.

Shermie shook his head. "She was one night only."

"Where is she tonight?"

Shermie got out his phone, tapped at it for a while. "She's off tonight. Next show's at the Junction in Lubbock, Texas, two weeks from tomorrow."

"I'd like to get in touch with her."

Shermie didn't reply, maybe because he was drinking from the hose. Even though I wasn't at all thirsty, I wanted to do what he was doing, and very badly, although I'd never drunk from the end of a hose and had no idea how to manage it, what with the water shooting so fast out the end. But could it hurt to try?

"Shermie?"

Shermie looked up, water dripping off his chin.

"You heard me," Bernie said. His voice was nice and quiet, even soft. For some reason, that often caught the attention of certain dudes, especially ones who'd been on the end of that sweet uppercut.

"Um," Shermie said. He turned a tap. The water stopped pouring out of the hose. "Is this about last night?"

"Got it on the first guess," Bernie said.

Shermie gazed down at the end of the

hose. A last drop dribbled out. "What about last night?"

"Shermie? Don't overthink — anyone ever told you that?"

"Nope. What's it mean?"

"It means don't let your mind twist itself in knots."

"That's never happened to me, Bernie."

"You're a lucky guy."

"Yeah?" Shermie beamed. "Never thought of myself that way."

"Now you can," Bernie said. "So what's the answer?"

Shermie blinked. "To what?"

"How to get in touch with Lotty Pilgrim."

Shermie's forehead started to furrow, but then it smoothed out. "Hey! Almost over-thunk right there."

"Good catch," said Bernie. "Remember — curiosity killed the cat."

Excuse me? Had I ever heard something so important? Why was I just finding out about it now? Question after question came tumbling into my mind. What was curiosity exactly? And how could I use it the next time a cat entered my life? Cats had entered my life more than once, never with good results. Here's the thing about cats entering your life: by the time you realize it's happened, they've already been there for a while.

I glanced around. We seemed to have moved inside the Crowbar, in fact into a small office near the front. Shermie opened a desk drawer, shuffled through some papers, handed one to Bernie. Bernie took a look at it, handed it back.

"Don't want to write it down?" Shermie said.

Bernie shook his head.

"You memorized it?"

Bernie shrugged.

"How?" said Shermie.

"I don't understand."

"How do you do that? Memorize written-down stuff?"

Bernie's eyes got an inward look. "I've never thought about it."

"Like it just happens?"

"I guess so."

"You're a lucky guy, too, Bernie," Shermie said.

Bernie was quiet for a moment. Then he said, "I know." And gave me a pat, not a long one, but very nice all the same.

"Dolly Parton has Dollywood," Bernie said, as we followed a long dirt drive to what looked like a little ranch house at the end.

But no cattle around? No horses? No sheep? All of them interesting to pal around with, at least for a while. What kind of ranch was this?

We parked in front of the house, actually kind of nice from close up, not so different from our own place, but smaller. Pink flowers that smelled like Suzie's perfume — I missed her! — grew on both sides of the door, and piano sounds came from inside, starting, stopping, starting up again.

We stood outside, but Bernie didn't knock. Instead he cocked his ear. I do the same thing — don't forget we're a lot alike in some ways — but only to pick up sounds from far far away. What we were hearing now came from inside the house, or actually just behind it: the piano, then Lotty sort of half-singing, and after that the piano again.

I turned and started around the house. Bernie didn't say, "Chet?" Or, "Where you going, big guy?" He just followed. We're a team, me and Bernie, and a real, real good one. If you're a perp, we'll find you. If not, you've got nothing to worry about. But feel free to come say hi. A treat would be nice.

More piano. Then Lotty half-sang, ". . . lonesome road that brought me . . ." She paused, began again: ". . . lonely road that took me here, to . . ." I felt Bernie go still, so I went still, too. When Bernie gets really interested in something, a look comes over his face that makes him much younger, actually reminding me of Charlie. That was the look I saw now.

". . . to," Lotty took up the half-singing again, "to anybody . . ." She grunted, muttered something I couldn't make out, then went on. "Not just to anybody, but . . . but anybody except for you." The sound of the piano rose higher and her voice strengthened with it. "I ended up on / this lonely road / that took me here / to not just anybody / but anybody else / from you, ol' darlin'." She went silent.

We walked around the house. There was a little patio at the back, partly shaded by an overhang from the roof, and in the shade of that overhang stood a piano, the upright kind. Lotty, wearing a bathrobe, sat before it, writing on a pink sheet of paper, glasses on the end of her nose, and a cigarette between her lips. Bernie started clapping.

Lotty looked up, startled. She lost her balance, for a moment seemed about to topple off the piano stool.

Bernie raised his hands, palms up, sometimes the signal for don't shoot, although probably not now.

"Didn't mean to scare you," he said.

"Well, you did." Lotty took off her glasses and gave him a close look. "The big tipper from last night."

"First time I've been called that," Bernie said.

"It's a compliment," Lotty said. She glanced at me. "Chet, right?"

"Right," said Bernie.

"He's a stunner."

Bernie cleared his throat. "I'm Bernie."

"I remember."

"Great show last night."

"Thanks," said Lotty. "But I get alarmed when fans show up unexpectedly."

"I'm sorry about that. Doubly so since you were composing."

Lotty stubbed out her cigarette. "That's a fancy-pants word for what I do."

"What would you call it?"

Lotty shrugged. "Just fiddling around."

"How come you didn't play the piano on your records? You're really good."

"Far from it. The piano's set up for right handers and my right hand's a slug."

That was strange. I knew slugs from several gardens I'd . . . explored, you might say, and they looked nothing like Lotty's hands, quite nice hands, in fact, although not in Bernie's league.

". . . wondering why you changed 'lonesome' to 'lonely'?" Bernie was saying.

"You're the snoopy type."

"True."

"Why do you want to know?"

"Just curious."

"You know what they say about curiosity."

I sure did! It couldn't have been fresher in my mind. I took a quick sniff: no cats on the premises, but I remained on high alert, in the picture as never before.

Lotty picked up the pink sheet she'd been writing on, stuck the glasses back on the end of her nose. "Hard to say," she said. "These things just happen. I get —" She looked up, met Bernie's gaze. "— a sort of warning bell that something's not quite right."

"So you got a warning bell about 'lonesome'?"

Lotty nodded.

"It seems more . . . poetic to me," Bernie said. "Speaking as an outsider."

"An outsider to what?" said Lotty. "Human emotion?"

Bernie laughed, just one short burst, not too distant from a bark. Did I love hearing that or what?

Lotty smiled, seemed to relax a little. "You're right about that — Bernie, was it?"

110

"Yes."

" 'Lonesome' is more poetic. And also what you'd expect in country music. So that's your answer."

"Thanks."

"Any other questions?"

"Two," said Bernie. "In no particular order, first — why would you arrange the car repair for the tip jar thief? Second, why don't you sing 'How You Hung the Moon' anymore?"

Lotty went still. She'd been starting to sound friendly, like they were having a nice chitchat, but now that was all gone. "Who are you?" she said.

"I'm a fan of your music."

Lotty batted that away with the back of her hand.

"And also a private investigator," Bernie said.

Her eyes widened and she shrank back a bit. Humans sometimes do that when they're scared, although not always. But their smell changes every time — sharpening in a somewhat oniony and not unpleasant way, as Lotty's did now.

"Working for who?" she said.

"Nobody," said Bernie.

"Then those two questions — who are you asking them for?"

111

"Myself."

"Why?" Lotty rose. "What the hell are you doing here?" She stabbed her papers at Bernie, like they were some sort of weapon.

"Offering my help," Bernie said.

"I don't need help from you or anyone else. Please leave."

That seemed strange to me, on account of how Lotty was shaking. The sun came out and shone down on her. She wasn't wearing makeup and all the lines on her face were suddenly visible. For some reason, that made me like her face better, and I already liked it a lot.

"Here's my card, just in case." Bernie stepped up, put it on the piano.

"Just go," said Lotty.

My tail started wagging, like . . . like it was trying to change her mind? Something like that. My tail has a mind of its own, sometimes even gets ahead of me. For example, it knew we needed a client. I agreed. Where else does the money come from in this business?

Lotty gazed at me, and the angry, scared look in her eyes softened a bit.

"Are you afraid of someone?" Bernie said.

"You," said Lotty.

"You've got nothing to fear from us," Bernie said.

112

She didn't answer for what seemed like a long time. Then, looking over Bernie's shoulder and into the distance, she said, "So long."

We went. My takeaway? Lotty was a big fan of mine, but maybe not of Bernie. She'd have to get to know him better.

NINE

We drove down the dusty road from Lotty's ranch. No horses, no cattle, no sheep. Not even a pig! Probably a good thing, the pig part. I'd once found myself alone in a barn with a pig. A locked barn, shouldn't leave that out. Plus this particular pig was very large, had long, sharp tusks, and possibly hadn't enjoyed a good meal in some time. At one point in our encounter, I got the strange idea — just from a certain way of grunting he had, but it made an impression on me — that he wanted to make a meal of . . . well, I'd rather not go there. I was happy to see that Lotty had no pigs. Let's leave it at that.

Bernie gazed at Lotty's fence as we passed by, many of the posts leaning and some down flat. "I just don't get it," Bernie said. "Looks like what they call rural poverty, but —"

The phone buzzed.

"Hello," Bernie said.

"Hi, Dad!" Charlie's voice came through the speakers. "Is it true? You're out of the hospital?"

"Couldn't be truer. I was going to come see you today."

"Can you come right away?"

Bernie's eyes got misty. You didn't see that very often. Also his voice got choked up, and that was a first. "Of course," he said.

"Whew," said Charlie. "I have to do a project for Ms. Minoso."

"She's your teacher?" said Bernie, no longer choked-up although still a bit misty-eyed, and also surprised. Something seemed to be going on inside him, but who could keep up with whatever it was?

"Of course, Dad! Jeez."

"What happened to Ms. Peoples?"

"She met a rich guy online and moved to Florida."

Bernie grinned. How happy he looked, those other looks now gone! "What's the project about?"

"Aquifers."

"Yeah?" Now he was beaming, his eyes on the road, but maybe not really seeing, because he didn't seem at all interested in a car coming the other way, meaning I didn't think he noticed the driver peering our way and looking not a bit happy to see us. The driver was Clint Swann, Lotty's . . . manager, was it? Boyfriend? I'd never gotten that clear. I turned to watch as he sped toward the ranch, his car disappearing in a dust cloud.

"Mom says you're the go-to guy."

"She does?"

"Only for aquifers."

"Good enough," Bernie said. "When's it due?"

"What's 'due'?"

"When you have to hand it in."

"Yesterday."

"Oh?"

"But I got an extension."

"How'd you do that?"

"I said can I have an extension."

"Nice. Till when?"

"Tomorrow."

"We're on our way."

I looked back again. The dust had settled. Far in the distance I could see the ranch house, a tiny squarish shape, and a metallic glare, maybe off the windshield of a car parked in front.

Leda and Charlie — plus Malcolm, the new husband, with the very long toes — live in High Chaparral Estates, maybe the fanciest part of the whole Valley, although not the nicest. Mesquite Road is the nicest, in case I haven't made that clear already. Charlie came running outside the moment we pulled into the drive. Sometimes — not nearly often enough, in my opinion — humans go out of their minds with joy. Hard to think of a better sight, especially when the human involved is still a kid. So the next moment, with Charlie in Bernie's arms getting hugged and hugged — both of them out of their minds in the best way — was very nice to see. I was just about to hop out of the car and get involved myself when flying out the open front door came . . . well, maybe I'd better back up a little.

But that turns out to be hard to do! Backing up and organizing a whole lot of — what would you call them? Facts? Bernie often talks about facts and I love listening, but the fact is I'm not sure what he means by facts. So right now all I can pass on to you is that running after Charlie was what still might be called a puppy, although now somewhat sizable, especially his paws. This puppy — Shooter, by name — and I went way back, even . . . even before there was a Shooter, as I had heard more than once. Also I'd heard more than once that Shooter was the spitting image of me. The spitting part confuses me, since we don't do that in the nation within. We're kind of like women in that respect. But the point is that Shooter had turned up in our neighborhood — of all possible neighborhoods! — and after a lot of events not so easy to remember, he ended up here with Charlie in this McMansion, except for the Mc part, as Malcolm always says. I think it's a joke of some kind, since he always laughs when he says it. No one else does, except for Leda, and maybe she's not laughing quite as hard as she used to. But don't trust me on things like that. Especially now, when I no longer seemed to be in the car. Instead I was on Leda's beautiful lawn, soft and green, joining in on all the running. Not that I was touching the lawn, except for when I was making my cuts. I was zooming along at pretty much my fastest, meaning my paws were hardly touching down. Was Charlie part of all this running? Perhaps not. I caught a glimpse of him over by the car, still hugging Bernie. But Shooter was a different matter. He was running, and not just running, but streaking right beside me, cut for cut! I bumped him! He bumped me! I bumped him good and hard so he'd stay bumped. And what was this? Shooter bumped me right back, the exact same kind of staying-bumped bump I'd just laid on him? Who did he think he was? I bumped him a bump that sent him flying and then tore around the house to the backyard, a lovely big yard with more lawn, flowers, bushes, trees, an outdoor kitchen, a fire pit, a swimming pool, and lots of other fun stuff.

But it was the swimming pool that reminded me of why we were here. Wasn't it all about the aquifer? Funny how the mind works. As I maybe mentioned already, I'd once seen the aquifer, a tiny puddle way down at the bottom of a construction site. That gave me an idea — one of my very best! — and the next thing I knew I was digging. Not that casual sort of front-paws digging, but all-out, all-paws digging, pedal to the metal. Digging didn't even describe what I was up to. This was excavating! I was excavating this — flower-bed, was it? — to get down to the aquifer, no matter how deep. Hard work, sure, but all for Charlie, so I loved doing it. Well, I already loved doing it, but because of Charlie I loved it even more! I was so full of love that when I happened to glance over and notice Shooter at my side, excavating away at full blast, enormous clods of earth flying high into the sky — what a fine digger he turned out to be! — I didn't mind a bit. The truth was at that moment I loved him, too. What a world! We dug and dug, digging ourselves deeper and deeper into the —

Leda has this scream, so piercing it's hard to believe a human can do it. I hadn't heard that scream in a nice, long time, but I thought I sort of heard it now.

After that came a calm interlude where Shooter got removed to the house and I sat like a very good boy while Bernie rolled up his sleeves and shoveled earth back into the hole. Malcolm stood nearby, saying, "Bernie. Please. I have people for that." Which only made Bernie work that shovel faster and faster.

"If you don't mind just smoothing that little section where the orchids were," Malcolm said when it was over. Is it easy to smooth earth with rough jabs of the shovel? Probably not, but Bernie managed. My Bernie!

"What we'll do," Bernie said, back in our kitchen on Mesquite Road and rooting through drawers, "is make a three-dimensional model."

"What's three-dimensional?" Charlie said.

"Well," Bernie said, "think of a box." He made a shape with his hands. "Length, width, height. Interestingly enough, Einstein —" He paused, looked at Charlie more closely. "When was your last haircut?"

Charlie shrugged. "Couple of days ago?"

"He didn't take much off."

"She," said Charlie. "Ambrosia. Her and Mom like it long."

"And you? How do you like it?"

"I don't know," Charlie said. "How do you like yours?"

"Hmm," said Bernie. "I don't think much about it."

"Same," said Charlie.

Bernie smiled, a tiny smile, here and gone, but one of his best. "Okay — where were we?"

"The bagel guy," Charlie said.

"Bagel guy?"

"Einstein."

"How about we skip that part?"

"Sure," said Charlie. "Got any snacks?"

"In the cupboard. Help yourself."

Charlie helped himself to snacks. He helped myself to snacks, too. Plus I myself helped myself to some of his snacks. Bernie, busy with all sorts of materials — colored pencils, papier-mâché, scissors, even for a while the blowtorch from the garage — didn't have time for snacks. We got that project done, baby! What a team!

■ ■ ■ ■

"You talked about the aquifer," said Dr. Bethea, who used to be called Doc and was now Eliza, if I'd been following things right. We were at one of the picnic benches out back of Max's Memphis Ribs, Bernie and Eliza sitting across from each other, and me perhaps closer to the smoker by the wall, where Cleon Maxwell was laying down another row of ribs. Cleon's an expert chef, but even the best can slip up sometimes, for example by accidentally dropping a rib or two on the deck.

"In the hospital?" Bernie was saying.

"Especially after you first came to," Eliza said.

"I don't remember."

"That's not uncommon. Although the aquifer subject at a time like that was a new one on me."

"What does it mean?" Bernie said.

"I couldn't tell you."

The waitress came with beer for them and water for me. They clinked glasses.

"But here's to mystery in life," Eliza said.

"Within limits," said Bernie.

Eliza laughed, just at the moment she was taking a sip, giving herself one of those foam mustaches. She licked it off. That caught Bernie's attention for some reason.

"Charlie's a great kid," she said.

"Thanks."

"There was some discussion, also especially in the early days, about whether he'd be allowed to come see you."

"I didn't know that."

"Leda was against it. So was Suzie. Malcolm got them to change their minds."

"Malcolm?"

Eliza nodded.

"I don't remember much about his visits," Bernie said. "Actually nothing."

"Charlie came twice. The first time you were asleep and he stood in the doorway and looked at you, but wouldn't come in. You were asleep the second time, too. That second time — you were off the ventilator by then — he came up to the bed and said, 'Dad? Are you asleep?' Your eyes stayed closed but you said, 'Sit on the fastball.' Charlie said, 'It's T-ball, Dad. There's no pitching.' You didn't say anything. This is according to Suzie — I wasn't there. You just smiled. A tiny smile she said, there and gone, but she was sure of it."

Bernie stared into his glass. There was only beer to see — not a particularly interesting sight, in my opinion — but it held

Bernie's attention for what seemed like a longish time.

"How is Suzie?" Eliza said at last.

"Good," said Bernie, looking up. "As far as I know. We're not together anymore."

"She told me that might happen."

"She did?"

"I wouldn't be here otherwise." Eliza looked Bernie in the eye. "These are the basics: I'm divorced — once — no kids, very picky, and come from a family of long-lived folks."

Bernie held her gaze. "Anything else I need to know?"

Eliza gave him a look I've never understood, where one eye closes a bit and the other doesn't. Does it mean *Easy there, podner*? That was my best — and only — guess. "Want, maybe," Eliza said, "but not need."

"You're not the close-to-the-vest type," Bernie said.

"Not when it comes to the important things," Eliza said. "What's the point?"

"It's an occupational hazard in my line."

Eliza thought about that. "Tell me more about your line."

"What do you want to know?"

"Everything," Eliza said. "Especially the part where personal courage comes in."

Bernie grunted. Eliza waited for him to go

124

on but he didn't. He never does after a grunt like that.

"Your friends all mentioned it," Eliza said. "Your bravery."

"What friends?"

"Sergeant Torres. Captain Stine. An odd character named Otis DeWayne who made a fuss about leaving his weapon at security. A number of odd characters, in fact. One — I didn't catch his name — might have just escaped from Central State Correctional, if I understood him properly."

"Putting you on, most likely," Bernie said. "They all were, about the so-called — about that other part. My job's more like yours — following a trail of symptoms to the guilty diagnosis."

Eliza laughed.

"What's the joke?"

"No joke. It's just that I haven't had this much fun in ages."

"Um," said Bernie. He raised his glass. "Well, then, here's to —"

What was coming next? Here's to more and more treats? Here's to fetch forever? I never found out what. Not because Cleon slipped up with the spareribs. None of the ribs even came close to getting loose before he had them all arranged and closed the big lid on the smoker. But at that exact moment, Bernie's phone buzzed, and he took it out of his pocket and gave it a glance, the kind of glance that meant this was an annoyance and he wouldn't even take the call.

Except he did take the call. "Hello? Lotty? I can hardly — Lotty?"

He rose. "Sorry, Eliza."

"You're leaving?"

"I . . . ah . . ."

Some surprises are happy, some not. This was the unhappy kind: I could see that all over Eliza's face. I had a very good viewing angle because by then I was in my place beside Bernie, ready for anything.

"Right now?" Eliza said.

"Afraid so."

She took a long look at Bernie. Her mouth opened and closed. And opened again. "And Lotty is . . . ?"

"A client. Sort of."

"Sort of."

Bernie laid some money on the table.

"That won't be necessary," said Eliza. Somewhere down the street a door closed.

TEN

Once we raced Zippo Zatarian, the best wheelman in the Valley, up and down the Sagebrush Mountain switchbacks for no reason. The way Bernie was driving after we left Max's Memphis Ribs reminded me of that day, although then he'd been laughing most of the way — *No reason's the best reason, big guy!* — and now he wasn't laughing at all. Did that mean we were about to win nothing again? I sat up my tallest, in a very good mood, and I'd been in a very good mood already.

We fishtailed off a stretch of two-lane blacktop and onto a narrow dirt road, almost a track. "Should save us time," Bernie said. "I didn't like the sound of her voice, not one little bit."

Whose voice might that have been? Eliza's? I had a clear memory of her voice, could hear it in my head: an easy-on-the-ears kind of voice, but it had the hint of a

127

low throb that meant plenty of oomph in reserve. Who wouldn't like a voice like that? I gave Bernie a long look. Most dudes, when they're driving like this, meaning the motor is shrieking and the up-ahead view is piling in way too fast, tend to hunch forward and squeeze the wheel so tight you can see all the bones in their hands, but not Bernie. He was actually kind of sitting back, and his hands were loose on the wheel. That didn't mean he wasn't concentrating. I could feel his concentration, like the air just before lightning. Bottom line: we were doing great. The only problem was the lack of any other cars in sight. Did that mean we were racing nobody? For no reason? Human behavior sometimes has . . . how would you put it? Gaps? Yes, gaps. Human behavior sometimes has gaps in it, no offense.

We swung onto another dirt road, this one wider, with a falling-down fence on one side. That seemed familiar, and when we topped a slope and a small, square ranch house appeared not far away, I was suddenly in the picture, if the picture was about paying another call on Lotty. Fine with me. I liked Lotty, a big fan of Chet the Jet. Maybe that would mean a treat this time.

Bernie hit the brakes. We skidded to a stop in front of the ranch house and hopped out of the Porsche, me actually hopping and — and Bernie hopping, too! Or just about. We ran up to the front door, which was hanging open. Bernie halted and raised his hand. I froze and didn't make a sound.

"Lotty?" Bernie called. "Lotty?"

No answer.

"Lotty?"

Silence. Bernie glanced at me. "Hear anything?" he said in a low voice.

Well, of course, but not from inside the house. Smells? That was different. A tiny indoorsy breeze flowed through the doorway and it carried an important smell. When I pick up that particular smell I sit straight up, facing the direction the smell is coming from. Which is what I did now. Bernie pushed the door open. I like to be first when it comes to going through doorways, and almost always am — but not this time. Bernie put his hand on my neck, not heavily, just a touch. From Bernie and only Bernie, that was enough.

Everything was nice and tidy inside Lotty's ranch house. No dust on the living room coffee table, no towels on the bathroom floor, no dishes in the kitchen sink — not even any drying in the dish rack, just one lone knife, the big kind Bernie uses for carving the turkey on Thanksgiving. Normally just the thought of Thanksgiving turkey makes me want some, and if not turkey then anything at all, but that didn't happen this time, here in Lotty's quiet house.

We entered the bedroom at the end of the hall, me because I was following the smell I'd smelled from out front, Bernie — on account of the shortcomings of his nose — probably for other reasons, maybe that it was the only room left, for example.

Also nice and tidy, this bedroom. There was a dresser with one of those makeup mirrors — Leda had had one, although not Suzie — and a guitar stand with two guitars, and a window with a view of the piano out on the patio. Plus a big bed, all made up. Clint Swann lay there on his stomach like he was taking a nap, eyes closed, face toward us. He was fully clothed, even wore his snakeskin cowboy boots. Lots of humans napped in their clothes, but only drunks, in my experience, kept their boots on.

But booze wasn't the smell I was picking up. Booze is one of the easiest, by the way, so don't go fooling yourself on that score.

"Clint?" Bernie said. "Clint? Wake up. Where's Lotty?"

No answer from Clint. He just lay there. One of his cowboy boots was twisted to the side in a way that couldn't have been comfortable. Bernie seemed to notice that. His mood changed. I could feel it darkening within him.

"Clint?"

Bernie moved forward, leaned over Clint, gripped his shoulder, gave it a shake, not particularly gentle.

"Clint!"

Nothing from Clint.

Bernie rolled him over. Clint flopped in a loose, rag doll way. I'd had one experience with a rag doll, possibly belonging to the daughter of a rich dude from LA who didn't quite become our client, so I knew how rag dolls moved. But that's not the main point, the main point being what we saw when Clint was rolled over. Namely blood, which I'd been smelling from the get-go.

Blood is something you get familiar with in this line of work. I'd seen a lot more than this, and plenty of times. With Clint, we had a roundish red splotch on the bedspread, and a smaller one in the middle of his chest, both still a bit damp. His shirt — one of those western shirts you see a lot of in these parts, although not on Bernie, who prefers Hawaiian shirts, like the one with surfing coconuts that he wore today — had a small tear, short and narrow, where the blood had leaked out. Bernie put his finger on Clint's

131

neck, and shook his head. At that moment I heard a siren, distant but coming our way. Should I also mention that I picked up the tiniest aroma of hair gel? There. It's done.

Bernie reached into his back pocket, took out surgical gloves, and began opening one of Clint's hands, which was closed tight. Hey! I hadn't noticed that! What can you say about Bernie? Better than the best? Is that a thing?

But he never did get that hand open, instead went still, which had to mean he'd finally heard the siren. I gazed at his ears: they were doing the best they could.

Bernie straightened, took a careful look around the room, went to the closet. He stood there for a moment or two, then suddenly flung the door open, real quick.

There was no one in the closet, living or dead, which I already knew. Had Bernie known, too? In which case, why was he looking in the closet? He seemed to be interested in the clothes hanging on the rail, all of them cowgirl dresses of the fancy kind, with lots of fringe and sparkles. Why? I had no idea. The siren grew louder. Bernie closed the closet door.

We went back outside, Bernie pocketing the surgical gloves. A squad car, green and yellow with lights flashing on top and the

siren going BWAA BWAA — a horrible
noise I'd had to get used to in my job, but
still hated — pulled up. The siren did one
of those quick fades, like a screamer getting
choked — oh, what a terrible thought!
Where had that come from? And the driver
stepped out of the car.

He was a big old guy in uniform, a uniform that included a cowboy hat and a
sidearm on his hip. Some of the faces out in
the desert have seen lots of sun. This guy's
face was like that, leathery and sort of
saddle-colored. His bushy mustache looked
extra-white. He gave us a squinty-eyed look
and then his hand moved — the smooth,
sure movement of someone younger — and
rested on the butt of that sidearm.

"Name's Grimble," he said. "Sheriff of
this county."

"Bernie Little," Bernie said. "And this is
Chet."

Sheriff Grimble, maybe not a fan of me
and my kind, didn't look my way.

"And what brings you here, Bernie Little?"

"A social visit," Bernie said. "But we
found a body inside. I assume you got a
call."

"Is that a question?"

"No."

"Sounded like a question to me," Sheriff

133

Grimble said. "I'll ask the questions."

"Okay," Bernie said.

"What you said about getting a call — that's a cop-type remark. But you're not a cop."

"No."

"What are you?"

"A private investigator, based in the Valley."

The sheriff held out his hand. Bernie came forward, opened his wallet, took out our license — we've been through this before — and gave it to the sheriff. There's a picture of Bernie on it, but you can see me, too, in the background and sort of on my way into the photographer's room. The sheriff looked at the front, then the back.

"Got a reference at Valley PD?"

"Do you know Lou Stine?"

"Met him," the sheriff said. "Stay put." He got back in the cruiser, took out his phone. He spoke, listened, grunted, put the phone away, climbed out of the car. "Social visit?" he said.

"Correct."

"Not working a case?"

"No."

"Got a client? Lotty Pilgrim, for example?"

"Why would she want a private detective?"

"Another question," said the sheriff. "Makes two. One more and we won't be friends."

"How will I cope?" said Bernie.

The sheriff gave him a long gaze, unfriendly for sure. Bernie gazed right back, not in a friendly or an unfriendly way, in no way at all: one of my favorite Bernie looks, although the sheriff didn't seem to like it. I got my paws under me. From where I was I could have jumped right over his head. But that wasn't the plan.

The sheriff finally turned away from Bernie and nodded toward the house. "Is it her in there?"

Bernie shook his head. "Clint Swann," he said. "The manager."

"Manager, hell," said the sheriff. He handed Bernie our license, actually kind of slapping it on Bernie's palm. "Let's see the bastard." He motioned for Bernie to go first. Usually I go first, as I mentioned quite recently, but in a case like this I prefer last. I followed along, right at the sheriff's heels. He glanced back, taking his first real good look at me, and made a face like: Whoa!

Life is so much more comfortable when two beings come to an understanding.

135

We went into the bedroom and looked at Clint. The dead keep changing, which is kind of strange if you think about it, which I don't. Clint, for example, was turning a bit waxy and giving off more — and stronger — smells. The sheriff snapped on his own surgical gloves and saw what we'd already seen, namely the opening — like a little tear — in Clint's chest.

"This is when I hate the job," the sheriff said. He pointed his chin at Clint. "An abuser — emotionally for sure and maybe more than that. Plus a parasite. The latest — and last, I guess — in a long line of abusers and parasites. Who can blame her? Everyone snaps eventually."

"You're talking about Lotty?" Bernie said. The sheriff nodded.

"Quick on the draw, Sheriff," Bernie said. "Unless you know things I don't."

"Makes two of us," the sheriff said. "You show me yours. Where is she? And what brought you here?"

"Can't help you with the first one," said Bernie. "As for the second, I met her the other night. She had a little problem with her tip jar. We got it sorted out."

"So that's why you're here? A tip jar problem, whatever the hell that is?"

Bernie nodded.

"You're expecting payment?"

"I'm a fan of her music."

" 'Cause payment ain't happening. Lotty's got no money, never did."

"How's that possible? 'How You Hung the Moon' was big. George Jones sang it, for god's sake."

"Don't ask me to explain the music business," the sheriff said. He glanced down at Clint. "But I've known Lotty a long time. Leastwise, I knew her way back. She's from around here — Fort Kidder — and so am I. She was friends with my big sister Jean — rest in peace — in high school. This was before she went to Austin. Austin, Nashville, Santa Fe, other places in New Mexico, maybe — meaning decades went by. But she moved back here last year and we had coffee once or twice. Know what she told me?" He pointed to Clint. "That she was madly in love and in hate with him. Exact words — in love and in hate. Ever heard that one before?"

"No," Bernie said.

"She's an artist, of course, maybe explains a lot," said the sheriff. "She also told me that if she was a man she'd probably end

137

up killing him one day."

"Kind of an old-fashioned remark."

"Lotty's an old-fashioned gal," the sheriff said. At that moment, his gaze went to Clint's hand, the tightly closed one. He leaned forward, opened the hand, held up a pink earring. "You one of those hipster types? Sport an earring every now and then?"

"Now you're wasting time," Bernie said.

The sheriff didn't like that. A muscle bulged in his jaw, like . . . like he was a biter? We'd see about that. "Happen to notice that bejeezus-size knife in the dish rack?" he said.

"It's not that big," Bernie said.

"Didn't wash it off or nothing like that, by any chance?"

"No."

"Ever had it in your hand?"

"What are you getting at?"

"You're a man. Maybe the kind an old-fashioned gal might employ to do the things old-fashioned gals don't do."

"Are you going to arrest me?"

Whoa! What was this? Weren't we having a nice little back-and-forth? And now arresting Bernie was in the cards? How was the sheriff planning to do that with me around? I checked his gun hand, just hanging by his side. Could that hand reach for the gun and draw it before I had his wrist between my teeth? Care to place a wager?

But none of that happened. The sheriff's jaw muscle stopped bulging. "Not after what Lou Stine said about you," he said. "Hadn't taken him for the effusive type." He brushed off his hands, took out his phone, called his crime scene dudes. After that, he turned to Bernie and gave him a still-here? look. "Nice meeting you," he said. "Safe journey."

"Where am I going?"

"Wherever you like. But I wouldn't want to trip on you."

"Then I'll need to know where you're headed so I can stay away."

"You're almost funny," Sheriff Grimble said. "I'll be tracking down Lotty. And not looking forward to it."

ELEVEN

"One good thing about all that hospital time," Bernie said, "I gave up smoking. Gave it up forever."

Wow! I hadn't known that! And he'd been trying for so long! I laid a paw on the steering wheel, which made sense to me at the time.

"Che—et?"

I took my paw off the wheel, and then had some trouble figuring out where to put it. Had that ever happened before? I tried the dashboard, the armrest, the gear shift —

"Che—et?"

— and finally my paw came down on the edge of my seat, more or less by accident, and stayed there.

"What gets into you?"

Nothing. Nothing gets into me. We rode along in silence. I'd never been more silent in my life. You wouldn't have known I was there.

"I even got to the point," Bernie said after a while, "where I didn't have the urge. But today I'm past that point. Do you see what I mean?"

I did not.

Soon we came to a little town. Bernie parked in front of a convenience store and went inside. When he came out, he was . . . opening a pack of cigarettes? Getting past the point of not having the urge meant you had the urge again? What a complicated thought, way beyond my usual abilities. It vanished without a trace, and none too soon.

Bernie stuck a cigarette in his mouth and tossed the pack — still filled with all the other cigarettes — into a trash barrel. What a confusing day we were having! He got into the car and lit up.

"Ah," he said, sitting back in his seat and blowing out a cloud of smoke. I could feel how relaxed he was, relaxed a bit myself, even though I'd already been relaxed. Hadn't I? I tried to remember and all of a sudden felt very unrelaxed.

"So many questions," Bernie said. "We need to think." He tapped some ash out the window. "Question one — who tipped the sheriff? Question two — why did Lotty call us? Question three — where is she?"

I waited for more, was very glad when no more came. These questions were hard enough already.

Bernie took another drag. "There's the bread crumbs approach and there's the psychological approach."

A tough one. Bread crumbs didn't do a whole lot for me, but I had the feeling that the psychological approach had nothing to do with food at all. Was there a steak-tips approach? I leaned toward the bread crumbs, but I wasn't excited about it.

"The psychological approach seems more interesting to me, Chet. Maybe it always has, but now more so." He puffed at the cigarette. "In this case, it means understanding Lotty, her whole life. After that, her whereabouts should be obvious."

He thought for a long time, smoking the cigarette down to almost nothing, and finally said, "But the crime-solving tradition is all about bread crumbs."

The phone buzzed and Nixon's voice came through the speakers.

"Hey, Bernie. That Civic? With the steering wheel situation?"

"Go on."

"It got picked up — thought you'd want to know."

"Picked up by who?"

"The owner. Rita Krebs is her name. And one fine-lookin' —"

"Was she alone?"

"Yeah. Left twenty minutes ago."

"How did she get there?"

"Huh?"

"Did someone drive her?"

"Musta. Or it coulda been a taxi. Then there's the ride sharing companies, Uber and —"

"So you didn't see anyone else?"

"Nope. She walked in alone."

"Did she mention Lotty Pilgrim?"

"Nope."

"Or anybody?"

"Did she mention anybody? Is that the question?"

"Yes."

"Let me think." Time passed. Bernie tapped his foot. "Jayne Mansfield. She mentioned Jayne Mansfield. Zoltan was putting the finishing touches on the Girlie World shuttle van and the young lady said, 'Is that supposed to be Jayne Mansfield?' I told her it was more of a generic thing. Then we had a brief discussion about Jayne Mansfield's movies. Rita hadn't seen any. I made the point that she was a better actress than most people think. After that she paid and drove off."

"Paid how?"

"Cash."

"How much?"

"Four hundred seventy-three dollars. That was after a ten percent discount. For being so young and knowing who Jayne Mansfield was. Makes no sense, I know."

"It does to me," Bernie said.

"That's what I like about you."

They hung up. Bernie turned the key. "Let's go with the psychological," he said.

I felt hungry right away.

We drove back toward Lotty's ranch, but just as it appeared in the distance we hung a turn onto a smoothly paved road that took us past what looked like a military base and into what looked like the kind of town you find next to military bases.

"Fort Kidder," Bernie said. He shook his head and glanced at me. "Learned to fly helos here. I was no star, believe me."

What was this? Bernie could fly helos? I was just finding this out now? Of course I knew he'd been in the Army — that's where his leg wound came from — and sometimes we ran into old Army buddies who hugged Bernie and thumped him on the back showing they loved him, although not as much as I do, meaning I generally squeeze myself

144

in between pretty quick, but he could fly helos? Were we getting one? Soon, I hoped?

"What's all that panting? Thirsty?"

Not in the least. And then extremely.

We parked by what looked like a glass-fronted store in a strip mall. Bernie read the sign. " '*Frontier Gazette.* News you can trust since 1901.' " He filled my portable water-bowl and I lapped it all up, then he refilled it and I lapped it all up again, and after that I gave myself a real good shake, some water droplets flying from my mouth and making tiny rainbows in the air. There's all kinds of beauty in life. That was my thought as we entered what had to be the office of the *Frontier Gazette,* if I was following things right.

I'd been in a newspaper office before, back when Suzie worked for the *Valley Tribune* and she and Bernie were just getting started. And now it was over? I didn't understand. My tail drooped. I got it right back up there, and stat. We were on the job: I sent that message to my tail, and in no uncertain terms.

Where was I?

Right, newspaper offices. Normally real busy, with folks making calls, taking calls, typing so fast their fingers blurred. But not here at the *Frontier Gazette,* where we had

145

one lone man, on the youngish side, who was spreading peanut butter on a cracker. Charlie's a fan of peanut butter so I've sampled it, getting peanut buttery clumps stuck to the roof of my mouth every time, the taste for peanut butter ending up as one of those human mysteries.

"Hey, there," the young man said. "Help you?" He popped the whole cracker in his mouth.

"I'd like to speak to a reporter," Bernie said, "preferably one who's been here for a long time."

"There's only me," said the young man. Or something like that, what with the insides of his mouth practically glued together. "I'm the manager."

"Can you put me in touch with one of your veteran reporters?"

"We don't have veteran reporters," the young man said, spreading peanut butter on another cracker. "Don't have any reporters at all."

Weren't managers supposed to be on the older side? Was this dude going to be trouble? All at once, for whatever reason, he noticed me.

"Whoa! That's one sizable pooch!"

"He's very gentle," Bernie said. "Nine times out of ten. Back up a little, big guy."

146

Had I somehow gotten myself most of the way around the desk? Possibly. I made things right, nice and gentle, except for certain ungentle feelings in my teeth, totally controllable, no worries.

Maybe the young man sensed that. He seemed to relax. "No reporters," he went on, "being the cornerstone of our business plan." He handed Bernie a card.

Bernie read it. "Rob Tritle, PhD, Southwest Manager, Friendly Communications, Inc."

"Proud owner-operators of what used to be called community newspapers," said the young man, most likely Rob Tritle, unless I was missing something. "Just acquired this particular property last week. We're projecting twenty-three percent growth in year one."

"Growth of what?" Bernie said.

Rob Tritle blinked. "That would be revenue."

"How will you generate that with no reporters?"

Rob Tritle raised a finger, a smear of peanut butter on the end. Right away I had a strong desire to give that fingertip a quick nip. Very bad of me, but is it possible to keep your mind in line at all times? There was just something about him.

"You familiar with AI?" Rob Tritle said.

"I know what it means," Bernie told him.

Whatever AI was it had never come up in any conversation I'd ever heard. But Bernie somehow knew all about it? Was there no end to his brilliance?

"Friendly Communications has developed AI software that handles the entire reporting side of the news gathering business. Or will once the boys in India iron out the last few bugs."

"How can AI gather news?" Bernie said.

"That's proprietary," said Rob Tritle. "But put it this way — the news is out there. I like to think of it as dustballs under a bed. Our AI software just vacuums it up."

"And writes the stories?"

"That's the easy part — a few lines of simple programming and presto! The writing side turns out to be pretty much a no-brainer." Rob Tritle's phone went ping. He licked peanut butter off his fingertip and reached for it. "Anything else I can do for you?"

"How about the name of one of your former reporters? An older one."

"You could try Myron Siegel. He's older than dirt."

We had a quiet ride to Myron Siegel's place,

148

probably because there was so much to think about. Writing, for example, being a no-brainer. As I may have mentioned already, no-brainers were in my wheelhouse. Did that mean that writing was . . . possibly something I could . . . what a strange idea! I let it do what it wanted, namely slip away, and fast.

Myron Siegel lived in one of those condo developments you see out here, the kind for oldsters. We found him by the pool, a leathery little guy in a bathing suit, sitting in the sun and busy with a pencil and an open book. He didn't look at all dirty to me, Rob Tritle turning out to be like a lot of dudes we deal with, unreliable.

"I'm Bernie Little and this is Chet," Bernie said.

Myron Siegel clapped the book shut. "You're just in time," he said. "I was about to commit hara-kiri by means of sudoku."

"Ran into a hard one?" Bernie said.

"Hard? They're all easy as pie. The problem is I'm going out of my mind with boredom. Be interesting. I'm begging you."

Begging, of course, was very bad, but maybe Myron Siegel didn't know. I gave him the benefit of the doubt.

"I got your name from Rob Tritle," Bernie said.

"Tell me he's got a terminal diagnosis."

"Not to my knowledge," Bernie said. "He says you were a reporter there for a long time."

"A totally true remark. The bastard mustn't be in his right mind."

"Did you grow up here in Fort Kidder?"

"Affirmative. My father had a small transport company, supplied the base before the war."

"I wondered if you knew — or ever wrote about — a certain woman who also grew up in these parts."

"Name?"

"Lotty Pilgrim."

Myron Siegel gave Bernie a careful look. He had pale blue eyes, so pale there was hardly any blue at all. That could have been scary, but wasn't in his case, although I had no idea why.

"Bernard Little," Myron Siegel said.

"Yes, sir. That's me."

"That's a name not totally forgotten around here. I'm talking about Bernard Little, the Arizona Ranger from the turn of the last century — rode with Jeff Kidder himself."

"I believe he's an ancestor," Bernie said.

Myron Siegel leaned forward a bit. Muscles moved under his tough old skin. Not big muscles like Bernie's, or huge ones like Shermie's, but muscles all the same. His pale eyes got bluer, and now they had a gleam.

"When I started out, there were a few old-timers who'd known some of those Rangers. Bernard Little had quite a reputation as a marksman. How about you, Mr. Little? Handy with a gun?"

"I had some training in the Army," Bernie said. Now he would add the part about shooting dimes out of the air, or even put on a demonstration, if we were packing, which we actually weren't. That's not a smell I miss. In the end, Bernie didn't even mention the dimes! All he said was, "And call me Bernie."

"And you can call me Myron. Tell me something, Bernie — you in law enforcement?"

"No."

"Sell that one to me," Myron said. He tapped his nose. "This is saying something different."

What a stunner! I knew what Myron was talking about, but exactly! My nose often did the same thing, and was right every single time. Yet Myron's nose was a regular human nose, not even as big as Bernie's. What was going on?

"I'm a private detective," Bernie said. He handed Myron our card.

Myron glanced at it. "The flowers are a nice touch," he said. "Who's your client?"

"Don't have one."

"Not working for the police in some adjunct capacity?"

Bernie's posture changed a tiny bit — you had to really know him to spot it, and of course I do. "Has Sheriff Grimble been out here?"

"Well, well. I said be interesting and god-damn it, you came through." Myron rubbed his hands together. "You working with him?"

"I told you I didn't have a client," Bernie said. "If he said otherwise, he's a liar."

"That he is," said Myron. "But your name didn't come up."

"What did he want?"

"Same as you — to pick my brain on Lotty Pilgrim. The problem he ran into — same one you've got right now — is that my brain is a picker, not a pickee."

I was completely lost. For the first time since we'd arrived, I found myself considering a quick dip in the pool.

Bernie's eyes hardened but his voice stayed the same, nice and even, close to friendly. I loved seeing that one! It often meant we were on our way.

152

"Maybe this is the time for you to over-come that," he said. "Unless you're too old to change."

Myron sat back real quick, almost like Bernie had smacked him. That couldn't happen: I'd never seen Bernie lay a finger on an old person, and he never took a swing at anybody unless they unloaded on him first. Unloaded isn't the same as connect-ing, by the way. No one slips a punch like Bernie, just the tiniest head movement. When perps first see that is when they start to get the picture.

But back to Myron, now glaring at Ber-nie. He tapped his forehead. "I've still got it — still got it all up here, you son of a bitch. You're no better than that moron down at the office, replacing me with some goddamn robot."

Bernie smiled. "That's the worst thing anyone's ever said to me."

Whoa! I could think of way worse things that had been said to Bernie, even by some of our pals! And what about that time his mom — a real piece of work — flew in from Florida for a Thanksgiving visit and had one too many and said something I'm not going to repeat, even if I could remember it?

Myron laughed. This conversation was getting hard to follow. "Do you have any

153

idea where the world is heading?"

"Tell me," said Bernie.

"Slavery," Myron said. "Straight to slavery for ninety-nine point nine nine nine of the human race. Slavery of the unknowing, blissful kind — like sheep on Prozac."

"Then how about we do some good when we still can, you and I?" Bernie said.

Myron gave Bernie a look. It reminded me of the time — the one and only time — that I'd been in an art gallery. This was with Bernie and Suzie, and she'd gazed at a — what was the word? Sculpture, that was it. She'd gazed at a sculpture of a cat, a cat which had turned out to be made of glass — an important detail then, but surely not now, after all this time — in the same way Myron was gazing at Bernie.

"You're relentless," he said, "down underneath it all."

"Only when time's a factor," said Bernie.

Myron nodded to himself. I could feel his thoughts. They were big and fast, not unlike Bernie's. "Did Lotty finally kill that blood-sucking boyfriend?" he said. "Or is that just more of Grimble's bullshit?"

TWELVE

"Why 'bloodsucking'?" Bernie said.

I was with him on that. It sounded horrible.

"Before we get to your goddamn questions," said Myron, "explain your interest in this."

Bernie started in on a long story, going all the way back to Nixon's Championship Autobody, the tip jar, Rita and Jordan, how Lotty called in the car repair, and lots of other stuff I'd smelled with my own nose, heard with my own ears — and seen with my own eyes, although that part's not necessary, more like an add-on for me. The story was so clear, the way Bernie told it. I not only understood what had gone down, but even came close to knowing what was coming next! I could feel it! But just before that happened, the whole thing broke into little pieces, and all those pieces got away from me.

"Not a bad story," Myron said. "But what are you doing? You're a private detective with no client. What kind of business plan is that?"

Yikes! Our business plan: I'd had questions about that myself, and more than once. Hawaiian pants! Tin futures! Bad dreams about both of them sometimes bothered my sleep — hard to believe in the case of tin futures, since I didn't even know what they looked like. Hawaiian pants were a different story, on account of our self-storage in South Pedroia being packed to the ceiling with them. Everyone loved Hawaiian shirts, so why not Hawaiian pants? It made no sense. Uh-oh. Did that mean our whole business plan made no sense? For a moment or two I actually felt myself drifting over to Myron's side. Not that I moved at all, out there by the condo pool. This drifting was going on in my mind. But whoa! Drifting away from Bernie? Never! Not on any subject! Case closed! I opened my mouth nice and wide, showed Myron my teeth, just a hint of what was in store for him if he tried that kind of trick again. He didn't seem to notice. There are humans out there who aren't really aware of the nation within, even when we're right in front of their noses. It had taken me a long time to realize that. Myron turned out to be one of them.

"If I told you I was hoping Lotty would be the client, can we get past this?" Bernie said.

"Any truth in that?" Myron said.

"Yes."

"Did you ask her?"

"She turned us down."

"But you're still hoping."

"Lotty needs help," Bernie said.

"From a lawyer, not a detective," said Myron. "And soon. Where's someone like her going to hide?"

"Any ideas on that subject?"

"Grimble asked that exact same thing."

"And what did you tell him?"

Before Myron could answer, a sliding door opened in one of the condos and a woman — not nearly as young as Suzie or Eliza but also not nearly as old as Myron — looked out. This woman, who wore a towel around her head and another one around her body, or part of it, was the kind of woman who had an effect on Bernie. His mouth didn't fall open; he didn't stare at her with a dumb expression on his face — impossible, since dumb expressions never appeared there; he didn't say the kinds of things you sometimes hear on the street, like, "Hey, baby," or "Yo, junk in the trunk." But I could feel the effect all the same.

The woman leaned out the door, having a bit of trouble with the lower towel, and said, "Yoo-hoo, bunny, anything you need?"

Whoa! Bunny? No one had ever called Bernie that before, and why would they? Ever seen a bunny in a barroom brawl, for example? Or —

But I was way off course, because the next thing that happened was Myron saying in an irritated voice, "Damn it, Oksana, can't you see we're talking?"

"Then how about a nice cigar? You like cigars for when you're talking."

"Sure, sure, a cigar." Myron turned to Bernie. "Cigar?"

"Thanks."

"Make that two," Myron called to Oksana.

"As many as you like, Mister Man," said Oksana, and she pivoted in an interesting way and disappeared back inside the condo.

Their eyes met, meaning Bernie's and Myron's. Myron looked down. "Cigars are the one vice I've got left," he said.

Bernie nodded one of his nods, namely the nod for when he's trying not to laugh. Probably my very favorite of all the nods. For one thing, it usually meant we were in the driver's seat. As for why this had just happened between us and Myron, I had no clue.

Oksana came outside, wearing shorts, a halter top, and high heels, and carrying a tray with cigars and foam-topped beer mugs.

"Who said anything about beer?" Myron said.

"You'll be thirsty," said Oksana. "It's thirty-eight degrees."

"How many times do I have to tell you? Talk Fahrenheit."

"Fahrenheit is stupid."

Oksana stuck a cigar between Myron's lips, struck a match with her thumbnail, and lit the cigar. Myron blew out some smoke. "Oksana, meet Bernie. He's a private detective."

"Is he going to lock you up?"

"A *private* detective," Myron said. "Private detectives can't lock anybody up."

"Shut up! What a country!"

"Nice to meet you," Bernie said.

She turned to him. "So handsome," she said.

"Well, uh," said Bernie.

"What's his name?" Oksana said.

"Ber—" Bernie began, but Myron interrupted.

"She means the pooch," said Myron, now

more annoyed than ever.

"Oh," said Bernie. "Uh —"

"Of course I am meaning the pooch!" Oksana patted Myron's cheek. "Who's my little jealous fellow?"

"Don't call me little," said Myron.

Oksana threw back her head and laughed and laughed. Bernie started laughing, too. And finally Myron joined in. Why? I had no idea. When all that died down, Oksana picked up a mug and said, "Here's to this beautiful creature," she said. "His name?"

"Chet," Bernie said.

He and Myron took their mugs. Then clink, and Oksana said, "To Chet."

Well, how nice! My tail got going big-time, cooling off the whole outdoors. Bernie, Myron, and Oksana took a sip of their beers, except for Oksana, who chugged hers and went back into the condo.

A little cloud of smoke hung over our table by the pool. Myron had opened the umbrella and I lay in the shade.

"The first time I became aware of Lotty Pilgrim was in high school," Myron said. "Coronado High, now moved because of various mining pollutants that were ignored for years. Someone should be tracking the birth defect rate for the kids of all the girls

160

who —" He shook his head. "Forget that. Still makes my blood boil." He puffed at his cigar. "In those days Coronado was seven through twelve. Senior year I was editor of the school paper — wrote the whole thing, end to end. Naturally I covered the school talent show. In the auditorium, always a raucous affair. Lotty was a seventh grader. Just a little thing with a banjo, alone on the big stage. Raucous, as I said, on the edge of being a snakepit."

"What did she sing?" said Bernie.

"Don't rush me," Myron said. "I tell my stories how I tell them. Understood?"

"Got it."

"And spare me the undertones." He drank some beer, licked his lips. "She sang a hymn."

"Which one?" said Bernie. "If you don't mind me asking."

"Relentless," Myron said. "Relentless and a hard-ass — it's the damn desert that makes men like you. Ever considered that?"

"Yes."

"Well, then." Myron nodded in a pleased way. "Lotty sang 'Are You Washed in the Blood.' Familiar with that one?"

"I am."

"Hardcore, doctrine-wise, wouldn't you say?"

"But rousing," Bernie said.

"You're right about that." Myron gestured at Bernie with his cigar. "From the first note she sang till the end, you could have heard a pin drop. I felt chills. It was then and is still the most moving musical experience of my life." He knocked ash off his cigar. "I considered converting. My father would have killed me."

Bernie laughed. How I love when he enjoys himself! Maybe he was happy because Myron was about to become a paying client. I checked out his bathing suit: no pockets, meaning no wallet. A bad sign.

"I went away to college after that," Myron went on, "worked out of Houston for a while, and when I came back, Lotty was a senior herself. All grown up, the most beautiful girl in town. And already making a name for herself in the music world, singing every weekend in some club or other in southern Arizona or over in New Mexico. Her boyfriend was Boomer Riggs, the varsity quarterback, big handsome kid. He's up in the Valley now, made a lot of money."

"How?"

"He started a private security firm that got some big military contracts, based on connections from growing up here. His father commanded the base."

"Which private security firm?" Bernie said.

"Western Solutions," said Myron. "Heard of it?"

Bernie nodded.

"Doesn't matter," Myron said. "Boomer Riggs isn't important to the story — just threw him in so you could see Lotty reached the high school pinnacle. The relationship didn't last long. Lotty fell in love with a musician — Mexican, I believe — dropped out of high school around Thanksgiving, and left town for good."

"Who was the musician?"

"Lotty doesn't talk about him."

Bernie set his cigar down on the edge of the table. "You've been in touch with her?"

"Why the hell not? Retirement's going to kill me — haven't I made that clear?"

"You're writing an article about Lotty?"

"A book was what I had in mind. What I didn't realize was how the target would keep moving even at this late stage of Lotty's life."

"Is she cooperating?"

"To a point. I wish I'd started sooner."

"What do you mean?"

Myron shrugged. "She's been based out of that ranch for over a year but I didn't find out till last month."

"So therefore?" Bernie said.

What was this? The way we had things arranged, Bernie handled all the so-therefores while I brought other things to the table. But now he was looping Myron in on a so-therefore? This was something brand-new. I didn't like it.

"So therefore," Myron said, "if I'd found out sooner, maybe she wouldn't have done what she did."

"Maybe she didn't."

"The sheriff's convinced otherwise. He's a prick and a bully but he's not stupid."

"What do you think?"

Myron gazed at the smoking tip of his cigar. "Until recently, I wouldn't have believed her capable of something like that."

"What happened recently?"

Myron's head snapped up. "You're pumping me. I don't like being pumped."

"Then you find her," Bernie said.

Myron's whole body tensed up. He was real mad about something, but I didn't know what. Or why: Bernie hadn't even raised his voice. Now he spoke again, even quieter.

"We've found a lot of missing people, Chet and I."

Myron turned to me, sitting very still in the shade. At first he looked angry, and then

164

not. "Do all dogs have eyes like that?" he said.

"Like what?"

"His eyes give me the feeling he's following along."

Bernie smiled but he didn't say anything.

Myron turned back to him, took a deep breath, just a bit wheezy. "A few weeks ago, I made what might have been a mistake. For a good reason, of course, which is how the worst mistakes get made." His voice was starting to get a little scratchy. "I didn't factor in what a passionate woman Lotty is — still is. Like a character in one of her songs." Myron went silent, as though listening to something.

"What did you do?" Bernie said.

"It began with a chance sighting," Myron said. "Well, there was context, of course. I'd noticed — how could anyone not — the way that nasty pipsqueak had her wrapped around his little finger."

"You're talking about Clint Swann?"

"Hell, yes — try to keep up," Myron said. "It was pathetic and infuriating. I took the chance of raising the subject once with her, in a subtly understated way. Although Oksana will tell you that subtle understatement and I are ships passing in the night, or whatever the Russian equivalent is. She

165

often speaks to me in Russian equivalents." Myron glanced at the sliding door of the condo and his eyes warmed up for a moment.

"What was Lotty's reaction?" Bernie said.

"She told me to mind my own goddamn business, and if I didn't, the book thing was done. Fine. Her life, not mine, and who can know the heart of another, et cetera. But later that same day, moving ahead to the chance sighting, we — Oksana and I — were up in Pottsdale, having supper outside at Café St. Petersburg. Just an average spot in my opinion, but we're practically regulars. When Oksana needs blinis she needs blinis. So we're at this sidewalk table and a convertible passes by, Clint Swann at the wheel and a woman of his own age beside him. Not really beside him — more in his lap. Kissing him, running her fingers through his hair — get the picture?"

Bernie nodded. "And you told Lotty?"

"The next morning. We had a scheduled meeting at a coffee place here in town, to work on the book."

"What was her reaction?"

"At first, she went completely white. I was sure she was going to faint, but she mastered herself. Amazing to see. She got up and said, 'Please cancel my order, Myron. I'm not hungry after all.' And then she walked out, steady on her feet, but still white as chalk. That was the last time I had any contact with her. She stopped taking my calls."

"Did you tell that story to the sheriff?" Bernie said.

"No."

"Why not?"

"I'm not sure what I would have done if I'd been alone, but Oksana was here."

"So?"

"She gave me a look," Myron said. "Oksana despises cops of any nationality. She has great instincts in general."

"You're a lucky man," Bernie said.

"Lucky in love, anyway," said Myron, "even if it came so late."

Bernie got a faraway look in his eye. He reached for his cigar, puffed, but it had gone out. Myron struck one of the matches Oksana had left, leaned forward, and gave Bernie a light. Their faces were close together.

"I didn't tell Grimble a thing," Myron said. "Especially not about Leticia Wells."

"Who's she?"

"Lotty's daughter," said Myron. "Her only child. Lotty didn't mention her till last month. She's in the area but Lotty had hardly seen her in thirty years. I was actually hoping to get the details that morning at the coffee shop."

"Leticia Wells," Bernie said. "Any relation to Jordan Wells?"

"Who's he?"

"I thought he was just a fan of Lotty's," Bernie said. "Now I'm not so sure. Is Leticia in Phantom Springs, New Mexico?"

"How did you know that?" said Myron.

"Just a guess." Bernie rose. And so did I. "What we need is a client. It doesn't matter about the fee — a nominal amount will do. But any case goes better when there's a client in place, especially if the law's involved."

Myron stubbed out his cigar in the ashtray. "I'll pay the going rate," he said.

I checked his bathing suit one more time. No pockets, as I'd already seen, and therefore no wallet. Was I missing something? Also, what were blinis?

THIRTEEN

Bernie can find out all kinds of things on his phone, even without talking to anyone — just another amazing thing about him. Of all the human brains in the world, I ended up with numero uno! Who's luckier than me? I felt so happy — this was at a red light on the way out of Fort Kidder, Bernie tapping away on his phone — that I came close to jumping right out of the car. Good idea? Not good? I was going back and forth on that when Bernie looked up. "Leticia Wells, 299 Bluff Street. Should have been on top of that before."

On top of what? Why? The light turned green and we sped out of town.

"In fact," Bernie went on, "I bet we've already seen her face. Remember that photo I picked up off the floor — Lotty and Jordan with a dark-haired woman, the only one not smiling?"

I searched my mind and came oh so close!

Like a step or two away. Wow. I felt pretty good about myself.

"This is why I like the psychological approach," Bernie said after a while. "Ever notice how so many cases turn out to be about family?"

Weren't most of them about gunplay? Grabbing perps by the pant leg? Snapping up crullers at Donut Heaven? What did I know about families? Nothing came to mind. There was my own family, of course. Me and Bernie. Oops. Almost left out Charlie. That would have been terrible. I loved Charlie! What about Suzie? And . . . and Bernie's mom? Her new boyfriend, what's his name? Uh-oh — and Shooter? This was starting to get not totally comfortable. What was the other method again, besides the psychological? Any hope of going back to that?

We drove up Bluff Street, back into the sound of all those wind chimes chiming, and parked in front of the yellow house. Last time a big dude in a business suit had been on his way out. A light-on-his-feet big dude. For some reason I could see his face quite clearly, a face with strong features and eyes that were in no hurry. You could say those same things about Bernie, but this

170

dude looked nothing like Bernie. The inside part of humans is sometimes on their faces, and the inside part of Bernie is gentle. Also, you never smell hair gel on him and never will.

Meanwhile Bernie was knocking on the door and no one was coming to answer it. A car pulled into the driveway, not the direction we were looking in, which is why you've got to watch your back in this line of work. My eyes are probably positioned a little better than yours for doing that, no offense. As for the car, I recognized it right away: the little yellow number that Shermie had pulled the steering wheel out of.

"Matches the house," Bernie said, finally turning to look. "Maybe this case is color coded."

What did that mean? Were we entering new territory? I couldn't wait.

The car door opened and the driver got out. She was a big woman with black hair, curly and glossy, and wore jeans and a denim jacket with little birds — yellow birds! — embroidered on it. At that moment I knew Bernie was right about the case, and way ahead of the curve, as usual.

The woman paused in front of the open car door and gave us a look, not friendly. "Yes?" she said. Bernie says there's a yes that means no. Kind of puzzling but now at last I got it.

"My name's Bernie Little." Bernie stepped away from the door. "And this is Chet. We're looking for Leticia Wells."

The woman's eyes went to me, then back to Bernie. The expression in them changed, that change you see when something in the human brain clicks into place. Once Bernie told Charlie that the human brain is very complicated and down at the bottom is the reptile part. "What's reptile?" Charlie had said, the exact same question that had risen in my own mind. "Like lizards," Bernie had said. "Or snakes." I'd never forgotten that, even though I'd tried. There were snakes in the human brain? I feel so bad for all of you.

Back to the woman. Somewhere in her brain — I hoped not in the snake section — something had clicked into place. She stood by the yellow car, arms folded across her chest. "Why?" she said.

We moved closer to her, across the tiny yard — mostly dirt and pebbles with a dried-up bush or two — and stopped maybe one leap away; a leap of mine, not Bernie's.

"I think you know who we are," Bernie said. "We want to help."

"I don't need any help."

172

"That's what your mother said, Leticia. Just before things went south."

"I don't have a mother," said the woman, almost certainly Leticia since she hadn't said she wasn't. That was just another of Bernie's many techniques, not as good as shooting dimes out of the air, but still nice. "And things went south long before you," she added.

"Oh?" said Bernie. "How?"

"Forget it," Leticia said. "Running my goddamn mouth."

"I told you — I want to help," Bernie said. "Among other things, that means getting to Lotty before Sheriff Grimble does."

Leticia's voice rose. "Otherwise he won't pay you?"

Curtains parted in the house next door — sliding curtain rings make a sound that's hard to miss, at least by me. A woman in curlers appeared in the window. Women in curlers scare me every time. I made my low, rumbly bark. Bernie's gaze went to the window, and so did Leticia's.

"What is wrong with people?" Leticia said.

The curtains closed. "How about inviting us inside?" Bernie said.

"I'm inviting you to leave."

"Because the house is a mess?"

Leticia pointed her finger at him. "Was

that your doing?"

Bernie shook his head. "You're in an urgent situation. We deal in those. And we're not working for any lawman."

"Then who are you working for?"

"Someone who's worried about your mother."

"Stop calling her that!"

"Why? Isn't it true?"

"None of your goddamn business," Leticia said. "Who's this supposed client of yours?"

"I'm going to protect the client's identity for now," Bernie said.

"Then we're done." Leticia walked past us toward the door.

Bernie walked after her, not in an aggressive way. I did the same, also not aggressively, at least not very. Leticia whirled around.

"You're trespassing. Do I have to call the police?"

"This is complicated enough already," Bernie said. "You have nothing to fear from us. We're on Lotty's side. She's not capable of murder."

Leticia gave Bernie a look, a little less angry but still unpleasant in other ways I didn't understand. "Oh?" she said. "You can see into the human soul?"

174

"No," Bernie said, "but I've dealt with dozens of murderers. She just doesn't fit. I think she's protecting someone. Possibly you, but maybe Jordan."

Leticia's eyes narrowed. She was a big, strong woman and now looked dangerous. "You stay away from him."

"He's your son, isn't he? Did Clint beat him up the other night, or hire someone to do it? And Jordan, already primed by how Clint treats his grandmother, finally boiled over?"

Leticia pointed her finger at Bernie again and then did something I'd only seen once before. She jabbed him in the chest, good and hard, and not just once but twice, the second poke harder than the first. "Stay away."

Oh, what a terrible mistake she was making! But how could she know what had happened to the last chest jabber, an enormous dude who'd been flat on his back and eyes rolling up a single moment later? Would this be that sweet uppercut? The right cross was always a possibility, or what about the left hook? Poor Leticia!

Except nothing happened, not in the punching department. In a quiet voice, Bernie said, "Let's go, Chet." We walked down to the street, got in the car, and pulled away.

Jabbed in our chest and we were just going to take it? We were almost down at the bottom of the hill before it hit me that although we'd dealt with some bad women — poisoners! brakeline cutters! even a parachute rigger! — I'd never seen Bernie use the uppercut, right cross, or left hook on any of them. What was up with that?

At the bottom of the hill stood one of those boarded-up gas stations you see from time to time. We pulled in — a bit of a puzzler, since boarded-up means the pumps are empty — and parked in a weedy strip behind the building. Bernie glanced around the car, felt under his seat. "Did I really throw away that pack of smokes?" he said.

Poor Bernie! There's a gaze I have for making him feel better. I tried it out now, but he wasn't looking my way.

He sighed. "Do you think it's true — some people really are incapable of murder, in any circumstance?"

I didn't know, although I sort of thought I understood the question.

"Is it graphable? One of those curves with two little tails and a big fat part in the middle?"

Uh-oh. Maybe I hadn't understood after all. What was he talking about? Some

176

strange creature with two tails? Did that mean no head? It sounded so awful.

"At one end would be the murderous types, with an appetite for killing and no consciences at all. At the other end, the saints, no appetite, and consciences in command of all they do. And in the middle are the rest of us — no appetite, middling conscience, and therefore capable of murder in the right circumstance. No reason to believe that Lotty's a saint. But I just don't see —"

The little yellow car appeared, making the turn at the bottom of Bluff Street and heading out of town. "That was quick," Bernie said, turning the key.

An eighteen-wheeler went by in the same direction, not far back of the yellow car. We're real good at following cars without being spotted, me and Bernie. We can follow from way back, from different lanes, even from in front. Following from behind an eighteen-wheeler is as easy as it gets. We could do it with our eyes closed, a strange human expression since they're helpless with their eyes closed. Meanwhile, my own eyes seemed to be closing. Was it just because the idea of closed eyes was suddenly in play? I was too sleepy to even think about it.

■ ■ ■ ■

I chased javelinas for a while, always fun, especially if you knew how to fly, which I did. It was actually more of a gliding since I had no wings to flap. I glided over the desert, taking my time, glancing around: and what was this? Way down below a tiny car, all alone, was moving along an endless strip of two-lane black-top. Something familiar about that car, and a moment later I was hovering right above it. A Porsche? Yes, and more specifically, our Porsche. With Bernie at the wheel, smoking a huge cigar, almost the size of a baseball bat. And beside him, sitting up straight and tall, was . . . was a member of the nation within . . . who looked . . . looked a lot like . . . Shooter. And was! It was Shooter, for sure, riding shotgun in the Porsche! Oh, no.

"Chet? Hey, big guy, you all right? Wake up."

I opened my eyes and saw I was in the Porsche, in the Porsche with Bernie and curled up in the shotgun seat. No sign of . . . any other party. Bernie was patting my shoulder.

"A nightmare?" he said. "You were whimpering pretty good there for a while."

Whimpering? How embarrassing! But . . . but another party in the shotgun seat! Not me! Then came a sound a lot like — oh, no — a whimper!

"Chet. What's wrong?"

I sat up. All these strange pictures in my mind faded away. I gave myself a little shake, the best I could do in a small space.

"Back to normal?" Bernie gave me a big smile. "Reason's a thing we dimly see in sleep, as they say."

That one — which I'm pretty sure I'd never heard from nobody — zipped right by me.

Bernie opened his door. "Come on, Chet. Let's get to work."

I hopped out of the car. We were somewhere new! Somewhere that smelled of the open desert and also sounded like the open desert, a still and empty sound I loved, although this particular spot wasn't empty. We seemed to be parked a little way off a dirt track, behind a big cottonwood on the bank of a dry wash. Bernie headed up a steep, rocky slope, and therefore so did I, following him in this way I have of getting wherever we were going — in this case, the top of the hill — first.

"Down," said Bernie, in a low voice.

179

I crouched behind a row of prickly pears, and so did Bernie, as soon as he caught up. Together we took in the scene below. The dry wash made a long curve, widening a bit, and at the widest spot even had a glint of water in it. We have mirages out in the desert, but not when it comes to smell, and I smelled water. On each bank by the watery part was a grove of cottonwoods, and in the grove on our side of the wash stood an RV, not the real big kind. Parked nearby, at the end of a dirt track leading back toward the base of the hill, was the little yellow car.

Hey! We were on the job, and doing well! What a team!

Time passed. A big black bird circled over the cottonwoods, then spread its wings and drifted higher and higher, drifting in a gliding sort of way that . . . that reminded me of Shooter? What a strange thought! Where had it come from? It made no sense.

The back door of the RV opened and a person stepped out. We were too far away to make out the face of this person, but men and women move differently, and this was a woman. She moved between the cottonwoods, sunshine lighting up her hair, black and glossy. Had to be Leticia! Wow! Was I on fire or what?

Leticia got in the yellow car, drove out of

the cottonwood grove and up onto the dirt track. It led her to the bottom of the hill — she was leaning forward, both hands on the wheel — and then veered into the desert, headed toward a low black smear on the horizon, possibly a town. We jumped up, ran down to the Porsche, swung onto the dirt track, and followed —

But no. None of that — none of the usual things we do at a moment like this — happened. We just stayed where we were. I watched Bernie. His gaze was on the RV, but after a while he looked my way. "I'm getting a funny feeling."

That sounded interesting. I waited for more, and when more didn't come, made a quick check for funny feelings of my own. Nope, not a one, from nose to tail and back again. All of me felt tip-top.

By that time, the yellow car was just a tiny speck, the only movement in all there was to see — except for the black bird, now circling over the RV. Bernie rose, and so did I. After he looked all around, we made our way back down the hill — side by side with me in front — and got in the car. Bernie steered us out from behind the big cottonwood, around a clump of jumping cholla — I once had a problem with jumping cholla, and had learned to keep my distance, learned that lesson very well and many times — and onto the dirt track. Then came a bit of a surprise. We didn't go zooming after the yellow car, but headed the other way, toward the RV.

We parked right where the yellow car had been and walked up to the RV. Sometimes Bernie speaks in this low voice that means he's talking to himself. I love when he does that, and always listen in.

"What if I'd said, 'Suzie, let's sell everything, take off in an RV, and just live?' "

What a brilliant idea! As long as we towed the Porsche behind the RV, of course. Was this the RV? I was all set to take possession, when Bernie called through the door.

"Lotty? We need to talk."

FOURTEEN

Silence from inside. Then came footsteps, very soft, but there's no such thing as footsteps too soft for my ears. Also I could hear breathing on the other side of the door. Plus there were smells of cigarette smoke, coffee, and perfume — and the specific smell of Lotty Pilgrim, which had an interesting milky quality. The door might as well not have been there.

At least in my case. Did Bernie realize Lotty was standing pretty much right in front of us? He raised his voice. "Lotty? Lotty?" Raised it to a level that meant the answer to my question was no.

No answer from Lotty. The milky smell changed, went the tiniest bit sour. I've tasted milk both sour and not, don't like either kind. Water's my drink. The best I ever tasted came right out of a rock, but no time to go into that now.

Bernie raised his voice even more. "You're

headed in the wrong direction. You know that."

Silence.

"And if you'd let us help before, maybe —"

The door opened. "Stop shouting," said Lotty, although for a moment I hardly recognized her face; it looked so old. Plus she'd been doing a lot of crying. Crying signs stay on a woman's face for some time after the crying's over.

She stepped aside. We walked in. She looked past us, into the distance, then closed the door.

We were in a tiny kitchen. Lotty sat at the tiny table, a cup of coffee in front of her. We sat, too. She wore pink sweats and pink slippers. In case you're interested, Bernie wore jeans and a Hawaiian shirt, the one with the laughing pineapples, hard to describe, and I wore my everyday collar, the one made of gator skin, a long story, even longer than the one about the water from the rock.

She gave Bernie a look. "Proud of yourself?"

"For what?" Bernie said.

"Being such a sneak. Following Leticia out here. God knows what else."

"She's your daughter?"

"That's no secret," Lotty said.

"And Jordan's your grandson?"

"That's not a secret either."

"There's a difference between not a secret and common knowledge," Bernie said. "For example, I'm guessing Clint didn't know about Jordan, maybe didn't know about Leticia either. Is that true?"

"Stop interrogating me," Lotty said, her eyes tearing up. "Is that what I need? Where's this help you keep promising? You want up-front money? Is that it? I have none."

"I don't want your money," Bernie said. "But how is it possible you don't have any?"

"Nothing's more possible." Lotty wiped her eyes on the back of her sleeve. "Most folks have no money."

"But most folks haven't had a long career in the music business. Most folks didn't write 'How You Hung the Moon.' "

"You want me to explain the goddamn music industry?" Lotty said. "How's that going to help?"

"You never know what will help — that's something you learn in our business."

Lotty's eyes shifted my way. "When you say 'our' you mean Chet and yourself?"

"I do," said Bernie.

Well, of course! What could be more obvious? I had the feeling, a bit disturbing, that

185

we weren't getting anywhere. What was this case about? A whole strange back-and-forth with a C-note. And Clint, the boyfriend or manager or whatever he was, laid out in Lotty's bed. Was there anything else? Not that I could think of. I felt a little better about the case. C-notes and dead bodies were our bread and butter. All at once, I was hungry. Does that ever happen to you, out of nowhere and for no reason? I sniffed the air for scraps, came up with zip.

Lotty stuck her finger in her coffee, stirred it around, seemed to calm down a little. "I had a dog named Patsy once."

"Named after Patsy Cline?" Bernie said.

Lotty tilted her head, checked Bernie out from that angle. "Well, well," she said. "I even formed a company with her — Lotty and Patsy Songs, Limited."

"Is it still in existence?"

Lotty shook her head.

"What happened to it?"

"Now you're in the weeds," she said. "Sure you do this for a living?"

"I can give you references."

"And then I'd call them? How smart would that be at the moment? But if you do it for a living, why aren't you charging me?"

"We have a client."

Lotty sat back. "Someone's paying you to

help me?"

Bernie nodded.

"Who?"

"I'd rather keep that private for now."

"Then that's the end of our powwow."

"It's a friend."

"I have no friends."

"Sure you do — think of all the people who love your music."

"You're very naïve," Lotty said. "Those aren't friends."

"Maybe not," Bernie said. "But our client has your interests at heart."

"The name," said Lotty.

It got very quiet in the RV. For a moment I thought I heard a car, but far away. Lotty sat motionless, her arms folded across her chest.

"Myron Siegel," Bernie said at last.

"Damn it to hell," Lotty said. "Everything's always about money. I never learn."

"Myron's about money?"

"Sure. With me — how would you put it? — on the run, his little book or whatever he's got in mind suddenly gets a bump in value." She sucked in her breath, started to rise. "Have you told him I'm here?"

"No," Bernie said. "That won't happen. And you're wrong about his motives. It goes back to high school."

Lotty's face went pale. The sour milk smell got more sour. "High school?" she said.

"Coronado High, down in Fort Kidder. Weren't you and Myron there at the same time?"

"So he says. I don't remember him at all."

"But you made a big impression on him."

"How?"

"When you sang 'Are You Washed in the Blood.' "

Her eyes shifted. For a moment or two she seemed not to be with us, just a feeling I had, hard to explain. Then she gave her head a tiny shake, like she was snapping herself out of something, and said, "The talent show? That's the connection to high school?"

"Yes," Bernie said. He ran his thumb along the side of his chin. I'd never seen that before from Bernie. What did it mean? Something amazing, I knew that much. "What else could it be?"

Lotty shrugged. Color came back to her face and the sour milk smell weakened down to almost nothing. She took a sip of coffee. "All right. Let's hear your advice."

"First I need to know more," said Bernie. "Start with the last time you saw Clint."

She looked at Bernie over the rim of her

188

cup, first a hard look, and then with no warning, tears were flowing down her face, although she made no sound. I eased myself over a little bit and sat on her foot. No idea why. Things happen in life. I felt her hand on my back, very gentle, but there was a tremor in it.

"What if I told you I was guilty?" she said, her voice thick.

"Of murdering Clint?" said Bernie.

Lotty looked down, stroked my fur. "That, too," she said.

"What do you mean?"

"Nothing. I have no meaning."

"Explain."

Lotty shook her head. "There's no explanation. I killed Clint."

"I don't believe it."

"No? Didn't your pal Myron supply you with the motive?"

"The girlfriend in Pottsdale?" Bernie said. "Maybe a motive for some, but not for you."

"Why not? You don't believe I loved him?"

Bernie just sat there.

"I did," Lotty said. "I do. I always will."

"That sounds like a bad lyric, Lotty. The kind you wouldn't write."

Lotty's hand went still. Some hands might have gripped my fur at that point, even in a too-strong grip, but hers did not. There are

189

humans — not a whole lot — with no violence in them.

"Do you treat all your clients like this?" she said.

Bernie rose, lifted the coffeepot off the counter, filled her cup. "It's nothing compared to what's in the sheriff's plans."

Lotty's hand, still on my back, seemed to go colder. Bernie raised the pot in one of those little human gestures that sometimes — not often enough, in my opinion — take the place of talk.

"Help yourself," Lotty said.

Bernie opened a cupboard, took out a mug with writing on it. Bernie checked out the writing. "Michigan State," he said. "Who owns the RV, Lotty?"

"Why does that matter?"

"It probably doesn't." Bernie sat down, set his mug on the tiny tabletop.

"Friends of Leticia's from up north," Lotty said. "They won't be back till November. Do you ever ask questions that matter?"

"Let's start now," Bernie said, "with one finite problem, a small one, but maybe a building block. What went on with the tip jar?"

Lotty shook her head. "You'll only come to the wrong conclusion," she said.

190

"Try me," Bernie said.

"Every time a man says that, trouble comes next."

"For example."

"Good lord, you just keep pushing," Lotty said. "The ruthless type."

"So I keep hearing," said Bernie. "But somehow you got past that yesterday. You called me. You must have wanted something."

"It was a moment of weakness."

"Or clarity," Bernie said. "How about I handle the tip jar story myself and you jump in with corrections?"

Lotty blew air through her lips in a way that makes a flap-flap sound, a neat human trick, but she didn't say anything.

"I put a hundred-dollar bill in the tip jar," Bernie said. "Your grandson Jordan stole it. We got it back but when we tried to give it to you Clint grabbed it. Was it just that he was in charge of safe-keeping your money? Or has he been scarfing up every penny you earned?"

"What are you saying?" said Lotty. "That he didn't really love me? That I'm a hag, therefore beyond love?" Her eyes, which had been close to tears, cleared up. Teary eyes have a smell, by the way, a smell that had been in the air around the tiny table, but now was not.

"I'm just trying to get a handle on the money part," Bernie said.

"I couldn't care less about the money," said Lotty. "My money got stolen long ago."

"By whom?"

"Ruthless types. Like yourself, not like Clint."

"Did these ruthless types have names?" Bernie said.

"No," said Lotty. "No name."

"No name singular?" said Bernie. "Meaning there was just one?"

"You're way off course."

"Then help me."

"How?"

"By giving me facts. Even just one. For example, Jordan was at the Crowbar but I didn't see any sign that Clint knew him. Am I wrong?"

There was a long silence. Actually not a complete silence: I heard an engine again — in fact, now more than one — but still far away. Then, quite suddenly, the distant engine sounds cut off.

"No," Lotty said at last. "You're not wrong."

I moved out from under her hand and went to the window. Outside I saw the cottonwoods, the dry wash, the dirt track curving around the bottom of the big hill, and high above the big black bird hovering in the empty sky.

"Meaning," Bernie was saying, "that when you came back to Arizona you didn't tell Clint about Jordan."

"That's right."

"Or Leticia."

"Correct."

"So I'll ask you again," Bernie said. "Why the big secret?"

Lotty gazed into her mug. "Better to keep these things separate."

"What things?"

Lotty looked up. "The good from the bad."

"I don't understand," Bernie said. "Was Clint bad after all?"

"He loved me," Lotty said. "No matter what anyone thinks."

"Then there's something bad about Jordan and Leticia?"

Lotty shook her head. "It's me. I'm the bad one."

"How?" Bernie said.

At that moment the big black bird suddenly flapped its wings and took off, disappearing behind the hill. I barked.

Bernie came to the window, peered out. "Chet? Something wrong?"

I couldn't tell. It was only a feeling.

Bernie turned to Lotty. "Who knows you're here?"

"Leticia."

"What about Jordan?"

"Maybe."

"Rita?"

"I don't know."

Bernie moved toward her. "Pack your things."

"Why?"

"This isn't safe."

"What makes you think so?"

"Chet," Bernie said. "He senses something."

Lotty looked my way. I looked her way. She rose. "Where are we going?"

"I'll tell you on the way," Bernie said. Lotty moved toward the little bedroom at the back of the RV. I turned from the window and saw her pick up a framed photo of her and Clint, and stick it in a pink suitcase. Bernie saw that, too.

"Is it possible Clint found out on his own?" he said. "About your family?"

Lotty went still. "There's my motive," she said. "My family."

"Motive for what?" said Bernie.

Lotty closed the suitcase and came forward. "Doing what I did."

194

"I don't believe you killed him," Bernie said.

Lotty met his gaze. "Bad things happen in the blackness. In the blackness I'm a stone killer."

"What blackness?" said Bernie.

"If you don't know, I can't explain," Lotty said.

Bernie opened the door. Light gleamed on her earring, a pink one that seemed familiar. "Where's your other earring?" Bernie said. Hey! He was right! No surprise there. The surprise was Lotty's other ear being earringless. Not a huge surprise, since lots of folks rocked the one-earring look. But if Bernie thought it was important, that was that.

We stepped outside, me first, waiting on Lotty's answer to the earring question. There was no time for an answer, even if one was in the works. Out in the yard stood Sheriff Grimble and a whole string of deputies, all of them drawing down on us.

Oh, no! How had this happened? There wasn't a cruiser in sight. Whoa! They'd moved in on foot? Footsteps too soft for me to hear? My tail dropped right down into the dirt.

"Hands up," Grimble said, mouth mostly hidden by his mustache. "Just you, Lotty.

Bernie, you're free to go. Thanks much."

Lotty gave Bernie a look I'm going to have trouble forgetting. I forced my tail to smarten up, all I could think of to do.

FIFTEEN

A bunch of cruisers came up the dirt track and stopped in front of the RV. Sheriff Grimble and a deputy helped Lotty into the backseat of the lead cruiser. Then they all drove away, leaving a big cloud of dust, plus me and Bernie. Nobody had even glanced at us.

Bernie gets mad sometimes, but hardly ever during a fight. It's more when he gets pushed around. Getting pushed around in the nation within means you're actually getting pushed around. When that happens I push back, and way harder — even way way harder if necessary, or even if I'm simply in the mood! — just to show the pusher what's what. In the human world, you can get pushed with no pushing to be seen. That makes Bernie mad. When he gets mad, I can feel it, a sort of pressure inside him, like . . . like some bigger Bernie is trying to get out. Whoa! A scary thought, because if that ever happened what would become of my Bernie? My Bernie was big enough. I moved over and pressed against his leg. He scratched between my ears, not his best effort but better than none at all. His mind was somewhere else. I could feel the anger going on inside, which was how I knew we'd been pushed around. Had I let that happen? I was pretty sure I had, although I couldn't think how, even though I suspected that I had in fact known how at one time, perhaps not so long ago. But one thing was very clear: I no longer had a clue. And if you couldn't think how you'd messed up, what was the point of getting upset about it? None that I could see. And just like that, I was back to feeling tip-top! I shifted slightly so I could paw at Bernie a bit, maybe rev him up.

He glanced down at me — not really down, since at that moment we were pretty much eye to eye — took a deep breath and let it out slowly.

"Let's get out of here," he said.

What a great idea! Who's smarter than Bernie? No-body, amigo, and you can take that to the bank, although maybe not our bank where there'd been some recent problem with Ms. Mendez, the manager.

This time we didn't climb the hill, but followed the dirt track around it, all the way to the Porsche, parked in the shade by the dry wash. I hopped right into the shotgun seat, but Bernie lingered outside, gazing at the car in a strange way. Was he having second thoughts about those painted martini glasses on the fender, and how often we got pulled over? I was going back and forth on that, when all at once Bernie got down and crawled under the car.

That was a first! Normally we at least try turning the key before starting in on repairs. I hopped right out, wriggled under the car myself, squeezing in as close as possible to Bernie. When new things are in the works, you want to be close, as I'm sure you know already.

"Hey, big guy, a little space."

I heard him and totally sympathized, but there was nothing I could do, not in these close quarters. He grunted a few times, squinted up at the underside of the car, then suddenly reached up and grabbed a little plastic gizmo. "Can't even think when they planted it," he said. Bernie rolled out from under the car. I scrambled after him. "Got to raise our game," he said. And then he reared back and flung that gizmo into the blue sky, high and far, over the dry wash and out of sight.

Raising our game — anything at all about games — sounded good to me, and was there a better game on earth than fetch? I took off after that gizmo at top speed, shredding some spiky little plant under my paws, and another and another.

"Chet, no, come back here! This isn't fetch!"

Then what did you call it? I must have heard wrong.

"Chet! We're not playing!"

And when you're hearing wrong the only thing to do is not listen. Otherwise you get confused, and what sort of life is that? I tore across the dry wash, up the bank, past the charred remains of a campfire, snapped up the gizmo — easy to find, what with Bernie's lovely scent all over it . . . and also a hint of Sheriff Grimble's not-so-lovely scent. How was that possible? I considered that question as I sped back to Bernie.

I dropped the gizmo at his feet. He picked it up. "You're right, Chet. Might need it someday, in a courtroom, for example."

No problem. I was familiar with courtrooms, had even been Exhibit A. The judge had slipped me a chewy from under her robe. I hopped back in the car, my mind on chewies, and soon.

Bernie has only one suit, but it's a beauty, soft and black with a powerful mothball smell that clears your head big-time. He took the suit out of the closet, gave the jacket a good shake, held it up to the light.

"Think these lapels are back in style?"

Of course I did, depending on what lapels were, exactly, and also style. Bernie got dressed — white shirt, black socks and shoes, black suit.

"Which tie?" he said, eyeing the ties in the tie rack, of which there were two: plain blue, and the gold number with the dice. That was the one he reached for, changing his mind at the last second. "Might strike the wrong note," he said, which zipped right by me, Bernie not capable of doing wrong.

Not long after that, we were in the part of Pottsdale where the fancy stores peter out and the golf courses begin, parked outside a white church — churches always easy to spot on account of the steeple with the cross on top. As for what went on inside, that was a bit of a mystery, since I'd never been in one. Was today the day?

Bernie switched off the engine and turned to me. How beautiful he looked in his suit and tie! Was the collar on the tight side? Kind of making his face a bit purplish? No problem. Purple looked good on Bernie.

"Need you to be on your best behavior," he said.

Went without mentioning! I hopped out, spotted a fire hydrant close by — couldn't have been more convenient — raised my leg, marked that hydrant so that it would stay that way till the end of time, washed clean of all those other annoying marks; and then we were good to go.

There wasn't a big crowd inside, maybe similar to the crowd at the Crowbar, although no one here smelled boozy. We sat all by ourselves at the end of the last row, Bernie in a seat, me in the aisle. I didn't move a muscle. You wouldn't have noticed me.

Up front, some sort of speech was going on, hard to understand. The speaker stood on a platform, and below the platform was a long wooden box, painted white with lots of black curlicues. A complicated smell rose out of that box. The strongest part of that smell reminded me of a chemistry lab I'd visited — very briefly — on a divorce case involving husband, wife, and boyfriend chemists, one of our very worst cases, and that was before the explosions. The next strongest part of the smell was also familiar from my job, namely the smell that humans give off after they're no longer among the living. But way more interesting was a scent so weak I almost missed it: the scent of snake. Whoa! A snake was in that box, alongside or . . . curled up with! — a dead human? I was starting to scare myself. But just then I remembered: snake-skin boots. And presto! Clint Swann was in that box, and probably looking pretty cool, at least footwear-wise, for wherever he was headed next. Wow! First time in a church and I already had it down pat. Would we be doing this again? You can always hope, and I always did.

As for Bernie, he didn't seem to be interested in the box, the speech, or anything else happening among the little group of unhappy-looking people in front. Instead he was glancing around, mostly in the direction of a youngish woman sitting a few rows ahead of us, over in the section across the center aisle. Did that mean he'd left it up to me to figure out who was in the box? The Little Detective Agency, folks. Remember that name.

I checked out the youngish woman, blond, and with that certain something that always had an effect on Bernie, although maybe not this time. Was it because she was crying softly to herself? That was my only guess.

Meanwhile up front, whatever was going on kept going on, and on. The human voice can sometimes be droning, no offense. Droning makes me sleepy. I would never sleep on the job, of course, an absolute no-no. But were we on the job? I decided to have a good think about that. For good thinks I do better lying down.

I felt a hand on my back. Ah, Bernie's hand. The world was my oyster, although in truth I'd had more than my share of trouble with —

My eyes snapped open and I was up and at 'em at once. Where were we? Still the church? A bit disappointing but the droning had stopped and everybody was filing out. We followed the last person out the door.

The youngish woman was walking toward a small convertible parked all by itself at the far end. We went that way, too, and just as she was opening the door, Bernie said, "Sorry for your loss."

The woman's head snapped around, and I got my first good look at her: a pretty woman, maybe not much older than Rita Krebs, with a red nose and teary eyes. Those teary eyes went to Bernie, then me, and back to Bernie.

"Who are you?"

"My name's Bernie, and this is Chet."

"I . . . I don't know you," she said.

"Mutual," said Bernie.

"So . . . but . . ." The young woman glanced across the parking lot, where people were getting into cars and driving off. One or two of them shot a hard look at her on the way out.

"Clint's family?" Bernie said.

"They hate me," she said, still watching them go.

"Why?" said Bernie.

She turned to us again, redid the whole looking thing — Bernie, me, back to Bernie. "You're friends with Clint?"

"We've spent time together," Bernie said.

"What was your name again?"

"Bernie. Bernie Little. And this is Chet."

She frowned. "Why do you keep introducing him? He's a dog."

"With a name," Bernie said.

Of course I had a name! Poor woman. She must have been having a rough day. I decided to cut her some slack. Most humans need at least a little slack, a surprising number needing a whole lot.

Meanwhile the woman was biting her lip, a sign that serious thinking was going down.

"Were you . . . implying you know about me and Clint?" she said.

Bernie nodded. A simple little down and up, but one of his best nods, in my opinion.

"He told you about us?"

"Not in so many words," Bernie said. "But obviously I know — why else would I be offering condolences?"

"You're the only one," she said, and burst into tears. She covered her face and sobbed. Bernie reached out in a hesitant sort of way and touched her shoulder. The next thing I knew she had her arms around him and was doing her crying against Bernie's chest.

"There, there," he said, looking at me over her head, his eyes . . . terrified? That was a first. No way I could stand Bernie being terrified. He needed help, and stat. I squeezed in between them, perhaps more a barging than a squeezing. Bernie's very quick for a human, as I may have mentioned, and caught the young lady before she fell.

"Oh my god," she said, as Bernie brushed her off, "he's so powerful." She wiped away her tears. "Was he jealous?"

"I wouldn't really put it that way," Bernie said.

"Maybe I should get a dog myself," the woman said.

"It's a thought," Bernie said.

The woman gazed at me. I happened to be scratching myself at that moment, in a particularly itchy place. Itchiness is very demanding, as you must know.

The woman turned to Bernie. "Did he ever mention me?" she said.

"Not by name," said Bernie. He smiled. "Although I don't actually know your name yet."

"Adele Marr," said the woman.

"Pleased to meet you," Bernie said. He held out his hand. After a moment or two Adele reached out and shook it.

"Am I being selfish?" she said.

"How?" said Bernie.

"Thinking about myself at his goddamn funeral." Adele's eyes were drying up. "But I can't stand not knowing if he even loved me at all."

"What did he tell you?" said Bernie.

Behind the church was a nice little garden, with stone benches and a fountain. Bernie and Adele sat on one of the benches. I lapped up fountain water, fresh and cool. Humans like to say they're getting their money's worth. We were getting our money's worth from this garden, no question! Would someone be around to hand over the cash on our way out? I glanced around, saw no one but us.

"Clint told me he couldn't wait till we could be together," Adele was saying.

"What was stopping him?" Bernie said.

"His work."

"Which was?"

"Artist management, of course," Adele said. "I thought you knew him."

"I knew he had something to do with the music business," said Bernie.

Adele nodded. "Clint was totally into the music business, country music especially. He'd even owned a bar in Nashville — that's how he met Lotty Pilgrim."

"What was the name of the bar?"

"I don't know. The point is that's how he got involved with her. Musically, I mean."

"Naturally," Bernie said. "When did you meet Clint?"

"Last year," said Adele, "when they moved here from Nashville. At the time I was pitching a whole bunch of musical acts, all over the southwest."

"Pitching what?"

"My services."

"Ah."

Adele gave Bernie a funny look. "I'm an influencer."

"Oh?"

"A social media influencer. I promote things on the Internet."

"You get paid for that?"

"There's a sliding scale, depending on what click levels are reached according to agreed-on metrics," Adele said. Or something along those lines. I can't be counted on when it comes to talk like that. "In Lotty Pilgrim's case even the lowest level turned out to be a fantasy."

"Why was that?"

"Have you ever seen her?"

Bernie nodded.

"Then you know that she's way way over the hill," Adele said. "If she was even on the hill in the first place."

"So what was Clint hoping to gain?" Bernie said.

Adele bit her lip again. "What are you saying?"

"If she was a has-been that never-was what was he hoping to accomplish?"

"That's what I asked him. Clint said she'd been cheated out of her whole career and he was going to make it right."

"Cheated how?" said Bernie. "By who?"

"He was still working on that when . . . when . . ." She came to a stop, and just gazed into the fountain. That was the moment I realized that I myself seemed to be actually in the fountain, standing motionless, the water just touching my belly, a very nice feeling. What a stroke of luck!

"What did he tell you about Lotty getting cheated?" Bernie said.

"Nothing. He was still gathering facts. But it happened a long time ago."

"He told you that?"

Adele shook her head. "I figured it out. If she was cheated out of her whole career then it must have happened way in the past. She doesn't tell her age, but Wikipedia says it's either sixty-five or sixty-eight." Adele shivered. "Christ," she said. "An old crone but quote, 'still hot-blooded.'"

"Who are you quoting?"

"The sheriff — Gamble, or Gumble or something," Adele said. There was a slight change in Bernie, not a movement or anything like that, but inside him. You'd have to know him well to spot it, and I do. "I may have to testify if there's a trial."

"How did the sheriff find out about you?"

"From Clint's family. I told you — they hate me."

"Why?"

"Because they thought I was a homewrecker."

"What home are we talking about?"

"Clint and Lotty were living together,

210

down at her crummy ranch," Adele said. "Didn't he tell you?"

"No," Bernie said.

Her eyes narrowed. "Bernie, was it?"

"Yes."

"He never mentioned a Bernie."

"Not surprising," Bernie said. "I always had the impression he was going pretty fast."

"You got that right," Adele said. "But that didn't mean he was sleeping with her."

Bernie didn't say anything, just waited. Standing in the nice cool water, I waited, too. Waiting was one of our best techniques at the Little Detective Agency.

"The sheriff says it was a crime of passion," Adele said at last. "Lotty found out about me and . . . did what she did. But I hope he's wrong. I hope she's innocent."

"Why?"

"Isn't it obvious?" She gazed at Bernie. "Maybe not to a man."

"Walk me through it," he said.

"It's simple logic," said Adele. "If she's innocent that means she wasn't jealous, and if she wasn't jealous they weren't involved. And if they weren't involved, then Clint didn't lie to me."

That was simple? But Bernie seemed to get it. "I'm with you," he said. "I hope she's innocent."

"Thanks," said Adele. "But don't hold your breath. The sheriff thinks she's going to plead guilty."

SIXTEEN

"Logically," Bernie said as we drove away from the church, the shotgun seat possibly a little on the damp side, "we should be looking into Adele's whereabouts on the night of the murder. But I'm just not feeling it, Chet. Is that the feminine side of me?"

What was this? Feminine side of Bernie? I'd never been so baffled. Feminine Bernie? Was it possible we'd been partners all this time and I'd missed something like that? I gave him a real good sniff and —

"Hey, Chet, knock it off!"

— and detected not a trace of feminine. He was one hundred percent male, practically as male as me. So what was going on? I thought about that my very hardest, right to the edge of making my head hurt, and came up with not just one but two possibilities, a new record. First possibility: this was one of Bernie's jokes, Bernie being quite the jokester at times. Second possibility: he was tired and needed a nap. Human beings sometimes have a way of getting so wound up they don't know what's good for them. For example: a nap. To give Bernie a hint, I turned to him and yawned the biggest yawn I could.

"Yikes!" said Bernie. "What's up?"

Wasn't it obvious?

"Tired? Or are you fixing to take a bite out of somebody?"

What? No, no, no. This wasn't about me. Was I the problem? Not that Bernie could ever be the problem. So maybe there was no problem.

"Curl up, Chet. Take a load off. No pressure."

I did not want to curl up. In fact, all at once, I sort of did want to take a bite out of someone. Bad of me, I know. I stuck my head out the window and right away spotted . . . a dog walker? I've never had a dog walker, of course, but that didn't stop me from not liking them. This particular dog walker was walking a mob of tiny members of the nation within. The whole scene was very bothersome. As we rolled by, I barked the kind of bark that gets your attention. Some of those tiny dudes flipped right over, like they'd been hit by a strong wind, and a

214

leash or two, or maybe all of them, slipped out of the dog walker's hand. I felt better immediately, sat up tall in my seat, facing forward, nice and still.

"What gets into you?" Bernie said.

Nothing. Nothing gets into me. We were good.

We drove downtown, through the campus where the college kids seemed to be having a busy day, what with playing Frisbee, smoking weed, and downing beers — how did they ever fit in all that activity? — and past the office towers, their tops vanishing in the brassy haze we had downtown, not a subject you want to touch on with Bernie, and into the research park. We'd worked a case in the research park, all about stolen DNA and twin sisters, a case about which I'd understood nothing. And then we'd gotten paid by the wrong twin, which Bernie discovered when her check bounced, although I'd known from the get-go on account of their smells being very slightly different. And now we were back in the research park? I got ready for anything.

Bernie parked in front of a coppery-colored building — not a tower, but not small — with coppery windows I couldn't see through. We sat in the car for a bit, me because that was what Bernie was doing, and Bernie for reasons of his own.

"Does this case go all the way back to high school?" he said after a while. "Maybe not surprising in theory — high school has a kind of power that college just doesn't."

Whatever that was it had to be brilliant. I loved when Bernie got into these moods, and we wrestled with the big questions in life, just the two of us. Did high school kids play more Frisbee than college kids, smoke more weed, throw down more cold ones? That was as far as I could go on my own.

"Take baseball," Bernie said. "High school was where I really fell in love with the game." He got a faraway look in his eyes. "And then there was Annie Roberts."

Annie Roberts? A new one on me. A teammate, maybe? Possibly the catcher, catchers being very important to pitchers, with that big mitt of theirs, swallowing up the ball? I waited to hear more, but there was no more.

"Let's take a trip back to Lotty's high school days," Bernie said, opening the door.

Fine with me! We walked to the entrance of the coppery building. Bernie read the sign. " 'Western Solutions' — not very descriptive, is it, big guy?"

I had nothing to offer on that, whatever it might have been. Was Lotty inside this building? Annie Roberts? I was a bit confused.

We went in, came to a security gate, sort of what you might see in cattle country, but nicer. The guy behind the desk said, "Help you?"

"Here to see Boomer Riggs," Bernie said.

"Is Mr. Riggs expecting you?"

"No."

"Name?"

"Bernie Little."

"One moment."

The guy tapped at a keyboard, gazed at a screen we couldn't see. His eyebrows rose slightly. He looked up. "Elevator three," he said. The gate swung open and we walked through.

"Is that a service dog?" the guy called after us.

"Very much so," said Bernie.

"He's not on a leash."

"No."

We came to some elevators. One opened by itself. We went in, Bernie first and then, not quickly, me, elevators not being my best thing. He rested his hand on my head, very lightly. The door closed. There were no buttons to push. The elevator rose — I guess that's one way to put it. But the truth was I felt like I was getting pushed down.

Wouldn't that make anyone pukey? I felt a bit pukey right away, and soon more and more and then we came to a stop and the door opened.

"Good boy," said Bernie.

My pukiness vanished, so fast I could hardly remember it. We stepped out of the elevator and into an enormous office with an enormous desk at the far end. A big man with a full head of white hair and a deep tan rose from behind the desk and waved us over.

"Well, well," he said. He had a strong, deep voice. "Bernie Little. And this must be the famous Chet."

Whoever this was, I liked him already. We headed toward him, my claws clicking on the polished wooden floor. The idea of doing some serious floor scratching rose up in my mind. I made one of my quick decisions: maybe later.

The man came around the desk, a big man, as tall as Bernie, and wider. Softer, too, but not that soft. They shook hands. "Wilder J. Riggs," the man said. "But my friends call me Boomer, and I'm friends with everybody." The shaking part of the hand shaking was over, but Boomer Riggs was one of those guys who doesn't let go right away. "Friends with everybody," he went on, "although you're the very first person who ever got in to see me without an appointment. Know why that is?"

"You were having a boring day?" Bernie said.

Boomer Riggs went still, his smile frozen, but that frozen moment went by so fast you had to be watching closely to catch it, which I was. Then his face came alive and he started to laugh, a big, booming laugh — hey! just like his name! — and he clapped Bernie on the shoulder.

"Heard a lot about you, Bernie Little," he said. "And now I know it's true. Damn good thing, because I just hate being disappointed." He let go of Bernie's hand.

"What have you heard?" Bernie said.

"That you're a son of a bitch," said Boomer, "who'd be a real big asset if we could ever get you on the Western Solutions payroll. Even though your pardner here" — he gestured toward me — "is the brains of the outfit."

Bernie laughed. "They're right about that part."

Whoa! I was the brains of the outfit? What did that mean, exactly? I went around on it, and around again, and then began to lose the thread, in a way that makes me nice and peaceful inside.

"Which is why I had them send you right up," Boomer said. "Name your price."

"I'm not here about a job," Bernie said.

"Even after I just said I hate being disappointed?"

"So does everybody."

Boomer shook his head. "Not true. Most people get used to being disappointed and finally just accept it. I've always hated it and still do, more than ever."

"My guess is you haven't dealt with a whole lot of it," Bernie said.

"That's the point!" Boomer said. "Cause and effect, Bernie. They work both ways for some people — and now that guessing is on the table, my guess is you're one of those people. Just like yours truly."

"Someone who hates being disappointed so much that others will do anything to not disappoint him?"

"Couldn't have put it better myself," Boomer said. "Hatred is a tool, one of the best tools in the box, as every successful man on earth could tell you." He gestured at a chair. "Take a pew. Something cold?"

"No thanks."

"Bourbon your drink, by any chance? I've got some twenty-year-old bottled special by an old buddy in Bardstown, Kentucky."

"I don't —"

Boomer pressed a button on the desk. "Two bourbons," he said. "And a dog treat."

A voice came out of a speaker. "What kind of dog treat, sir?"

"The best," said Boomer.

Boomer was making a very good impression on me so far. He pulled up a chair on our side of the desk. He and Bernie sat down. I sat, too, fairly close to Bernie but not too far from Boomer, in case the treat passed that way. You've got to think ahead in this life. All the more so if . . . if you happen to be the brains of the outfit! Wow! Could it be true? And if I was the brains, what was Bernie? My mind backed up to a more comfortable spot.

"So if you're not looking to get hired, what brings you here?" Boomer said.

His eyes opened extra wide, bright blue eyes, very lively, except for the black circles in the middle, which seemed empty. Were everybody's like that and I was just noticing now? Or . . . or . . . Or what? Nothing came to mind. I gazed at the door. Why the big holdup on my treat?

"I get it," Boomer was saying. "You've come to hire me!"

"I've come for information," Bernie said. "I'm prepared to pay."

"Well, well," said Boomer. "Music to my ears."

Oh? I myself heard no music. I checked out Boomer's ears. Not small for a human — actually not unlike Bernie's — but in the end only human ears, and therefore low-end when it came to listening. Still, this case seemed to have something to do with music, so —

The door opened and in stepped — oh, no. A robot. I knew robots from a visit I'd made to the science fair at Charlie's school. "Let's see if we can get Robie to scratch Chet between the ears," some kid had said. And the next thing I knew I was back outside in the car.

This particular robot was bigger, and walked instead of rolled. It smelled like our TV and had a hand like a platter. On the hand-platter rested two glasses of bourbon — a very familiar smell — and something that reminded me slightly of a Slim Jim, except it was bigger and had an aroma that made me sit up straight right away, even though I already was.

"Say hello to the future," Boomer said.

"I'm not looking forward to it," said Bernie, reaching for his glass.

"Nice to meet you, too," the robot said.

Bernie hardly spilled anything at all. The

robot served Boomer, and then came my way, walking, yes, but in a slightly rolling way that reminded me of Nemo Sparks, a perp who lived on a boat and robbed banks across the seven seas, wherever those happened to be. How hard would it be to tip this . . . what would you call it? Contraption? Yes. How hard would it be to tip it over? I was trying to decide how happy that would make me — somewhere between delighted and out of my freakin' mind — when the robot extended its platter hand in front of my face and I caught a real good whiff of that Slim Jim thing.

"White truffle–infused Kobe beef jerky treat," the robot said.

By far the most interesting words I'd ever heard! And coming from a robot. Calmly and politely, I helped myself to what was being offered.

"Enjoy the day," said the robot, and left the room, the door closing behind it.

Calmly and politely, I moved off a little way by myself. No sense in tormenting anyone with the sight of what I had and they did not, and sure as hell would never get. As for this job offer, when could we start?

Bernie and Boomer clinked glasses and drank.

"It's very good," Bernie said.

"I'll send you a bottle for Christmas."

"Thanks, but you don't —"

"Now how can I help you?"

Bernie set his glass on the armrest. I tried my very hardest to chew slowly.

"It's about Lotty Pilgrim," Bernie said.

"I saw the news," Boomer said, also setting down his glass. "Just terrible. I hadn't thought of Lotty in years, but I knew her way back when — as I'm guessing you know."

"In high school, correct?"

"Yes, sir. She made a big impression on me at the time, but the truth is I forgot all about her over the years. Honestly couldn't have told you whether she was still alive, I'm ashamed to admit." He picked up his drink, swirled it around, downed a nice, healthy slug. "Of course, as soon as I heard the news, I had Research dig for anything we had on her or this manager of hers, Clint somebody."

"Swann," said Bernie. "Did you find anything?"

"Zip," Boomer said. "I see Grimble purportedly has a confession. Hard to believe."

"You know him?"

"Sure."

"What do you think?"

"Of Grimble?"

224

"Yes."

"You already know, Bernie."

"Because you said 'purportedly'?"

Whoa! This conversation was getting hard to follow. But way more disturbing was the fact that all I had left of my treat — the tastiest treat of my career! — was one last tiny morsel. I chewed the smallest possible chew. But still too much! And just like that, my treat was gone. I turned to the door. How to make the robot return: that was the question, the big question, my one and only.

"You know and I know we could do big things together," Boomer was saying. "Feel free to revisit your decision any time. Agreed?"

"I'll agree to that," said Bernie.

"My man." Boomer raised his glass. "Sorry I don't have anything on Lotty. But very smart of her to hire you."

"Actually, she hasn't."

Boomer sat back. "No? You're confusing me."

"I have a client, but it's not her."

"A client who hired you regarding Lotty's present situation?"

"Yes."

"I won't ask you the name of this client —"

"Good."

"— but what's the goal?"

Bernie thought for a moment or two. "To find out what happened. And why."

"Don't tell me we're philosophers all of a sudden."

I waited to find out, hoping the answer was no. We'd worked a complicated case involving two philosophers over at the college who got into a fistfight about something called free will, or maybe a perp called Will Free — I never got that straight. Two roly-poly bearded dudes in a fistfight! If you could still call it that when no actual punches landed, although they both got chest pains and had to sit with their heads between their knees for a bit.

"Certainly not me," Bernie said.

"So what's going on?" said Boomer. "Especially if she's going to cop a plea."

"Maybe there are mitigating circumstances."

"Such as?"

"It's just a feeling so far," Bernie said. "But that's why I'm here. You knew her in high school. What can you tell me about her?"

"Going way way back, Bernie, my friend."

"Humor me," said Bernie.

"All right." Boomer gestured with his glass at Bernie. "But you owe me."

"I said I'd pay."

Boomer shook his head. "Just squeezin' your nuts. Your money's no good here."

Uh-oh. That first part sounded horrible. But Bernie and Boomer were still sitting in their chairs, pretty far apart, nothing much happening, definitely not anything horrible. Sometimes humans just could not be understood. That was one of the first and most important things I'd learned about them.

Boomer downed another slug of bourbon. Bernie had hardly touched his. What was up with that?

"High school and Lotty Pilgrim," Boomer said. "Every boy in the goddamn place was in love with her."

"Including you?"

"Hell, yes. She was the most beautiful girl in town, plus that voice. We all knew she was special. I even dated her a time or two."

"You were QB on the football team?"

Boomer smiled. "You're very thorough."

"Not really. That fact happened to come up."

"In conversation with your client?"

"Yes."

Boomer nodded. "He — or she — got that right. But none of that football hero shit cut any ice with Lotty."

"How long did the two of you go out?"

227

"I wouldn't say we went out at all — not on an exclusive basis. As for intimate details, don't go there. Back then a gentleman protected a lady's honor."

"Admirable," Bernie said. "Although chivalry means you're in the power position."

"Point taken," said Boomer. "You're an interesting guy, Bernie — even more interesting than I was led to believe." He drained his glass, licked his lips. "How does one hundred and twenty-five grand to start sound?"

"Way too much," Bernie said. "How did the two of you break up?"

"Me and Lotty? There was no formal breakup, not that I remember. We weren't an item — thought I made that clear." He gave Bernie a steady look.

"Got it," Bernie said.

"Meaning we just drifted apart," Boomer said. "I headed over to Lubbock right after graduation to catch the tail end of spring practice. Had a full ride at Texas Tech, sat for three years and then broke my goddamn leg in my first game as a starter. Typical college football story. Far as I remember, Lotty left town as well, maybe for Nashville."

"When was the last time you saw her?"

"Most likely at that graduation." Boomer's

watch made a little chiming sound. He checked it, and looked up. "Afraid I'll have to cut this short, Bernie."

"You've given us a lot of time already." Bernie rose. And me, too — goes without mentioning.

"Whoa!" Boomer pointed at Bernie's glass. "Turning down my money and my liquor, too?"

"I get into these ruts," Bernie said. Boomer laughed. Bernie drank up, set his glass carefully on the armrest. "Do you recall anything about Lotty dating someone after you?" he said.

Boomer was silent for a moment or two. Bernie turned to him. Boomer scrunched up his face. For a moment he looked almost like a kid thinking his very hardest. "Nope," he said.

"Possibly a Mexican," Bernie said.

"Doesn't ring a bell," said Boomer.

His watch chimed again. Chimes yes, bells no. I was keeping up with the humans, maybe even nosing slightly ahead of them. Nosing — that's a little joke, just between you and me. It won't happen again.

SEVENTEEN

"Here's a theory," Bernie said, as we headed out of town, roof down and the wind in our hair. "Clint beat up Jordan after the C-note incident. Can't see Clint as much of a fist-fighter, but Jordan's probably worse. Maybe Clint took him by surprise. And after, what if Jordan snapped? Or Rita convinced him that any man with a backbone should snap after that kind of provocation? So Jordan goes over to Lotty's ranch to settle the score. Rita goes with him to make sure it gets settled. Things get out of hand and the knife comes out of the drawer. And now Lotty's taking the fall for her grandson. It's like a distant cousin of 'Long Black Veil,' or some other murder ballad."

Bernie's always the smartest human in the room. There shouldn't be any disagreement on that by now. But sometimes he soars up to such a high level that he's like a super Bernie. I went over what I'd just heard:

230

backbone, knife, murder. It made total sense. Any moment now I'd be grabbing a perp by the pant leg and then we'd be celebrating at the Dry Gulch Steakhouse and Saloon, where I had many friends among the waitstaff. I gazed at the face of super Bernie. Super Bernie looked just like my Bernie, meaning you'd never guess the brainpower just humming away inside. Sitting there beside him, I listened for that hum, but heard nothing, surely on account of all the highway noise.

He glanced over and smiled. "Your mind on Kobe beef and truffle oil?"

Most certainly not! And then it was! Stuck on Kobe beef and truffle oil and nothing but. And suddenly I made an astonishing mental leap: we needed a robot of our own! Did you go somewhere to buy robots? Or did you just meet them in a bar and get friendly? Either sounded fine to me. I barked a bark that meant *Let's get cracking on this!*

Bernie laughed and said, "I knew it."

Bernie turned on the radio. "Two-lane blacktop and country music — who can resist?"

Not me, amigo. Especially when Bernie's doing the suggesting, but even if he's not, resisting is not my best thing.

He fiddled with the buttons. "Should be able to pull in that little country station from Silver City, unless some big outfit —"

There was a crackle and then a woman's voice came through the speakers.

". . . strange news from over in the Valley today, where one-time country songbird Lotty Pilgrim has been arrested in the stabbing death of her manager, Clint Swann, both of them residents, it says here, of Rancho Corazon, Arizona. Some of you old-timers might remember her big hit 'How You Hung the Moon' — the Loretta Lynn version's my personal fave — but here's the locked-up lady herself with 'One Bad Day.' "

"Locked-up lady — for god's sake," Bernie muttered. And then came Lotty's voice.

In a little border town
Where we were staying
You went out to make a call
And that's not all,
Cause when you came back I knew
That you'd been straying,
And I grabbed your shootin' iron
Down off the wall.

"Whoa," said Bernie. "Didn't know about

this one." He leaned in closer as the pedal-steel player started up. I love pedal steel myself — it does something to my ears I couldn't possibly explain — but just as Lotty's voice came in again, the sound got all fuzzy and then faded away completely. Bernie tried the radio buttons again but it was no use.

"Damn." He fished a pen out from under his seat and wrote on his hand, at the same time saying, " 'One Bad Day.' "

"But," Bernie said after a long silence — maybe very long since we seemed to be back in Phantom Springs, "what about the fact that Leticia's house got trashed? Didn't that big slick dude do the trashing? And leave the courtesy call note? Could he have been working for Clint, sending Jordan a warning through his mom? Did that set Jordan off?" Bernie shook his head. "I bungled that encounter at Leticia's house, big guy."

Which had to be one of Bernie's jokes, since he'd never bungled anything and never would. As for this big slick dude, I had no idea who he was talking about. But then I remembered — hair gel and baby powder! — and it all came back to me. I could even see him in my mind — that strong-featured face and eyes in no hurry — and hear him, too: *Have a nice day.* You hear that all the time. Once Bernie and Rick Torres had a whole discussion about have-a-nice-day, over a beer or two, or more. "Some folks mean it," Bernie had said. And Rick had replied, "And some mean the exact opposite." That had completely lost me the first time around, but now I sort of got it. If you just hang around long enough, does everything become clear? Wow! I had a game plan at last!

"And another thing I bungled," Bernie said, as we pulled up in front of the yellow house on Bluff Street — Leticia's house, if I hadn't forgotten the facts of the case, at least not all of them — "was that lunch with Eliza."

Lunch with Eliza? At Max's Memphis Ribs? There'd been no bungling at all — Cleon's ribs were perfect every time. I gazed at Bernie. Was he okay? He looked okay on the outside, easily the best-looking human on the planet. So why worry? I stopped at once.

"Maybe I should call her, straighten things out." Bernie took out his phone. "What's a good way to start?" We sat in silence. Before a good way to start occurred to him — I myself was thinking about other things, namely ribs — the phone buzzed. Bernie checked the screen and said, "Whoa." Then he touched a button.

"Uh," he said, "hi."

"Hi, Bernie."

Hey! It was Suzie! Hadn't heard her voice in way too long. Was there a reason for that? I tried to remember, but it wouldn't come.

"Busy?" she said. "Hope I'm not bothering you."

"Yes," said Bernie. "I mean no. No bother."

"But you're busy."

"Yes. No. I mean no."

"Chet with you?"

"Oh, yeah."

Suzie laughed. "What's he doing?"

"Right now?" Bernie gave me a quick glance. "Looking highly alert."

Suzie laughed again. Then she said, "Wait — you're not in danger?"

"Oh, no, nothing like that."

"Working on a case?"

"Yeah."

"An interesting one? Not that any of them are dull. I love what you do."

"Really?"

"It's so firsthand. Unlike mine. Anyway, I won't keep you. Just wanted to say hi. Hope you don't mind."

"Uh, no. Why would I mind?"

There was a pause. Then Suzie said, "I can think of reasons."

"Well, there's that," said Bernie.

Suzie laughed one more time, a different laugh from the others. I liked the others better. "Anyway, I won't keep you," she said. Which she'd said already. In fact, there'd been lots of that kind of thing in this conversation. A helpful development, from my point of view, made it easier to understand.

"Bye," she said.

"Bye," said Bernie. And then, "Hey — where are you?"

But too late. She was gone.

"Wonder what that was about," Bernie said, as we walked up to the front door.

I thought that over, came to the conclusion it had been mostly about me. How nice of Suzie! I missed her.

Leticia's chimes, hanging by the door, chimed in the breeze. There was a lot of chiming in this case. Bernie knocked. No one came to the door. "I really hope," he began, but then a car came climbing up the street.

Not the little yellow car that had been part of this case from the get-go? Or just about from the get-go, the actual timing of get-gos not always clear in my mind. Forget all that,

236

the point being it was that little yellow car, and with Jordan at the wheel. He stuck his fuzzy, baby face — still a bit swollen — out the window for a good look at us. His eyebrows rose way up.

"Jordan!" Bernie raised his hand in the stop sign. "We need to —"

Jordan didn't stick around to find out what we needed to do. Instead he booked, tires smoking as he zoomed up the hill, maybe not zooming on account of the hill being steep and the car being what we motoring types would call a shitbox. I'd run into some confusion when first learning that term, but that was long in the past, remembered by nobody, least of all me.

We hopped in the car, Bernie coming close to hopping himself, deciding to use the door at the very last second, or even later, maybe why he got his tie stuck in it — yes, still in his suit and tie from the church, what a long day we were having, but so much fun! — and took off after Jordan. At the top of Bluff Street, the pavement ended, as we already knew, becoming rough and narrow, as it zigzagged down to a distant highway, shimmering below. Jordan was zigging and zagging down with surprising speed, raising a long zigzaggy dust cloud.

"Not bad at all," Bernie said. "Or maybe

that's just desperation — the desperation that comes with guilt." Wow! One of his most brilliant puzzlers, but no time to spend on it now. We stepped on the gas, Bernie doing the actual stepping, and started after Jordan. Zigzagging up and down steep mountain roads was one of our best things, right up there with shooting dimes out of the air and grabbing perps by the pant leg. Maybe we'd be doing them all at once, and soon! Except I wasn't smelling the .38 Special, meaning it was back home in the safe and we weren't carrying. There are disappointments in life. You just have to find a way. For example, was there any reason I couldn't grab Jordan — or any perp — by both pant legs at once? Wow! Why had it taken me so long to think of that?

We roared down the back side of the mountain. Was it the mountain all that silver got taken out of? I kept an eye out for silvery glints but saw none before we were caught up in the dust cloud and I couldn't see a thing. Could Bernie? It didn't matter. Bernie's the best wheelman in the Valley, as you must know by now, and doesn't need to see. The Porsche roared its lovely roar. I howled my lovely howl. Bernie laughed his lovely laugh. Life gets no better!

Down and down we went, the yellow car

closer and closer with every glimpse we caught through the dust. But surprise! Just before the highway, Jordan made a sharp turn — fishtailing so much the car slid sideways — and took another track I hadn't spotted, even rougher than the one we were on, and headed back up the mountain. We made a sharp turn of our own — but no fishtailing with Bernie at the wheel — and stuck to Jordan like glue. I myself once had a bit of a problem with glue, but no time for that now. One of those things that smells better than it tastes, let's leave it at that.

"Knows he can't match us on the straights, big guy."

Well, of course not! Not on the straights, the crookeds, or anyplace else. He was dealing with the Little Detective Agency, my friends.

Back up the mountain we roared, closing in on Jordan, and big-time. On a ridge line near the top, he glanced back — and, oh yeah, glanced back again in that uh-oh way we love to see — then hit the brakes and tried the right-back-attya! Had to admire him: the right-back-attya, where you wheel around and zoom back in the direction you'd just been zooming from, is an expert move. Was Jordan an expert? At first I thought yes, but it ended up being no, easy to see the moment the yellow car began doing donuts, which means spinning round and round. As for donuts, Donut Heaven, crullers, and bear claws, we'll have to get into all that later.

The here-and-now problem was Jordan, donutting down upon us along the narrow track with a cliff on one side and — what was this? — a cliff on the other? When had that happened? Sometimes, especially when you're having fun, things go by so fast you can miss a detail or two. I glanced over at Bernie, just to make sure we were doing all right. And there he was, one hand on the wheel — actually only a couple of fingers of one hand — and sitting, well, pretty, like we were on our way to a picnic. Was that possible? This day just kept getting better.

That was how I came to be thinking about picnics as Jordan barreled down on us, the yellow car spinning in the center of a boiling cloud of dust and blue smoke. I caught a glimpse of Jordan's face, eyes and mouth opened wide like he was screaming, although the scream itself was lost in all the noise. I could actually see that weird pink thing that hangs from the back of the human mouth! And then — KA-BOOM!

All of that went down, except for the KA-BOOM. At just about the exact moment of the KA-BOOM — or even later! — Bernie's fingers made a little movement, and so did his feet, and the yellow car thundered right through the space we'd just been in. As for us, we zipped along the edge of one cliff — and then the edge of the other! — on only two wheels, and maybe none. We were free, me and Bernie, free as the wind. Don't you want to be like us? I'm not sure that can happen.

Free as the wind until we came down to earth, landing softly on the dirt track, slowing and turning, so smooth, just in time to see the yellow car whack a big boulder on one cliffside and come to a rocking stop. Everything got very quiet. We pulled up alongside the yellow car.

"Jordan?" Bernie called. "You all right?"

No answer. In fact, no sign of Jordan.

"Jordan?"

And there he was, popping up into view and wriggling out through the passenger-side window.

"Jordan? You okay?"

No reply from Jordan.

"Aw, Jordan. Try thinking ahead, just a little."

But maybe he couldn't. Instead he took off down the mountain on foot.

"For god's sake, Jordan — how's that going to work?"

Jordan kept running. A fine runner for a human, as I think I mentioned, and this time he was in sneakers, not flip-flops. Well, one sneaker, the other flying off. We hopped out of the car. Jordan's legs churned away so fast, a pleasure to see. But did we have all day? No. You have to get down to business in this life. I loped after him, stuck out my head, grabbed him by the pant leg. He went down, wriggled around, tried to crawl, wriggled some more and — good grief! His pants were coming off again? What was with this dude and his pants? Wriggle, wriggle and all at once he'd wriggled himself right to the edge of the track and over the cliff. I hung on by that pant leg, but Jordan was slip-slipping away. He screamed, maybe at the sight of where he was headed, a long way down to a rocky landing. And then Bernie was beside me, reaching with one hand and hauling Jordan back up. Still with one hand, he sat him down on the track with a thump.

Jordan gazed up at us, bloody, dusty, scared, angry, young. That was my first impression, more than good enough, in my opinion. No point in working yourself to exhaustion. Bernie looked angry, too, an unusual sight.

"We've run out of patience, me and Chet," he said.

We had? Good to know! Was it time for me to give Jordan a nip or two? I waited for a signal from Bernie.

"So before things get regrettable," Bernie went on, "let's have the truth. Did you kill Clint?"

"You out of your fuckin' mind?" Jordan said. He spat out a little blood, and also a tooth. The tooth sparkled in the sunshine and disappeared over the cliff. I was just thinking to myself that there's all kinds of beauty in life, when Jordan started to cry.

EIGHTEEN

Women cry more than men, but some men cry quite a bit, and lots of men cry at least once or twice. I'd even seen Bernie's eyes tear up, the day Charlie's things got hauled away to Leda and Malcolm's place in High Chaparral Estates. Also it was okay for men to cry. I'd heard it right from Bernie's lips, one day when Charlie started crying because of some bully in school.

"It's okay to cry, Charlie," he'd said. "But first try not to."

"Huh?" Charlie had said.

"Never mind," Bernie had told him. "Make your hands into fists and stand like this. Are you a righty or a lefty?"

"Dad!"

"Just kidding. I'm going to teach you the simple right cross. It starts in your legs —"

"Legs?"

"Actually the balls of your feet. And finishes smack on some ass — some jerk's

244

nose. No one likes getting hit on the nose. They try to avoid situations where it might happen again." He'd held up the palm of his hand. "Here's some jerk's nose." And Charlie'd thrown a punch. Smack. "Nice. Now punch like you're punching something a little behind the nose, so you have to punch through to get there."

SMACK.

"That should do it."

And Bernie had been right about that, except for an angry call from the bully's mom a few days later. But back to Jordan, crying on this mountaintop overlooking Phantom Springs and the desert all around. A lovely sight, and the air was lovely too, cooler than down below. Take away Jordan and we'd have been enjoying a peaceful little break.

Bernie crouched in front of Jordan, who was kind of sobbing now, hands over his face. "Uh, there, there," Bernie said. "What are you crying about?"

The crying stopped at once. Jordan peeked at Bernie through spread fingers. "You and your fucking hound tried to kill me — is that good enough?"

"It's actually problematic on multiple grounds," Bernie said. "First, any neutral observer would say we saved your life.

Second, Chet has very little hound in him, if any. Third, and most important, you can't use language like that about him."

Jordan lowered his hands. His face was an unpleasant sight. Was there any way to make the sobbing start again, get his hands back up there?

"I can't say fucking hound?"

"Neither one about him. You know I'm right."

"I do?"

"Sure. You're basically a good person," Bernie said. "But I've known some basically good people who've killed other people, usually basically bad ones, like Clint."

Jordan raised his voice to a screechy level that my ears just hate. "You're trying to hang that on me?" His eyes got squinty. "I don't get it — weren't you the one who set her up? Led that goddamn sheriff right to her door?"

Bernie's voice got low, but with this throb in it, hard even for me to hear. "I got set up myself. The point is I don't believe Lotty killed Clint."

"Neither did I," Jordan said.

"Can you prove it?"

"My word's not good enough?"

Bernie laughed.

A crafty look came over Jordan's face, a

246

look we sometimes see from perps who think they're about to put one over on Bernie. What fun we have at the Little Detective Agency! And we also get paid! At least some of the time!

"If I'm basically a good person," Jordan said, "then how come my word's not good enough?"

"Uh-oh," said Bernie. "That's the kind of question the basically bad ones ask."

The crafty look shifted around and turned confused, always a pleasant sight.

"Where were you the night Clint got killed?" Bernie said.

"Home. Home on fucking painkillers from him beating me up. Or can't I say fucking painkillers?"

"I'd actually prefer not, but no biggie," Bernie said. "Who can vouch for you?"

"Rita was there the whole time."

"Anyone else? Someone not so invested in you?"

"Invested?"

"Someone who doesn't care about you so much."

"You think she cares a lot about me?"

"Isn't she your girlfriend?"

"Yeah, but we fight a lot."

"What about?"

Jordan took a deep breath, then shivered

like it was cold outside, which it wasn't. "All this shit," he said.

"With Clint?" said Bernie.

"That, too."

"What else?"

Jordan shook his head. "Just all the shit." He gazed past us, beyond the edge of the cliff, and shivered again.

"Let's stick with Clint for now," Bernie said. "What went on with the tip jar?"

Jordan turned, took a look at Bernie. I got the strange feeling that he was really seeing Bernie for the first time, actually getting to know him.

"Are you rich?" he said.

"No."

True, but I knew we would be someday, possibly soon.

"Then how come you put in a C-note?"

"I like Lotty's music," Bernie said. "And I didn't like the way that guy was treating her."

"The one who wanted 'How You Hung the Moon'?"

"Yeah," said Bernie. "Why doesn't she sing it?"

"She won't talk about it," Jordan said. "Rita thinks that's the key to the whole thing."

"What whole thing?"

Jordan opened his mouth like he was going to say something, but he ended up just sighing. "It's hopeless. And even if I had the facts, why would I tell you?"

"Because I care about Lotty. Your grandmother's in jail right now, arrested for a crime she didn't do."

"You keep saying that, but how do you know?" said Jordan.

Bernie, still crouched in front of him, reached out and touched his chest, very lightly. "What are you telling me?"

"Nothing."

"Do you have reason to believe she killed him?"

"Goddamn right," said Jordan. "He's a parasite — was a parasite, charming this old lady to fall in love with him and robbing her blind. And meanwhile he's got a real girlfriend in the Valley."

"Those are reasons for motive, not reasons for guilt."

"What's the difference?"

"You can figure that out," Bernie said. "Did Lotty know he was robbing her blind?"

"She doesn't say it that way. He just worked on her weakness, made it like he was doing her a big favor."

"How so?"

Jordan shrugged. "Like it was her fault

she was broke, on account of being careless. Or if he was in a good mood, on account of her being an artist. 'You're an artist, Lotty. Artists can't be managing the money, not with those imaginative minds of theirs.' " Hey! All at once Jordan sounded just like Clint, except an even meaner version. Whoa! Could a mean Clint somehow be inside him? For a moment I was more scared than I'd ever been in my whole life. But then Jordan kept going in his normal voice, and I went back to being my normal self, just sitting near the cliff edge minding my own business, keeping watch on Jordan's ankles.

"But, yeah," he said, "she knew."

"So that's what your tip jar caper was all about?"

Jordan nodded. "The bastard was even taking the tips."

"Whose idea was it?" Bernie said. "Hers or yours?"

"Mine."

"Planning to keep it for yourself?"

"Hell, no. Stealing from my own grandma? What do you take me for?"

Bernie gave him a long look, and then nodded slightly.

"She's a great artist," Jordan went on. "Even if hardly anybody knows."

"I know," Bernie said.

"Yeah? You're into music?"

"Hers, for sure."

"Poor Grandma. Got off on the wrong foot and never really . . ."

"Never really what?"

"Got to where she shoulda been."

"But how come? Got off on the wrong foot in what way?"

"Maybe there were drugs involved, but I don't know, man. No one talks in this family — not about the big things."

"Drugs involved in what way?"

"Don't know that either," Jordan said. "This one day she caught me — not caught me, just sort of saw me with a beer and these pills of Rita's. Legitimate pills, left over from Rita's root canal."

"What kind of pills?" Bernie said.

"OxyContin. Lotty read the label and got real mad. 'Want to knock holes in your mind like I did?' That was all she said. But it's where I got the idea — like, her and drugs."

Bernie thought about that. Then he said, "Did you take the pills?"

"Not then," said Jordan. "After she left."

Their gazes met. Jordan looked down.

"Is your father in the picture?" Bernie said.

Jordan shook his head. "He's a sperm bank."

There's a look that comes over Bernie's face when he gets real interested in someone. I saw it now.

"What about your mom's father?" Bernie said. "Your grandfather."

"Not in the picture."

"What do you know about him?"

"Nothing. It was some brief thing. Lotty doesn't talk about it."

"Does your mom?"

"Just that it was a brief thing."

Bernie walked over to the edge of the cliff, gazed into the huge distance. I eased over a little closer to Jordan and watched Bernie from there.

"This dog of yours is kind of part of the team, huh?" Jordan said.

"You should be crystal clear on that by now." Bernie turned to him. "Who killed Clint?"

"I don't know."

"What's your best guess?"

Jordan just sat there, said nothing.

"Are you the uncurious type?" Bernie said. "Hard to believe — the uncurious type doesn't send away for an Arizona PI application."

Jordan's heart started beating faster. Hearing human heartbeats was no big deal, but I was close enough to feel Jordan's as well.

"How the hell do you know that?"

"I'm an Arizona PI myself."

"Yeah, but . . . but you all share applications?"

Bernie walked over to him. "PIs investigate things. What do you want to investigate, Jordan?"

Jordan looked up at Bernie, tried to meet his gaze and . . . did! "My grandma thought you were a good man — from how the dog acts with you. Before you set her up."

The expression in Bernie's eyes changed. Jordan caught that and added real quick, "Or didn't."

But way more important was this news that some member of the nation within was suddenly part of the show. When would I be meeting this newcomer?

"Does Lotty know about your investigation?" Bernie said.

Jordan shook his head. "And there isn't any investigation, not yet. Not by me."

"Then by who?"

"Nobody now."

"Is that your way of saying Clint?"

Jordan nodded.

"What was Clint investigating?"

"Maybe some guy who works at a dude ranch."

"What dude ranch?"

"I never found out. All this was from just one time I heard him on the phone."

"With who?"

"I don't know."

"How about the name of the ranch hand?"

Jordan shrugged. "Might have been Flaco."

"Did Lotty know about Clint's investigation?"

"Not that she ever said to me."

"What about your mom?"

Jordan made a small sound, like a groan but very soft. "My mom and Lotty don't get along. More like my mom kind of hates her."

"Why?"

"Lotty wasn't around much when my mom was growing up. Since she came back they were only at the beginning of making things right, if that's what they were doing. And now this."

Bernie gestured with his chin, down at Phantom Springs. "Why were you going to your mom's house just now?"

"To pick up some of her things."

"And take them out to the RV?"

"Yeah."

"Why is she out there?"

"That break-in at her place," Jordan said. "She doesn't feel safe."

The wind rose and ruffled Bernie's hair. Which was the whole point of the wind rising at the moment — just to see that sight. That's the kind of thing I like about the desert: sometimes you get to look inside the mind of the wind.

Bernie extended his hand. "Let's see if you've still got a functioning ride."

Jordan gazed at Bernie's hand, finally held out his own. Bernie pulled him to his feet. Was cuffing him next? That was my preference, but it didn't happen.

No question the yellow car was dinged-up pretty bad, but Bernie did some nice work with the tools — even throwing in a good solid kick that made all the difference — and Jordan drove it back down the mountain with us following behind, not real close but never losing sight of him.

"Got to keep him safe, Chet. Him and the whole family."

I went over that in my mind a few times while we swung by Leticia's house, trying to make sure it would stick. And just when it was about to stick forever, I smelled a lizard, of all things!

"You stay here," Bernie said. "First sign of trouble, let me know."

Aha! We were working separately. Not my

favorite technique but perfectly doable, as long as it was over real quick. Bernie and Jordan went into the house and came out again just as I was starting to get — let's not say agitated, more like slightly concerned — Jordan now carrying a suitcase. Bernie managed to unjam one of the back doors of the yellow car and Jordan put the suitcase inside, then sat behind the wheel.

Bernie spoke to him through the open window. "I'm going to describe someone — big guy, six five, two fifty, well-dressed, well-spoken, uses hair gel. Recognize him?"

"Sounds a bit like that bouncer at the Crowbar," Jordan said. "Excepting for well-dressed, well-spoken, and hair gel."

"Not to mention that Shermie's more like six two, three hundred. But the male part is bang on."

Jordan thought about that, then smiled a quick, small smile, actually kind of sweet, like a kid's. "You saying I'm not cut out to be a PI?"

"Not in so many words," Bernie said. He tapped the roof.

We drove up to the RV, first Jordan, then us. Cottonwoods, dry wash with that blue trickle among the rocks here and there: a peaceful scene. The door of the RV opened and Rita stepped out: ponytail, bare feet, metal-blue eyes, plus the shotgun again, muzzle down. What wasn't to like, except for that shotgun being with her at all times?

"Her, do you think?" Bernie said.

Her in what way? I had no clue, hoped that one might come along.

Jordan walked up to Rita.

"What the hell are you doing?" she said to him.

"Couldn't help it, babe," Jordan said. "They were waiting at the house."

"Christ," said Rita. "And don't call me babe."

"But you like when I do. Remember when you said —"

"Jordan?" Bernie said. "Go inside."

"Huh?"

"I'm going to have a quick word with Rita."

"Yeah, but —"

"Do what he says," Rita told him. "Make your mom some coffee."

"Instant okay?" Jordan said as he entered the RV. "I have trouble with the —" The door closed behind him.

Bernie faced Rita. He glanced at the shotgun. I thought he was going to say something about it, but he didn't. I changed my position a little bit.

"Your dog going to attack me again?" Rita said.

"Attack's a strong word for what happened," said Bernie. "Chet likes things peaceful, that's all. Someone that seems wedded to a single shot 410 — that makes him uneasy."

Rita gave Bernie a look. She leaned the shotgun against the RV and turned to me. "Happy now?"

I was! And I'd been happy before. And would be happy again. This visit was going very well so far.

Rita stepped away from the RV, walked over to the yellow car. Was it hers? I had a feeling that was a strong possibility. She ran her eyes over all the new dings — more like dents — from up on the mountain.

"Not really his fault," Bernie said. "He's actually a pretty good driver."

"He's incompetent at just about everything, like most men," Rita said. "What do you want from me?"

"Your help," Bernie said. "Who killed Clint?"

"I have no idea."

"Do you think it was Lotty?"

"It's possible."

"Any possibility it was you?"

Rita's eyes shifted toward the shotgun, just

258

the slightest bit. "Why would I do that?"

"Because he beat the shit out of your boyfriend, and you're . . . you."

Rita nodded. "I considered it."

"And?"

"What do you think? I'd use a knife? Cheat on my wedded husband over there?" She pointed to the shotgun, just leaning in the shade.

NINETEEN

The door to the RV opened and Leticia came out. "What does he want?" she asked Rita.

"He *says* he wants to find out who killed Clint," Rita said. "I don't know what he really wants."

Jordan called from inside. "Rita? I can't get this goddamn thing to work."

Rita and Leticia exchanged a complicated look, not particularly friendly. Rita went inside and closed the door. Then she came out, grabbed the shotgun, and went back in.

Leticia turned to Bernie. Her glossy black hair didn't seem so glossy today, and her face was a bit puffy, like she'd been sleeping. Also she had a crease on one of her cheeks, the kind of crease you often see on a human just after they wake up. So: my guess was that Leticia had been asleep when we'd showed up. Wow! Had I figured that out all by myself? Was this how it was to be Bernie? At that moment, I felt a big yawn coming on. There's no stopping big yawns, as I'm sure you know.

"My son says you almost got him killed," Leticia said.

"I wouldn't put it that way," said Bernie. "Did he mention the part about saving his life?"

"He said that was mostly the dog's part."

Suddenly they were both looking at me, still in mid-yawn. I tried to hurry it along, but it was no go.

"Chet, right?" Leticia said. "We had a dog when I was a kid."

"Patsy?" said Bernie.

"How do you know that?"

"Your mom mentioned it," Bernie said. "Where were you at that time — you, your mom, and Patsy?"

"It depends what 'my mom' means."

"Lotty, of course. What are you saying?"

Leticia walked away, into the cotton-woods. We followed her. Cottonwoods smell like that fizzing drink humans sometimes down when they wake up and find they're hungover. A nice smell, which I was enjoy-ing when Leticia stopped and gazed across the wash.

"Lotty wasn't around much during my

childhood. I thought I mentioned that."

"Just the bare fact," Bernie said.

He stood beside her. I took my place in the middle. We all gazed across the wash. Nothing moved on the other side except the air, shimmering a bit, meaning it was hot out there. But nice here in the shade, almost cool. Leticia wore a green and silver necklace that caught a ray or two shining down through the leaves. A fine sight, but she wasn't happy. I could feel it.

"Why does it matter to you?" she said.

"She's the central figure in this case. I need to understand her."

"What case? Her lawyer said she's pleading guilty."

"You spoke to her lawyer?"

"I saw him yesterday."

"Where?"

"At the public defender's office in the Valley."

"How is it possible she can't afford a lawyer?" Bernie said.

"She's broke," said Leticia. "Like most artists."

"But she wrote 'How You Hung the Moon,' for god's sake."

"Old news."

Bernie kicked a little stone. I went and picked it up, dropped it at his feet, but he

262

didn't notice.

"Do you think she killed Clint?" he said.

"I don't know."

"Anyone else who might have done it?"

"Not Jordan, if that's what you're thinking."

"I'm not," said Bernie. "How did you feel about Clint yourself?"

"I never even met him. Lotty keeps people in separate worlds."

"Why?"

"Part of her mystique."

Bernie gave her a sidelong look. "Jordan never met Clint either, but he hated him."

"Jordan's a big fan of Lotty's. Not just the music, but Lotty the person." Leticia gave Bernie a sidelong look of her own. Their sidelong looks met.

"What went wrong between you and your mother?" Bernie said.

Leticia blew air between her lips, making that lip-flapping sound. I can do that, too, although only by accident. The human lip flap means something, but I've never figured out what. "Where to begin?" Leticia said.

"How about your earliest memories?" said Bernie.

Leticia stared at Bernie, kind of like she was studying him. Her face was no longer puffy; the crease in her cheek had disappeared. "Are all detectives like you?"

"We — the good ones, at least — probably share some basic traits."

"Name one."

Bernie thought for what seemed like a long time. Then he happened to see me, still standing over the stone I'd brought back. "Doggedness," he said.

Whoa! That sounded so important, like maybe the biggest thing I'd ever heard. I wished I'd been listening just a little closer to what had gone down, so maybe all would be clear. And if not all, then at least part.

Meanwhile Leticia was nodding yes, like doggedness was the right answer to her question, whatever that had been. "Okay, Senor Detective," she said. "First memory — me and Aunt Rosita, out back with the chickens. I had names for all of them — Foo Foo was my favorite. She'd peck grains from my hand. Then this blond woman is standing over me. I'd never seen anything so lovely in my life. Like a storybook queen, or something. She says, 'Well, well, my little Mexican baby. Mama's come to take you home.' " Leticia glanced at Bernie. "Glad you asked?"

I sure was! Otherwise I'd never have found out about Foo Foo. A chicken, unless I'd missed something. Chickens can be fun.

They're like tennis balls in some ways. Would I be meeting Foo Foo anytime soon?

"And the storybook queen was Lotty?" Bernie said.

"Correct. From soon after I was born — can't tell you exactly how long because Lotty has several versions — until that day, I lived with my aunt Rosita in Tesabe."

"Down on the border?"

"Yes. But not long after that scene — might have been the same day — Lotty plunked me in this two-tone Caddy — she had a thing for Caddies, still hasn't grown out of it — and drove us to Austin. She had a new quote 'manager' and things were looking good. She explained on the ride, talked practically nonstop, talked and sang. Even made up a song called 'Leticia' right off the top of her head." There was a long pause. "Her voice was . . . nicer in those days."

A jackrabbit appeared by a bush on the far bank. Jackrabbits have been an interest of mine going way back. Those ears! Bernie says they can hear sounds from the next county, wherever that may be. And what great leapers and hoppers they are! I've had no success when it comes to —

I felt Bernie's hand on my collar, very gentle, but there. So friendly of Bernie! I sat down, got nice and settled. When I looked across the wash again, the jackrabbit was gone.

"Do you remember the song?" Bernie said.

"That doesn't sound like a detectivey question," said Leticia.

Bernie spread his hands and said nothing.

"In fact," Leticia said, "I do remember a bit, really just a fragment." And then she sang, "Leticia, never gonna miss ya, again." I liked the sound of her singing voice — way better than her talking voice, the opposite of what usually happens — but Leticia didn't seem pleased. "Country music lyrics tend to be nothing but fantasy in my opinion," she said, "and Lotty's a fantasist if ever there was. Two years later there was a new quote 'manager' and I was back with Aunt Rosita in Tesabe."

"Is she still alive?" Bernie said.

"She died my junior year in high school," said Leticia. "I've been on my — I've made my own way since then."

"How did she die?"

"Breast cancer caught way too late. No doctor, no insurance — the usual ramshackle shit that goes with having no money."

"Sorry for your loss," Bernie said.

Leticia shot him a glance. "Kind of long after the event," she said. Then she added, "But why should there be a rule? Thank you. She was a fine person. Collected butterflies, which was a bit unusual for someone of her background."

"Did you inherit the collection?"

"That would have been nice," said Leticia. "But by the time I got home — I'd been on the class trip to the Grand Canyon — it was gone."

"How were you related?" Bernie said.

"We weren't," said Leticia. "She was an old friend of Lotty's. I just called her aunt — actually Tia, Tia Rosita."

"What was her last name?"

"Flores."

"Did she have children of her own?"

"No."

"Was she married?"

"I think she had been in the past. And there was a boyfriend or two before she got sick."

"Do you remember any of their names?"

Leticia shook her head. "We're not talking till-death-do-us-part type boyfriends."

Bernie went still. Why? I had no idea. Leticia was watching him.

"What?" she said.

He gave his head a little shake. Don't

267

forget we're a lot alike in some ways, me and Bernie. "Even a first name might help," he said.

"Was that what you were just thinking about?"

Bernie smiled at her, the kind of smile you see between friends. "Not exactly."

Leticia's eyes shifted very quickly and for no time at all to one of Bernie's hands, the hand that doesn't get to do any of the big jobs, like throwing balls or pulling triggers. I'd seen that glance before between men and women, but what it was all about remained a puzzler.

"I don't see the relevance," she said, "but one of them might have been called Flaco."

I could feel something rev up in Bernie's mind, but his face gave no sign of it. "You're probably right about the relevance," he said. He looked back at the RV. "Does this ring a bell — big guy, six-five, two-fifty, well-dressed, well-spoken, uses hair gel?"

"No," said Leticia. "And Flaco was just a little guy."

Bernie handed her our card. "Let me know if a big guy like that shows up," he said. "And just for now, staying out here's a good idea."

"Why?"

"Because of the break-in."

"I get that it was a warning," Leticia said, "but what about?"

"We're working on that," Bernie said.

"And meanwhile we're in danger?" She gestured toward the RV.

"I wouldn't put it that strongly."

"But," said Leticia.

"You got it." Bernie took out a pen. "We'll need the name of that public defender."

Leticia said the name. Bernie wrote it on his hand. While he was doing that, she gave him a close look, maybe trying to see the inner Bernie. She had a treat in store.

The courthouse, which I'd been inside of several times, including once as Exhibit A, stands across the street from a shady little downtown park, where Bernie and I sat on a bench with Haskell, the public defender, me actually not sitting but lying underneath so I had the shade of the bench as well as the shade of the trees. Why not be nice to yourself in this life?

We deal with public defenders sometimes at the Little Detective Agency, but all I know about them for sure is they tend to be on the young side. Haskell reminded me of Charlie's jittery little buddy Murrow, called Murrow the Minnow by all the other kids at our Fourth of July blowout until Bernie said, "Kids?" Haskell and the Minnow even had that same expression on their faces, like they'd just been surprised. I kept my eye on him through the slats of the bench seat and tried to concentrate on their conversation, not easy, what with my mind wandering back to that party. Sausages! Burgers! Frisbees! Steak tips! It checked all the boxes. The only negative were the fireworks, and one firework in particular called Rocket to the Moon that took a rather strange flight, at one stage possibly passing right through old man Heydrich's house.

Maybe more on that later. Right now Haskell was tapping his foot like crazy and saying, ". . . really doesn't want to see anybody."

"I get that, Haskell," Bernie said. "You've said it three times."

"Sorry, Mr. Little."

"Don't say you're sorry. And don't call me Mr. Little."

"Um, okay."

"Did you tell her specifically that I wanted to see her?"

"Yes, sir. 'Mr. Little wants to see you.' Those exact words. I didn't know not to call you Mr. Little at that point in time."

Through the slats, I caught an interesting gleam in Bernie's eyes, kind of menacing.

Haskell, busy picking up some papers he'd just dropped, missed Bernie's look.

"And," Haskell went on, licking his thumb and trying to wipe a dirt smear off a page, "Ms. Pilgrim said especially not him. Her exact words. Sorry. Oops. Not sorry. Sorry."

Now he caught Bernie's expression and quickly turned away, like it could actually hurt him.

"I need you to think," Bernie said.

"Sure," said Haskell. "What about?"

Bernie took a deep breath. "How to get Lotty out of this mess."

"Boy," said Haskell, "that's a tough one. The problem, Mr., uh, is she's dead set on pleading guilty. So I've been more or less strategizing the end game, if you will."

"Go on," said Bernie, his voice getting quiet.

Haskell wriggled around, got more comfortable. "Well, with no aggravating circumstances I can see, I think we can rule out the death penalty. That sets us up for negotiations with the DA. We've got a little time — there's two weeks till the arraignment."

"Negotiations for what purpose?"

"Why, to go for reduced prison time," said Haskell.

"Reduced to what?"

"Don't hold me to it, but I'd be happy with ten years, maybe twelve."

There was a long silence. "Do you have any idea how old she is?" Bernie said.

"That turns out to be a tough one," said Haskell. "There's conflicting evidence."

"But she's not young."

"No, sir — sixty-five at the very least."

"So plus ten would make —"

"Seventy —" Haskell stopped himself. "Uh, I get what you're implying." He shook his head. "But I just don't see the DA taking any less. Ms. Pilgrim totally ruled out self-defense. I also tried a crime-of-passion angle, involving . . ." He flipped through the papers. One fluttered, unnoticed, down my way. I gave it a few licks, not sure why.

". . . one Ms. Marr," Haskell went on. "Adele Marr. Ms. Pilgrim said the name was unfamiliar to her, and when I mentioned Ms. Marr's alleged involvement with Mr. Swann, she got . . . incensed, I would say, and asked for another defender."

"Oh?" said Bernie.

Haskell looked down. "But the boss said no one was available."

They sat in silence. My paper had become mostly wet shreds. I ate them up, just keeping things tidy, more than anything.

Bernie raised his hand, patted Haskell's

knee. "Do you think she's guilty, Haskell?"

"I can't see any other explanation for the death, especially with the confession."

"But leaving all that out, just in your heart, yes or no."

Another long silence. At last, Haskell said, "No."

"Then let's get her out on bail," Bernie said, "so we can work on changing her mind."

"Uh, Mr., um, Bernie?"

"Yes."

"There is no bail. The judge turned us down this morning."

"On what grounds?"

"Flight risk."

"For god's sake," Bernie said. "Who's the judge?"

"Hyde."

"He's still alive? A bottle-a-day man for decades?"

"I've heard that," Haskell said. "Maybe his liver's the only decent part of him."

Bernie laughed, gave Haskell one of those second looks.

"Speak of the devil," Haskell said, pointing to the courthouse steps across the street. A red-faced old guy with a cane was making his way to the street, and listening to a man at his side, a man I knew.

Bernie started to rise, then stopped himself. "What's he doing with Boomer Riggs?"

"Who's that?" said Haskell.

TWENTY

Soon after that, we were pulling into our own driveway on Mesquite Road. Out of all the places we might have gone, we turned up at home! Who's luckier than me? Nobody, amigo! We headed for the door, and right away Iggy's yip-yip-yip started up. And there he was, standing at the floor-to-ceiling window in the Parsons's entrance hall, his stubby tail a blur, like it too was yip-yip-yipping, only even faster! This was all just Iggy's way of saying hi. I was about to say hi right back atcha when I got hit by a strange thought, not me at all, that maybe Iggy wasn't saying hi, was in fact saying get me out of here, you blockhead. I was trying to wrap my mind around that when suddenly we had more action in the window. First, old Mr. Parsons appeared, clumping slowly toward Iggy on his walker. Second, Iggy noticed him. The way Iggy's eyes are set meant he didn't have to turn the slightest bit to see behind him, a big advantage he had over Mr. Parsons. And finally Iggy lowered his head and snapped up something off the floor. It looked a lot like a string of . . . what do you call those things? Pearls? I caught only a glimpse before Iggy darted out of sight.

Mr. Parsons reached the window, lips moving. His voice had never been strong since I'd known him, but now it was even weaker. Still, I could hear him through the glass: "Iggy, come, for god's sake. She loves that one."

"Is he asking us something?" Bernie said.

Meanwhile Iggy did not appear. I headed for the Parsons's door, Bernie following. Clump, clump, clump on the other side, and then the door opened. Mr. Parsons looked out. He wore a shirt and tie, and over that a bathrobe.

"Good to see you, Bernie," he said, an odd whisper in his voice. "We're so glad you're back safe from the hospital, me and Edna. She prayed for you." Mr. Parsons smiled a shy smile, an unusual sight, in my experience, on such an old face. "Edna believes in the power of prayer."

"Thank her for me," Bernie said.

"That I will," said Mr. Parsons. "She's in the hospital herself — slight infection at the site of the procedure, the second one — but she'll be home real soon."

"Happy to hear that. Is there anything that needs doing in the meantime?"

"Well, Bernie, I hate to impose, but —"

At that moment, things speeded up big-time. Iggy came flying down the hall — his weirdly big paws hardly touching down and a pearl necklace somehow around his neck, like he was wearing it — and zipped right between Mr. Parsons's legs, out the door and away into the wild blue —

But no. When Iggy was already in the wild blue yonder, at least in his own mind, Bernie reached out with his amazing quickness and grabbed the little guy by the collar. Iggy kept on running in that over-the-top way of his, but now held in Bernie's arms, not too tight, he got nowhere. Bernie handed the necklace to Mr. Parsons, no harm done, everything good.

Except for the fact of Iggy being in Bernie's arms. Some things must be stopped at once. Which is why I did what I did. You would have done the same. No need to go into the details, a good thing since they're not totally clear in my mind. Is it possible that I myself wore the pearls at one stage? Hard to believe. Forget I even mentioned it.

When it was all over, with me, Bernie,

pearls, and Mr. Parsons outside the closed door and Iggy on the inside, Mr. Parsons wiped away his tears, not the unhappy kind, and said, "Almost forgot — did that fellow get in touch with you?"

"What fellow was this?" Bernie said.

"Great big fellow, like an NFL lineman, but wearing coat and tie." Mr. Parsons paused, reached up an unsteady hand, felt the knot of his own tie, and frowned. "Possibly a real estate agent — he took loads of pictures."

"Of the house?"

"Yesterday, this was. He knocked on the front door, walked all around. Pretty sure I heard him knock on the side door, too, and maybe the back gate."

Bernie gazed down the street.

"Oh, dear," said Mr. Parsons. "You're not thinking of selling?"

"Never."

We entered our house, but not in the usual way. This was much more careful. We went slowly from room to room, me because that was how Bernie was doing it, and Bernie for reasons of his own. Everything smelled, sounded, and looked just fine to me. In the office, Bernie took down the waterfall painting — we have a bunch of waterfall paint-

ings, what you might call a collection —
and spun the dial on the safe hidden behind
it. Out came the .38 Special, a lovely sight.
Any perp with a brain would have sur-
rendered right then, but none appeared,
which proved . . . something important. It
might come to me later.

We went for a nice spin, first on the freeway,
then on two-lane blacktop, the sun on my
side of the car, and sliding slowly down the
sky. As for the car, it smelled its very best,
now with the .38 Special in the glove
compartment. Open country with no traffic, an occasional farm or ranch, distant
horses and sheep, a mailbox or two. I tried
giving Bernie a look that said, *Take a potshot
at one of those mailboxes.* But that was
something we never did anymore. Hardly
ever.

On a hilltop not too far away, a bunch of
tall antennas appeared, with a blimp floating overhead, meaning we were close to the
border. Around the next bend stood a
roadblock, with dusty white SUVs, speed
bumps, Border Patrol dudes in green. We
bumped to a stop and one of the Border
Patrol dudes came over.

"US cit—" he said. And then, "Bernie?"

"Fritzie?" said Bernie.

What was this? Fritzie Bortz? A terrible motorcycle driver with lots of crashes on his record, but that wasn't the point. The point was Fritzie rode for the highway patrol. So how come he was dressed in Border Patrol gear? Was he pretending to be in the Border Patrol when in fact he was really . . . a perp? Maybe a crazy idea, but why else would Fritzie be doing this? I noticed he had a gun, still in the holster, although for how long? I watched his hands. First sign of movement, even a twitch — and good night, baby!

Fritzie's hands, kind of pudgy, hung at his sides, motionless, almost like . . . like they were napping. What a strange thought! But then came another: Bernie's hands never looked like they were napping, even when he was napping. At that moment I knew that even though I was doing a very good job of understanding the world around me, I wasn't quite done.

"You're alive, huh, Bernie?" Fritzie was saying.

"Unless I've gone to a kind of disappointing heaven where you're with the Border Patrol," said Bernie.

"You can say that again."

"Which part?"

Fritzie glanced around, lowered his voice.

"The disappointing part. Highway Patrol canned me. Can you believe it?"

"You had another wreck?"

"I wouldn't even call it that," Fritzie said. "Those kids were all back at school the very next week!"

"You hit a school bus?"

"The other way around, Bernie. But the powers that be — you know how these things work — used it as an excuse. It's all politics." He glanced around again. "These people are nice, but it's not the same. I miss the open road. I'm meant to roam the land, ride the range — like the old-time cowpokes. It's in the blood."

"It is? Aren't you from Cincinnati?"

"Long, long ago, in terms of my development."

Bernie gestured at the surrounding country. "Plenty of open range around here."

"Not the same," said Fritzie. "We're either cooped up in one of these ginormous trucks or we're tramping around the middle of nowhere on foot. I hate being on foot. And would you believe it? Sometimes they run. Who runs when it's a hundred and ten?"

Bernie got a look in his eye like he was about to say something real interesting, but before he could a car pulled up behind us. Fritzie held up his hand in the stop sign, even though the car was stopped already. Then he glanced my way.

"Chet's looking good," he said.

"Also a lover of the open road," said Bernie.

"Maybe we could trade places, him and me," said Fritzie. "You guys headed for Mexico?"

Bernie shook his head. "Stopping in Tesabe."

"What for? It's a pit."

"You might be able to help," Bernie said. "Know any Tesabe old-timers?"

"You could try the bartender at the Hilltop Cantina," said Fritzie. "But it's never open."

We drove away, not nearly fast enough. Fritzie was making a play for the shotgun seat? Good luck, buddy boy.

I'd been down on the border before — and across several times, including a night that began with some interesting she-barking in an alley back of our motel room where Bernie was sleeping — the window partly open, although far from all the way — and ended with . . . uh-oh, am I . . . what's the word? Rambling? Back to border towns, of which I'd seen a few, but not Tesabe. That was all I wanted to mention. Funny how the mind works sometimes, or at least mine. Yours

282

may be different. Maybe you don't understand about the power of certain things, she-barking, for example. When I hear it, I — But there I go again! Who's at the controls, my mind or me? My mind needs to get one thing straight. Either it —

"Chet? What's all that barking?"

Barking? I listened, picked up a possible distant echo of possible barking. It didn't sound at all like me. Meanwhile we rolled into Tesabe, a border town I'd never visited, just in case that point hasn't been made already.

Tesabe looked to be very small, with just one paved street and a few dirt roads running off it. We rode up a steep, curving hill, not seeing a single human, member of the nation within, or even a chicken, and this was the kind of place where you'd expect a chicken or two. I didn't even hear any buzzing flies. They called this a border town?

At the top of the hill stood a gas station and a small pink adobe building. Adobe has a nice smell, in case you aren't aware, a bit like being in a pottery studio, an experience I'd once had — if very briefly — with Bernie and Suzie. Suzie! I missed her.

We parked. I hopped right out. Bernie opened his door and then paused. "Eliza and me — that could work," he said.

"But . . ." After a long silence, he went on: "With Suzie there was still this trace of young passion between us — not just me, but both of us." He took a deep breath. "There's no substitute for magic. Does that make any sense?"

Not to me. I was getting a little restless. Finally Bernie snapped out of it and finished climbing out of the car. We went inside the pink adobe building.

A bar of course, which I'd known while we were still in the car. Booze has a smell that travels a long way, and so does human piss. Those are the two building blocks of all bar aromas, from the fanciest bar to the crummiest. This particular bar wasn't the crummiest I'd been in, although definitely on the crummy side. And also very small: two scarred-looking wooden tables, a bar with enough room for maybe one carload of humans as long as they weren't Bernie's size, and a single dusty window. Also no customers. A man in a cowboy hat stood behind the bar, his back to us, watching baseball on a tiny TV, no sound. Too bad: baseball sounds great, and the crack of bat on ball is off the charts.

"What's the score?" Bernie said.

"Diamondbacks two, Dodgers one," the man said, and turned to us. He had skin that reminded me of old leather and a huge, pure white mustache that curled way up on both cheeks. His hair was also pure white, and reached his shoulders. What else? He wore a red shirt and a bolo tie. In short, there was lots to look at with this guy, all good.

"You're a fan?" he said.

"Love the game," Bernie said.

"They say it's too slow."

"I know."

"But —" The old man wagged his finger, twisted and bent. Right away, my tail got a funny feeling, like always when finger-wagging starts up. "— they're wrong," he went on. "Everything else is too fast. You follow?"

"I do," Bernie said.

"Good," said the old man. "Something to drink?"

"Beer," said Bernie.

"Bottle or draft?"

"Draft if you have it."

"I have ale from the new brewery in Guaymas."

"Sounds good. Didn't know that was for sale up here."

"Only at the Hilltop Cantina," said the old man. "Nowhere else in the land."

The old man filled a glass for Bernie and

set it on the bar. "Is the dog thirsty?"

"You never know," Bernie said.

The old man went to the sink behind the bar, filled a bowl, handed it to Bernie. Bernie set it on the floor beside me. I didn't even look at it. *You never know?* What was that supposed to mean?

The old man leaned over the bar. He smelled a bit like mesquite; also the water had that stony well water smell. Had I ever been in a better bar?

"This is one beautiful dog," he said.

There, the answer, and so quick in coming: this was the best bar, bar none. I got a bit confused. Bar none? Where had that come from? What did it mean? I turned and lapped up all the water in the bowl.

"His ears don't match," the old man said.

"Nope."

"But why should they?"

A new angle on the subject of my ears, and a brilliant one. They were no problem for him, maybe even a bonus.

"His name's Chet," Bernie was saying. "I'm Bernie."

The old man nodded a serious sort of nod. "Hernando," he said.

Bernie laid some money on the bar. "And one for you."

"Thanks."

Hernando poured himself a beer. They raised their glasses. Bernie took a sip. Hernando polished off half of his. Some excited movement started up on the TV. They both watched till things went still again, never a long wait in baseball.

"Did you play?" Bernie said.

Hernando nodded.

"How far did you get?"

"Generales de Durango."

"That's Triple A."

"Yes," said Hernando. "And you?"

"Nothing like that," Bernie said. "Played a bit in college."

What was that? Bernie'd been a star at West Point, would have gone pro except for blowing out his arm. On her last visit, the Thanksgiving with the wishbone incident, Bernie's mom — if you ever run into her, be prepared — said, "Bernard" — which is what she, and only she, calls him — "when will you learn to toot your own horn?" On the way back from dropping her off at the airport, Bernie had leaned on the horn like crazy.

Bernie drank more beer. "Very tasty. But I'm no expert."

"No," said Hernando. "You don't look like a big drinker to me."

"I got the big part out of my system."

"That's the secret," Hernando said. They touched glasses.

"Been here long?" Bernie said.

"Here meaning . . . ?"

"Tesabe."

"All my life."

"Maybe you can help us."

"Who is us?"

"Me and Chet."

Hernando peered down at me. "I had that once — us, with a dog and me." He turned to the mirrored wall behind the bottles, picked up a framed photo, held it up. Here was a much younger version of Hernando — I could tell from the mustache, the same as now except for being black instead of white — and a big and real toothy member of the nation within standing beside him.

"What was his name?" Bernie said.

"Diablo. We hunted boar together all over Sonora. Sometimes I never even got to pull the trigger, if you understand what I mean."

"He must have been something," Bernie said.

"My best friend," said Hernando. "How can I help you?"

"We're interested in a woman who lived here years ago," Bernie said. "Maybe you knew her."

"The name?"

288

"Rosita Flores."

Hernando didn't move or actually do anything at all, just somehow stopped looking friendly.

"How much are you paying?" he said.

"There's a going rate?" said Bernie.

Hernando met Bernie's gaze and held it. "What's so important about Rosita Flores? She was a very nice lady but she's been dead for a long time."

"What did the others tell you?" Bernie said.

"Others?"

"The ones who paid the going rate."

"There was only one."

"Clint Swann?" Bernie said.

"Clint, yes," said Hernando. "The surname he kept to himself. Like you."

TWENTY-ONE

"Little," Bernie said. He handed Hernando our card.

Hernando glanced at it. "You're a private eye?"

Bernie nodded.

Hernando took a closer look. "With these flowers?"

For a moment, Bernie's face had an expression you might call — whoa! I came real close to "hangdog," a strange word I would never have anything to do with. But then I could see him having a thought, and what was more, a thought he liked a lot. "Ever heard of deadly nightshade?" he said.

"Yeah, but I never seen it," Hernando said. He tapped the card. "That's deadly nightshade?"

Bernie nodded one of his nods. I'd seen this one many times in many situations, and come to believe it meant nothing.

"Clever," said Hernando. "Not like your

friend Clint — he was *furtivo,* as they'd say on the other side."

"There's no friendship between me and Clint."

"You're working for him?"

"No."

Hernando made a little wave with the card. "But you're working for someone."

"The name is confidential."

"And there we have the problem, Mr. Little. You want but you won't give."

"I said I'd pay the going rate."

"I didn't take his money."

"You gave him information for free?"

"I did."

"So therefore the going rate is zero?"

A so-therefore? Bernie's in charge of so-therefores at the Little Detective Agency. It's a mysterious area. You never know what to expect after a so-therefore. I waited and waited, and all at once Hernando threw back his head and laughed and laughed. It turned out that lots of his teeth were missing, poor guy.

He wiped his eyes on the back of his hand. Then his laughter started up again, but weaker, kind of like when your car is switched off but comes to life again for a few moments on its own. Maybe not yours.

"Here's what I told Clint for nothing,

since I'd rather have nothing than feel dirty," he said. "Rosita Flores had a boy-friend. He's still alive. This boyfriend worked for many years at Rancho de la Luna — kind of a cowboy legend. Retired now but he still lives out there. Ten miles west on the old Yuma Road."

"His name?"

"Flaco de Vargas."

"Did you tell Flaco that Clint was coming?"

"For that answer, I charge fifty dollars."

"I thought money made you feel dirty."

"Clint's. I've changed my mind about yours."

Bernie handed over some money. Hernando tucked it in his pocket.

"I did not tell Flaco," he said.

"Why not?"

"He has an unpredictable temper."

"Did you warn Clint about that?"

Hernando shook his head.

"Why not?"

"He's the kind of man who can look after himself."

"Yeah?" said Bernie. "How bad is this temper of Flaco's? Is he capable of murder, for example?"

"Murder?"

"Clint was stabbed to death a few days

ago, not far from Fort Kidder."

Hernando backed away. "I know nothing about that."

"Does the name Lotty Pilgrim mean anything to you?"

Hernando shook his head.

"Do you like country music?"

"Country music?" Hernando looked puzzled for a moment. "Tejano, yes. American country, no."

He gave Bernie a long look, then reached into his pocket and gave us back our money. Had that ever happened before? This interview must have gone very well. I scarfed up a dusty Cheeto from under a table on our way out.

The old Yuma Road turned out to be the kind of road we loved, me and Bernie — no pavement, no traffic, no nothing, except for open country, purple mountains on both sides, the sinking sun in front, a dust cloud in back. For a while we went pretty slow, lost in the beauty of it all, and then, coming onto a smooth stretch of road, hardly rutted at all, Bernie stepped on it. At the exact same moment I would have done the exact same thing!

"Wee-ooo!" Bernie shouted, and waved his hat in the air, even though he had no

293

hat, so just made the hat-waving motion. I would have done that exact same thing, too!

I've got this howl I can let loose if the moment is right, and it was. I howled. Bernie went "Wee-oo!" I upped my howl to the next level. Bernie upped his wee-oo. I upped my howl to the max, where no one can follow. But Bernie tried! Had to love Bernie, of course. We howled and wee-ooed, howled and wee-ooed, howled and —

And then up ahead, a figure — or maybe two figures, one small, the other a little bigger — ran across the road and disappeared on a bushy slope. We slowed down, stopped, got out. No one to see up the slope, but I picked up their scents right away, a woman and a girl.

Bernie shaded his eyes. *"Hola!"* he called. *"Hola!"* No answer, no movement. The wind rose, weakening the scent right away. "We probably frightened the hell out of them, Chet."

Us? I couldn't think how. Bernie took a big plastic bottle of water out from under my seat and left it by the side of the road.

The ranch gate was open, a solid gate with a yellow metal moon hanging over the drive — not the full, round moon, more the slivery kind.

"Rancho de la Luna," Bernie said. "Established 1913." He turned to me. "Guess what we're going to do."

Grab a snack? Take off on a hunting trip — one of my oldest and strongest desires? A long hunting trip, possibly lasting forever? Those were my guesses.

"We're going to book a room, just like any normal guests."

How disappointing, at least at first. But then I thought: Don't normal guests love snacks? And what if normal guests hanker for a hunting trip? The guest is always right — isn't that a saying? I felt much better.

"Well," said Bernie, as we checked out our room, "don't say we never stay anywhere nice."

Oh, I wouldn't even have the thought! This room — with its tile floor, some tiles blue, some with yellow flowers, plus the sunset-colored adobe walls, the dark wooden beams and dark wooden furniture, all of it smelling so old but in a lovely way, almost how certain things smell in dreams, at least mine — was the second best place we'd ever stayed. The very best was a cave partway up a stony hillside where we'd been caught in a monsoon, a very small cave with just room for me, really, but I'd squeezed over in the most accommodating way. Deepest sleep of my life, and I'm sure for Bernie, too — he stayed drowsy for days!

"What d'you know?" He was gazing at a framed photo on the wall. "Teddy Roosevelt stayed here. Looks like a hunting trip."

Wow! Who's luckier than me? Now it was just a question of how soon this Teddy character would show up so we could get started. I took a good look at him so I wouldn't forget — a moonfaced dude wearing glasses and laughing his head off, probably so happy about hunting — and sat down by the door.

Teddy still hadn't come by dinnertime. We ate on a terrace outside, steak for Bernie, kibble topped with bite-size steak pieces for me, not as many as I could have eaten, but no complaints.

"What a hungry boy!" said the waitress. She crouched near me and spoke in a baby voice. "Has nobody been feeding poor widdle oo?"

"I have," said Bernie. "He had a full bowl this morning and —"

Or something along those lines, my attention wandering a bit on account of the waitress producing a whole handful of more bite-size steak pieces. I knew one thing for sure: Rancho de la Luna was first-class all the way.

A bit later I was lying under the table, licking my muzzle from time to time but mostly just relaxing, while Bernie polished off a bourbon and signed the check.

"Staying long?" the waitress said.

"Don't know yet," said Bernie.

"We've got great riding trails," she said, "and fine horses down at the stable."

"Sounds good."

Horses were in the picture? I'd had plenty of experience with horses, prima donnas each and every one. I stopped relaxing, sniffed the air. Yes, horses. Horses everywhere. How had I missed that?

"We've got some great wranglers, too, if you prefer a guide," the waitress said.

"Probably best," Bernie said. "Any chance Flaco de Vargas would be available?"

She blinked. "You mean old Mr. Vargas? He doesn't ride anymore."

We went back to our room, and soon Bernie was in bed, snoring in his gentle way, a sort of music, and I was lying by the door. Then came a soft crunch of someone walking on gravel, approaching the door, slowing down, moving on. Teddy Roosevelt, perhaps? If so, he was a hair-gel fan.

"Done much riding?" said the head wrangler, her mirrored sunglasses blue from the morning sky.

"Some," said Bernie. "But not recently."

Bernie had done some riding? On horseback? I wasn't sure I liked that idea.

The wrangler looked my way. "What's your dog's name?"

"Chet."

"Know his way around horses?"

Totally! For example, if you mosey up behind them and suddenly bark real loud, they rear right up — neighing like crazy, eyes bugging out — and take off, unless they're tied to something. And that's just one of the things I know, the first horsey fact that popped into my head.

"Um," Bernie was saying. "Sure."

"Then let's pick one out," the wrangler said.

She led us into the barn. The smell of horse was so strong it came close to making me dizzy. We went from stall to stall, looking at the horses. They looked back at us, every single one of them getting nervous just from the sight of me, meaning this wasn't all bad.

"Here's Rusty," the wrangler said. "Very placid."

"Sounds good," said Bernie.

But at that moment, another, much big-

298

ger horse in the next stall stuck his head around the corner. Rusty shifted away, even though this other customer couldn't change stalls or even make contact.

"What about him?" Bernie said.

"Mingo?" said the wrangler. "I don't think Mingo would be right. He can be a mite headstrong with strangers."

Bernie moved over to Mingo's stall and — and stroked Mingo's forehead? If that empty space between those two ridiculously widely spaced eyes — kind of insane-looking eyes in Mingo's case — was indeed the forehead? This was not a good development, and was followed by several more, starting with the wrangler leading Mingo out to the front of the barn and taking a bridle off the wall.

"How about I handle that?" Bernie said. The wrangler, her sunglasses now perched on her head, gazed at Bernie. I got the feeling she didn't like him. So why not bag this whole thing, do it some other time, or even better not at all? But before anyone could make that sensible suggestion, Bernie said, "Just so we get to know each other from the start."

There was a long pause in which nothing happened except for Mingo rolling his crazy eyes. Then without a word, the wrangler handed Bernie the bridle. He took it in one hand, sort of wrapped his other arm around Mingo's head, made a soft grunt I'd never heard from him before, and the next thing I knew he had the bridle in place and that metal bar — never between my teeth, amigo, no matter who was doing it — in Mingo's mouth. After that came the saddle pad — which Bernie let Mingo sniff at, why, I didn't know, since it reeked of horse and nothing but, of no interest to anybody — and then the saddle. In a flash Bernie got the under strap thing all tied up, muttering, "Seven, four, one," as he did so, a complete puzzlement to me, and in one easy motion he swung himself up top. For a moment Mingo went out of his mind. It happened just like that. I could feel it, and also feel his tremendous strength. He was going to rear up and toss Bernie to the ground. And that rearing up actually started, but it turned immediately into a sort of circling trot that ended with Mingo snorting and coming to a halt. Bernie patted Mingo's neck, not for a long time you might say, and maybe not putting a whole lot of feeling into it, but still: this day was off to a terrible start.

The wrangler was looking up at Bernie, no longer disliking him so much.

"Not your first time," she said.

"Been a while, like I said." He took a deep breath. "Going way back, in more ways than one."

The wrangler nodded.

"Can you recommend a nice ride?" Bernie said.

"Depends," she said. "Will Chet here be able to keep up?"

Bernie laughed. "That won't be the problem."

Nice to hear, but not nearly enough. What we needed now was more, lots more, about, well, me. I was considering some wild run through the barn just to show the wrangler the kind of speed we were dealing with, when Bernie made a little clicking sound and Mingo walked out of the barn and into the sunshine. They got through the doorway first. I didn't even make a play for it! Could we move on to some other case? Even divorce work?

Outside, the wrangler started pointing out the different trailheads.

"Which one is Flaco de Vargas's favorite?" Bernie said.

"You know Mr. Vargas?"

"Know of him," Bernie said. "A legend."

The wrangler nodded. "You could say hi if you wanted."

"Yeah?"

She pointed. "Take that trail there — Hanging Moon — due west for two miles. You'll see a big one-armed saguaro, and just beyond that to the right is Mr. Vargas's casita. No Wi-Fi out there, no cell — he could use a visitor."

"Hanging Moon is the name of the trail?"

The wrangler nodded. "A mistranslation of the old O'odham name, according to an anthropologist we had here a while back. But I like it. Is it about the moon hanging in the sky, or a nice moon for a hanging?"

Bernie made that click-click and Mingo trotted toward the Hanging Moon trailhead. I know a little about trotting myself and was soon in the lead. Mingo snorted once or twice. I barked in no uncertain terms and barked again, just in case he missed the point I was making, namely that —

"Che-et?"

No barking? Was that it? Silence, perhaps? I can be silent, better believe it. I can be silent and do other things at the same time, for example run circles around some object, even if that object happens to be moving, tighter and tighter circles, tightening faster and faster, yet silent all the while, those circles growing smaller and —

"CHET!"

TWENTY-TWO

We halted in front of the one-armed saguaro. Nice friendly buddies out on a nice friendly desert excursion: that's what you'd have thought if you'd seen us, me, Bernie, and Mingo. Here's a tip in case you need it someday: horses' hooves can be dangerous — they wear metal shoes, for some reason — but they're not good at sideways kicking. I always bear that in mind myself, but do whatever you like. I'm not the type who needs everybody to —

"Chet, for god's sake. What am I going to do with you?"

Take me to a cookout? That was my first thought, but I was open to suggestions.

Bernie pointed. "There's the casita." He did the click-click thing and Mingo went into his lope, lope-loping up a gentle rise toward a small green house, the only house around. I can lope, too, by the way, lope with the best of them. I loped my way into the lead.

A man sat on a bench on the shady side of the house. He turned toward us as we got near: an old shirtless man wearing jeans and cowboy boots, maybe around Hernando's age, and with the same sun-baked skin, although he had no mustache, no hair on top, either. It was very quiet, except for Mingo's ridiculously loud heartbeat. The old man looked at us, but in a strange way, more like he was looking near us.

"Hi," Bernie said, dismounting and walking toward him, one hand on the reins. "Flaco de Vargas?"

The old man nodded. "I don't see so good."

"I'm Bernie Little," Bernie said. "Guest at the ranch."

The old man — Flaco, if I was following this right — sniffed the air. That caught my attention, big-time. "They sent you out on Mingo?"

"Yup."

Flaco looked toward Mingo, although actually over Mingo's head. "*Aquí*, Mingo," he said.

Mingo stepped forward, Bernie moving with him, still holding the reins. Flaco held out his hand and Mingo lowered his head and nuzzled it. Then he leaned closer and

304

nuzzled Flaco's bare chest. Flaco patted his neck. "Poor Mingo. He doesn't get out much."

"No?" Bernie said.

"He has his ways, different from the ways of the guests." Flaco sniffed the air again. "You have a dog."

"His name's Chet."

"The dog is with you?"

"He's right here."

From out of nowhere, Flaco got very angry. His voice rose, not in a booming way, but thin and high. "I don't see so good. Didn't I tell you?"

Mingo backed away, neighing and tossing his head.

"You did," Bernie said, his voice low and calm. Mingo — how would you put it? Got a grip? Something like that.

"Well," said Flaco, maybe getting a grip himself, "remember."

"I'll remember," Bernie said. "In fact, memory is what this visit is all about."

"Whose memory?" said Flaco.

A hitching post stood outside the front door. I know hitching posts. Leda and Malcolm have one at their place, possibly a sculpture called *Hitching Post* — I've heard several discussions about it, the one where Bernie said, "Are you going to hitch a horse sculpture to it?" freshest in my mind. Now he tied Mingo to Flaco's hitching post and sat at the end of the bench. I sat down myself, a little way off, where I could keep an eye on everybody.

"Your memory," Bernie said.

Flaco, who'd been sitting at the middle of the bench, shifted toward the other end. "My memory is very bad."

"I think you're being modest," Bernie said. "Do you remember Lotty Pilgrim?"

Flaco shook his head. "I don't know that name."

"From way back, Flaco. Lotty was a young woman then, beautiful, with long blond hair."

"We have many guests like that but the name you said is not familiar."

"That's odd," Bernie said. "Since she was Leticia's mother."

"Leticia?" Flaco was gazing over my head. His eyes were strange and milky.

"Leticia — the kid being raised by your girlfriend, Rosita Flores."

Flaco shook his head. "You're not making sense, whatever your name is."

"Bernie Little."

"Maybe you have me confused with someone else."

"Who are you afraid of?" Bernie said.

306

Flaco sat very still. We were all of us still, nothing moving except Mingo's tail, which swished at a fly, missed, and tried again.

"Stupid people," Flaco said.

"Name one."

Flaco turned his milky gaze on Bernie's face, and said nothing.

Bernie rose and went to a window, just a step or two away. He glanced inside Flaco's casita.

"What are you doing?" Flaco said.

"Educating myself," Bernie said. "So I won't be so stupid."

That was a funny one, Bernie always being the smartest human in the room, and if we were outside, then . . . then there was no end to it!

"For example," Bernie said, "I see you have some framed butterflies on your wall. I'm betting that's Rosita's butterfly collection."

Flaco's voice rose again. "You have no right to look in my window."

"Did Clint Swann know about the butterflies?" Bernie said.

"Of course not! Why the hell —" Flaco went silent.

But maybe a shade too late. I'd seen this before, one of Bernie's many techniques for getting the job done. Soon we'd be cashing a fat check. I tried to remember from whom.

"Forget the butterflies for now," Bernie said. "What did you and Clint discuss?"

Flaco didn't reply.

"Come on, Flaco. The introductions are over."

"I told him nothing."

"What did he want to know?"

No answer.

Bernie took a long look at Flaco and said, "I can find out from him if you don't tell me."

What a puzzler! Was it possible Bernie had forgotten the last time we'd seen Clint? This was turning out to be a difficult case. Was there big money waiting at the end? Or any? Suddenly I remembered! Myron Siegel was paying the tab. Older than dirt, and there were other old men in this case. Also Lotty herself was pretty old. And all at once, from being totally lost I found myself right on the edge of figuring the whole thing out!

"He's a friend?" Flaco said.

"Far from it," Bernie said.

"You don't work for him?"

"How could I work for someone who treats Lotty the way he does?"

"You've seen Lotty?"

"Yes."

"You're a friend of hers?"

"That's why I'm here."

Sunshine poked around the corner of the casita, shone on Flaco. His chest was lean and brown, with a long white scar running down the middle.

"She was good with horses, too," Flaco said. "Like you. I haven't seen her in a long, long time. How is she?"

"Not good," said Bernie.

"No. She was never the same."

"After what?"

Flaco shook his head. "Why dig up the past? It's dead and gone."

"Is that what you told Clint?"

"Yes."

"What was his reaction?"

"He offered money."

"Did you take it?"

"No. He went away — went away angry. I want you to go away, too."

"You really think the past is dead and gone?" Bernie said.

"Why not?"

"Because it keeps changing all the time. That's a sign of life. And living things need to be understood."

Wow! Had I ever heard anything so lofty? I didn't get it at all, not the slightest bit. Flaco's gaze was on Bernie. Seeing or not seeing? I didn't know. Mingo's tail tried its

309

luck with another fly, missed again.

Bernie was meeting Flaco's gaze. No question about Bernie's eyes seeing. He was very good at spotting things, like a windshield glare on a distant ridge, or a tiny tremor in a hand, just before some perp makes a play for his gun.

"I lied to you about Clint," he said.

Flaco went very still.

"Clint's dead — stabbed in the heart. They arrested Lotty for it. She's in the county jail. The case is a lock, but I don't believe she did it. I'm a private investigator, trying to help."

It was quiet beside Flaco's casita, no sound except the swishing of Mingo's tail.

"This is the curse," Flaco said.

"I don't understand," said Bernie.

Flaco rose. "You are right about the past."

Flaco walked past the window and entered the casita, leaving the door open. We followed him in — me and Bernie, not Mingo. I've only seen a horse inside a house once in my life, a horse, by the way, capable of climbing stairs, although not going back down. Why it was our fault I never got clear, but that was definitely Malcolm's take, and it was his and Leda's bedroom where the . . . climax? Would that be it? Where the climax of that little incident took place.

310

Flaco's whole casita could have fitted into Leda's bedroom. It was mostly one room, very tidy, part bedroom, part living room, part kitchen, a cool room although there was no smell or sound of AC.

"What curse are you talking about?" Bernie said.

Flaco opened a small footlocker and took out some sort of machine. I'd seen one like it before, on a case involving hipsters and a stolen truckload of PBR. It was a cassette player, some old way of listening to music, according to Bernie. Flaco fished around in the locker, found a cassette, stuck it in the player, pressed a button.

What came next was a man's voice, humming softly. But: beautiful, beautiful right from the very start. I've heard a lot of music in my time — "If You Were Mine" being my very favorite, Billie Holiday singing and Roy Eldridge on trumpet at the end, that trumpet doing things to my ears I can't describe — but I'd never heard a man's voice like this.

His humming grew louder, but very slowly. I felt like I was floating on a river, kind of strange since our rivers hardly ever have more than a trickle, so I've never actually had the experience. From the look in Bernie's eyes I knew he was floating on a

311

river, too.

And now, kind of on top of that humming, a woman began to sing. I had an idea I recognized that voice, although this woman sounded much younger.

> With one little smile
> And the touch of your hand
> That's how you hung the moon.

Then the woman took over the humming and the man sang. Not loudly, but my paws felt him through the floor.

> The sound of your voice
> The promise of your love
> That's how you hung the moon.

And then they sang together. A feeling went all the way down my back to the tip of my tail.

> And even in darkness
> I'll never forget you
> And how you hung the moon.

The singing stopped. There was a little laughter, his and hers. Then the woman said, "What do you think?" "Think?" said the man. "That's the enemy." More laughter. "But what about 'even in darkness,' " she said. "Maybe it should be —" "Shh," he said. That was followed by what might have been a kiss, and silence. Flaco pressed a button, put the player back in the locker.

"That was Lotty," Bernie said.

"*Si*," said Flaco.

"And the man?" Bernie said. "Incredible. Is he someone I should know?"

"The man is El Cantate," Flaco said.

" 'The Singer'?"

"Correct."

"His real name?"

"Hector de Vargas."

"A relative of yours?" Bernie said.

Flaco nodded. "My . . . my big brother. He was twenty-one years old in that recording. Lotty was still in high school, or maybe she'd dropped out."

"They were writing 'How You Hung the Moon'?"

"You know the song?"

"I love it," Bernie said. "I didn't realize Lotty had a cowriter."

"He was much more than that," said Flaco. "Hector was a visionary."

"In what way?"

"A spiritual way," Flaco said. "The music was only the voice."

Bernie got one of his thoughtful looks. His thoughts at that moment were very strong. I

313

could feel them in the room.

"That was how he put it," Flaco said. "Music is the voice of the spirit, so if we work on the spirit, the music gets better by itself."

"What was Hector's relationship with Lotty?"

"At first, teacher and student."

"And then?"

"In love."

"I'd like to speak to him," Bernie said.

"So would I," said Flaco. His milky gaze went to the window. "Hector died that same winter."

"What same winter?"

"When they made that recording. Maybe three weeks later, maybe four."

"How did he die?"

"Drug overdose," Flaco said. "Unfortunately — as I see it now — drugs were part of the vision. Peyote, at first. Well, no shame in that, not in these parts. But then they started in on other things, very pure, very powerful."

"Like what?"

"Mescaline for one," Flaco said. "I don't know the others."

"Why do you know mescaline, specifically?"

"Because I met the supplier a few times.

He was a doctor in the Valley."

"Do you remember his name?"

"Dr. Wellington."

"First name?"

Flaco shook his head.

"Where did Hector die?" Bernie said.

"Not far from here," said Flaco. "Lotty had a tent they were living in, at least some of the time. That was another part of the vision — to return to earlier days."

"Where was Lotty when he died?"

"With him."

"In the tent?" Bernie said.

"That's right," said Flaco. "She woke up in the morning and Hector was dead. He died in her bed."

TWENTY-THREE

Somebody died in Lotty's bed? Hadn't I heard that before? And then it came to me: Clint! Wow! I was on fire, so on fire that I attempted a so-therefore, all on my own: so therefore Clint died twice in Lotty's bed. Amazing. Not only a so-therefore, but a so-therefore with numbers in it. I gave myself a very energetic shake, as energetic as it gets.

Bernie shot me an odd sort of glance and turned to Flaco. "I'm sorry for your loss."

"A long time ago," Flaco said. "But yes, okay. I accept."

"A loss for music, too," Bernie went on. "Did your brother release any records?"

"Hector didn't believe in the music business. Maybe he would have changed his mind, but . . ." He shrugged.

"Did he and Lotty write other songs, besides 'How You Hung the Moon'?"

"I don't know."

"Who ended up with his estate?"

"Estate?"

"His possessions, after he died."

"Hector had no possessions. Some clothes, a guitar, just things like that."

"What happened to the guitar?"

"Maybe Lotty took it."

"And what about the song credit? Many of the big stars in country music sang 'How You Hung the Moon,' and Lotty had a hit with it herself."

"I don't understand," Flaco said.

"A song credit means there are royalties. There's supposed to be a payment for every play — very small per play, but a lot of plays add up to real money."

"I never knew this," Flaco said. "What does it mean?"

"We need more facts," Bernie said. "Maybe your brother wanted Lotty to have sole credit. Maybe they made some other arrangement. I'll have to look into the song's history, see how much time went by between that cassette recording and the first release. A year or two is my guess, might have been more."

"By then she was forgetting Hector a little bit?"

"That's possible," Bernie said. "Do you remember her reaction to his death?"

"Not right at the time," Flaco said. "I was

317

working on a ranch in Colorado, didn't get back until the funeral."

"What was Lotty like at the funeral?"

"Just the way you'd think. Sad and crying." Flaco turned again toward the window. Did his milky eyes clear a little? Or was that impossible? "But the next day, something happened where . . . where I saw maybe how she felt. In the evening I went with flowers to the grave, and Lotty was already there. She sat on the ground with her arms around the stone, sobbing and saying all kinds of crazy things. I left before she could see me."

"What kind of crazy things?" Bernie said.

"Like 'I'm so sorry, Hector,' and 'I was insane from the drugs,' and 'Take me, take me,' " said Flaco. "Crazy things."

"Did you ever talk to her about any of that?"

Flaco shook his head.

"Did she ever try to kill herself?" Bernie said.

Oh, no, not that. We've seen it happen twice, me and Bernie, this strange and horrible human thing, so mysterious to me. We just don't do that in the nation within. Those were our two worst cases, except for the broom closet case, where we'd arrived too late. We'd made the bad guy pay, me and Bernie, pay big-time, but afterward we hadn't felt any better. I'm a champ at forgetting, so why can't I forget the moment when we opened that broom closet?

"Try to kill herself?" said Flaco. "Not that I know. She left a day or two later."

"Did you go back to Colorado?"

"*Si.*"

"When did you and Rosita get together?"

"A few years after," Flaco said. "I'd known her all my life, but . . . things happen. All of a sudden she was the one."

"That must have been nice," Bernie said.

"Nice," said Flaco. "But it didn't last."

"Was she already taking care of Leticia when you came back?"

"That's right. How do you know all this history?"

"I don't know nearly enough," Bernie said, which was just him being modest. No one knows more than Bernie, in case I haven't made that clear by now.

"So your next question will be, who is the father of Leticia," Flaco said. "Am I right?"

Bernie smiled. "Actually my next question was going to be about the cause of Hector's death."

"But I just told you," said Flaco. "A drug overdose."

"Was there a medical exam?"

"I don't know."

"Did you see Hector's body?"

Flaco shook his head. "The coffin was closed."

"Where's the cemetery?"

"Cemetery?"

"You said you saw Lotty crying by the gravestone."

"The stone isn't in a cemetery," Flaco said. He gestured toward the window. "It's down the trail, maybe half a mile."

Mingo snorted, just out of sight.

"Right on the trail?" Bernie said.

"A little way off," said Flaco. "There's a eucalyptus grove. It has meaning around here, going back a long time. A beautiful place. I'm planning it for myself."

"Not anytime soon, I hope," Bernie said.

"The doctor doesn't agree," said Flaco. He was silent for a bit, then said, "And now you will ask about the father of Leticia?"

"You're better at this than I am," Bernie said.

"I hope not," said Flaco.

Bernie . . . winced. Was that the word? He winced like he felt a pain. I'd never seen that from him before, never wanted to see it again.

"As for Leticia," Flaco went on, "everyone just — how do you say it? *Asumieron?*"

320

Bernie took a breath, came back to the here and now. "Assumed."

"Everyone assumed Hector was the father."

"But?"

"No buts. Everyone assumed."

"What did Lotty say?"

"She never said. She just went along with all the assuming."

"Did she ever discuss it with Rosita? Weren't they close?"

"Oh, yes, and maybe they discussed it, but does that mean Rosita would tell me? You didn't know her. A very stubborn woman."

"But you talked about it with her?"

Flaco's voice rose again, so fast and unexpected. "Didn't I tell you that already? And she wouldn't say a goddamn word? Don't you listen?"

Outside the window came sounds of Mingo shuffling around, tossing his head, snorting — in short, doing horse-type things, probably just to annoy us.

"You're scaring him," Bernie said quietly.

Flaco opened his mouth. I waited for some more shouting, but that didn't happen. Instead Flaco hung his head and said, "He is a very good horse."

Then we just sat for a bit, until Mingo settled down.

"What's your opinion?" Bernie said. "Was Hector Leticia's father?"

Flaco raised his head. "Does it matter after all these years?"

"I think so," Bernie said.

"Life just gets messier and messier and then you die?" Flaco said. "Is that what it's all about?"

"Help me tidy up a little," Bernie said.

Flaco nodded. "Okay, senor. Maybe it makes sense that Hector would be the father, maybe that's the simple truth, but two things bothered me. First, the child looked nothing like my brother. A little bit like Lotty, yes, but even that not so much. Second, Lotty left her with Rosita, once as a baby, and the second time when she was older, starting to be a real person."

"She wouldn't have done that if Hector was the father?"

Flaco shook his head. "It was special, what they had."

We headed down the Hanging Moon trail, me, Bernie, and Mingo. Are there nightmares in the day? Even if there aren't I had one anyway, all about Mingo joining the Little Detective Agency.

"Hey, big guy," Bernie said from up in the saddle, "you're getting a little close."

322

Boy oh boy. I headed off the trail, did some crazy running, returned in a better mood, although not much. Not long after that we made our way down a gentle slope and into a grove of eucalyptus trees. No surprise: I'd been smelling them all the way from Flaco's casita, the smell of eucalyptus — lemony, woody, and also like a kind of tea Bernie's mom mixes with bourbon — is impossible to miss.

The smell got much stronger in the middle of the grove. A nice spot, shady and cooler than out on the trail. Bernie got off Mingo, tied the reins to a branch. Mingo chewed on a leaf. Just a small one but his chewing went on and on. Mingo! Snap out of it!

Bernie glanced around, took a deep breath. "This is one of those places," he said. "Where time doesn't reach."

Something about time? Were we in a hurry? I waited to find out.

A gravestone, not big but of a pretty sunset color, stood near the biggest tree. We walked up to it. " 'El Cantate,' " Bernie read. "No date, no name."

Did that make any difference when it came to marking the stone or not? It had been marked by a coyote and not that long ago, a rather bothersome fact. There's a duty in the nation within to mark over all coyote markings, and I'm not the type to let the team down. I moved toward the stone, even raising a leg a little, or at least giving it a twitch, but just then Bernie put his hand on the stone.

"I've got an idea, Chet," he said. "Not pleasant, but —"

KA-RANG! And then CRACK! A chip of gravestone went flying, leaving a hole in the stone right beside Bernie's hand.

"Chet! Down!"

And then we were crouched behind the gravestone, Bernie with his arm around me.

KA-RANG! CRACK! Another chip flew off the stone, over our heads and into some bushes.

Silence, except for Mingo — out of our line of sight — who started up on some of his neighing, now louder and more irritating than before. Very slowly, Bernie raised himself up just enough for peeking over the stone. I did the same — we're partners, after all — and just had time to spot someone moving on a distant ridge before Bernie said, "Chet!" And sort of pushed my head back down. Kind of gently, but a push for sure. Did that mean we weren't partners?

Bernie ducked back down with me. He took my head in his hands, looked right into my eyes. "I can't let anything happen to you, big guy. So be good."

Well, of course I'd be good. That was my MO. But things happened to me all the time. I lead a very busy life. Plus I make things happen, better believe it. Was Bernie not making sense all of a sudden, just because we were getting shot at? That wasn't the Bernie I knew. The Bernie I knew would be firing the .38 Special, blam, blam blam. Oh, no. Was it in the glove box? Mingo had no glove box. The Porsche was preferable in every way.

We stayed together behind the gravestone. Mingo had stopped neighing, begun what sounded like stomping and thrashing. Bernie raised his head again. I did the same. We're partners, after all.

"For god's sake, Chet! Why —"

Bernie broke off before I learned what was on his mind. Now there was no one to see on the distant ridge, and no movement at all. We rose. And just as we did, Mingo snapped the branch he was tied to right off the tree, and went prancing away.

"Mingo! Come back!"

Mingo did not come back. Instead he gave his head a powerful toss or two. The branch came loose from the reins and fell to the ground. Mingo seemed pleased about that. He pranced even more prancily, if that makes sense, pranced right out of the eucalyptus grove and into open country.

"Go get him, Chet."

I went and got Mingo. You don't want to know the details. Hot? Dusty? Never-ending? Kicks, nasty and sneaky? Yes, yes, yes, and yes.

We crossed open, trailless country, in several formations, finally settling on me in the lead, and Bernie on Mingo following behind, which seemed to work best. After that we climbed the ridge, switchbacking on the steepest parts. Mingo turned out to be not so bad at this. "Good boy," Bernie said, as we got to the top of that last rise.

I turned back to look at him.

"Uh, and you, too, Mingo," he said.

I kept looking.

"Just do what Chet does and you'll be fine," Bernie added.

I trotted on.

We came to a jumble of big rocks. As I picked my way through, I smelled a shell casing, followed the scent, coppery and smoky, couldn't be easier, and snapped it up. Then, beyond the rocks was a little surprise: two ATVs and a couple of Border Patrol guys wandering around, one thin, one chubby. The chubby one turned out to be

326

Fritzie Bortz.

"Bernie? You're on a horse?"

"No denying it."

"What are you doing up here? There aren't even any trails."

"Someone took two shots at us from this ridge," Bernie said.

"At *you*?" said Fritzie.

The other Border Patrol dude came over.

"You know this guy?" he said.

"An old pal," said Fritzie. "Must have been mistaken identity, Bernie."

"What do you mean?"

"These drug dealers sometimes take potshots at each other. There's a couple of rival gangs."

"Three," said the other dude.

"We got a report of gunshots," Fritzie said, "and drove out for a look-see. No one here, but that doesn't mean —"

A beep sounded from one of the ATVs. Fritzie's buddy went over to it, came back with a laptop. The two of them gazed at the screen. "Recognize him?" Fritzie said.

"Nope," said his buddy.

"What's going on?" Bernie said.

"We had a drone nearby, just co-incidence," Fritzie said.

He turned the screen so we could see. What was this? A pretty clear picture, but

327

not so easy to understand. We seemed to be flying high above a ridge, with a jumble of rocks at the top and open country down below. A human lay prone among the rocks, a rifle barrel sticking out over the edge of the ridge, the only straight thing in sight. Then came an orange flash from the muzzle, and after a pause, one more. Meanwhile we were on the move, passing over him and heading away.

"Right now's when he hears us," said Fritzie's buddy.

The human — a man — turned over and looked up at the sky. This was a man we knew — the big hair-gel guy we'd met coming out of Leticia's house, the yellow one with the chimes on Bluff Street. Real quick, he covered his face with his hands and rolled back over. We moved on, and in a moment or two he was out of the picture.

There was a hard look on Bernie's face. "Can you ID him?"

"The boys in the office'll give it a shot," Fritzie said.

"Never seen him before," said his buddy. "And I've seen 'em all. Let's get back to work."

"Doing what?" said Bernie.

"Looking for shell casings," Fritzie said. "Normal policing procedure, Bernie."

What was that? Something about shell casings? I dropped mine at Fritzie's feet, where he couldn't miss it.

TWENTY-FOUR

There are many good things about the
Porsche. One is that it's too small to fit any
characters of, say, Mingo's size. We drove
back to the Valley alone, me and Bernie, a
quiet ride except toward the end, when Bernie turned to me and said, "Do we now
know for a fact that Lotty didn't kill Clint,
or is it the exact opposite?"

What a great question! Nobody has better
questions than Bernie.

"But here's one sure bet — if we're on the
same road as Clint, we've passed him. And
we're still alive, big guy."

Totally alive! Bernie nailed it again. I really
couldn't have been any more alive than I
was at that moment. As for the road, we
were on the freeway coming into town. No
surprise that Clint had been here, too. It
was the busiest road in town. I couldn't
have been more in the picture.

We have experts for this and that at the

Little Detective Agency. For example, Otis DeWayne is our weapons dude. He lives with a member of the nation within name of General Beauregard, a huge buddy of mine you don't want to mess with, although I always do. Then there's Prof at the college, our go-to guy for anything about money. He used to have a fish called Beryl in his office. It was really too bad what happened to her, a strange sequence of events which in the beginning had something to do with thirst. For what Bernie calls living memory, we see Mrs. Beamish, a retired librarian who was actually fired, a subject Bernie never goes near except for once, where it soon turned out that Mrs. Beamish kept a Colt .45 in her drawer, a big surprise at the time.

"Hello, Mrs. Beamish," Bernie said as she opened the door of her apartment, a small apartment in a part of town where things needed freshening up.

"So you're alive," she said, the cigarette in one corner of her mouth bobbing up and down. "There were conflicting reports."

"It wasn't that bad," Bernie said. "You know how people exaggerate."

"They get things wrong in every way imaginable," Mrs. Beamish said, and then peered through her cigarette smoke at me.

"Is he going to behave?"

"Oh, of course."

"Don't of course me, Mr. Little. He makes Delilah very nervous."

"He'll be on his best behavior. Isn't that right, Chet?"

Then all eyes were on me. Well, not Delilah's. I hadn't spotted her yet, but she was somewhere close by. Cat smell is not something I miss. I had a sudden and powerful desire to mark certain objects in Mrs. Beamish's place, such as her hat stand. This was probably not the time. Instead I sat down and took care of an itch or two, scratching with one back paw and then another.

"Don't tell me he has fleas," said Mrs. Beamish.

"Never gets them," Bernie said.

Good to know! So those drops from the vet were for something else? This visit was a success already.

We went into the living room. Mrs. Beamish sat at her desk, Bernie on a stool. I lay down near the couch. From there I had a good view of the fireplace and the mantel above. Delilah lay on the mantel, curled up between two candlesticks. She was gazing down at me in an irritating way. I ignored her completely, put her clear out of my mind. The mantel itself was a high sort of mantel, but don't forget that leaping is my best thing.

"Coffee, Mr. Little?" Mrs. Beamish said, reaching for a coffeepot that stood on the desk.

"That would be good."

"Or bourbon?"

"Well . . ."

"Or coffee with a shot of bourbon?"

"A nice compromise," Bernie said.

Mrs. Beamish added shots of bourbon to two mugs of coffee, handed one to Bernie.

"What happened to the spirit of compromise?" she said.

"I don't know," Bernie said.

A cylinder of cigarette ash fell on her desk and smoldered on the wood, glowing orange. She wet a finger with her tongue, stubbed out the tiny fire, and took a nice big gulp from the mug.

"The conquest of the outside world marches on," she said. "The inside world is a shambles. Ever think there's cause and effect between those two statements?"

"No," Bernie said, "but the shambles part is why we're here."

She gave him a look over the rim of her mug. "You use the pronoun *we* a lot."

"I do?"

333

"Is it a royal we?"

Bernie smiled. "I'm a commoner."

"So we is you and — ?" She gestured my way with her thumb.

Bernie nodded. As for what they were talking about I had no clue, but I'd picked up one new fact. We were commoners, me and Bernie, and proud of it. Actually two new facts, then. Wow! Was I getting smarter with age? If I kept on living, say forever, how smart could I end up? Something to look forward to, for sure.

"Just clarifying," said Mrs. Beamish. "Now walk me through the shambles."

I rose, but no actual walking ensued. Instead Bernie started in on a long story about drug overdoses, death certificates, doctors, and a lot of other stuff that sounded familiar and also just out of reach. I glanced up at the mantel. Delilah was gone.

"So," Mrs. Beamish said, "Hector de Vargas — cause of death, criminal record, possible descendants, song credits?"

"That's a start," Bernie said.

She flipped open her laptop. Silently — I never want to disturb anyone at work — I made my way out of the living room, down the hall, and into the kitchen. No visible activity, but something quiet and at the same time . . . how to put it? Dramatic? And if not dramatic, at least something very interesting was going on behind the fridge, something that involved tiny frightened squeaks, not the kind of sound you ever heard from cats. I moved a little closer and out from behind the fridge came Delilah, a mouse between her teeth.

Delilah looked right through me, like . . . like I wasn't there! Like there was no Chet! Cats: a complete mystery. Then she dropped the mouse from her mouth. The little guy took off, possibly headed toward an air duct in one corner. Delilah watched him run. He was a pretty good runner, for a mouse. Was Delilah thinking something along those lines? Or —

But no time for any ors. Next came a sort of leaping blur, orange and white, and Delilah was suddenly standing poised right over the mouse. She batted him sideways with one of her paws, batted him back with another. Was it some sort of game, a bit like ice hockey, perhaps? I'd tasted puck once, but no time to get into that now. The point was that Delilah seemed to be playing a game, a game I'd never even dreamed of, where a mouse gets batted around in a lazy sort of manner. Was it a fun game? I didn't know. The only way to find out with games is to play! And playing is one of my best things, maybe not quite on the level of my detective work, but close. A voice in my head — my own voice! — said, "Play, Chet, play!" And I was bounding toward that mouse, no actual idea of what came next in my mind but not in the least worried about that, when all of a sudden there was another one of those leaping orange-and-white blurs and — OW!

That hurt. Well, not hurt. Forget I mentioned hurt. But it wasn't pleasant. Some parts of the body — the nose, for example — are more sensitive to pain than others, a lesson you learn — possibly more than once — if very sharp claws are in the picture, which seemed to have been the case. I licked my nose. Delilah watched me do that. The mouse lay on the floor, not moving. I considered letting Delilah know what was what.

And was still considering it as I went back to the living room. This was in no way a retreat. I don't even know what that means, and never will. Just think of my return to the living room as getting back to work. We were on the clock, me and Bernie.

He had pulled his stool closer to the desk, was peering over Mrs. Beamish's shoulder at the screen. They were both smoking cigarettes, a little hazy cloud over their heads.

"No evidence whatsoever of a musical career," Mrs. Beamish said. She tapped at the keys.

"What about —" Bernie began.

"Don't interrupt," said Mrs. Beamish. She tapped some more, squinted through the haze at the monitor. "The rights to 'How You Hung the Moon' are owned by QB Inc., an LLC registered in Grand Cayman."

"No mention of the actual writer?"

"Hold your horses," said Mrs. Beamish.

Oh, no. I glanced at the entrance to the front hall. No sign of Mingo. Were there other horses suddenly in my life, horses I didn't even know about? We'd done just fine without horses so far. Didn't Bernie always say, "Don't change a winning game"? We were winners, me and Bernie!

"Here you go," Mrs. Beamish said. "Writer credit — Lotty Pilgrim. But —" Tap tap, tap, tap. "— no evidence of any connection between her and QB. Inc. Nothing on QB Inc. at all, beyond the registration."

Bernie drummed his fingers on the desk. He does that sometimes, why, I'm not sure. But it's nice to watch, since his hands are so beautiful.

Mrs. Beamish glanced over at his drumming fingers. "Please," she said.

Bernie's fingers went still at once and he stuck his hand in his pocket. Maybe Mrs. Beamish was the kind of human who had no time for beauty. Some humans — a surprising number, in my opinion — were like that.

"Death certificate of Hector de Vargas," she said, pointing her chin at the screen. "Drug overdose." She sat back and reached for her mug.

Bernie leaned forward. His eyes went back and forth, back and forth. Then he grew very still. "It's signed by Dr. Wellington? Dr. Frederick Wellington?"

"All death certificates are signed by a doctor, Mr. Little. I'm surprised that's news to you, given your line of work."

Bernie looked at her. He said nothing but Mrs. Beamish nodded as though he'd spoken after all. "Ah," she said, "person of interest?" Her hands returned to the keyboard. More tapping, and then, "Frederick Wellington, MD, general practitioner . . . affiliated with Valley Hospital . . . retired twenty years ago and . . . died five years after that . . . liver cancer." She turned to Bernie, waiting with her hands over the keyboard.

"That should do it," Bernie said. "At least

for now." He rose. So did I, which was when I noticed that Delilah was back on the mantel, eyeing me in a contented sort of way. How could I show her what was what? I waited for an idea.

"I'll send you an invoice," Mrs. Beamish was saying. "Terms are thirty days, no exceptions."

"You say that every time," Bernie said.

"Correct," said Mrs. Beamish.

We went outside, hopped in the car.

"Hey," Bernie said. "What did you do to your nose?"

Nothing. I'd done nothing at all to my nose.

"Is it bleeding?"

Absolutely not. I ignored my nose completely, hoping Bernie would do the same. The only problem was that the more I ignored my nose, the more it wanted to be licked.

"What gets into you?"

Me? What gets into me?

We drove away. I licked my nose.

"Do we need to go to the vet?"

The nose licking stopped at once, and didn't start up again, hardly at all.

"It stinks," Bernie said as we took an exit ramp. "Stinks big-time."

It did? I sniffed the air, picked up many smells, although none could be called stinking, at least not to me. I studied Bernie's nose. It seemed the same as always, slightly crooked in a very pleasing way.

"Hector de Vargas's drug supplier and the signer of his death certificate were one and the same," he said. "The metaphor comes to life."

We pulled into a parking lot. What with waiting for the arrival of a perfect Delilah-related idea — or just any — I hadn't been paying attention in my usual way. I'm a professional, don't forget. But now I saw that this parking lot was familiar: the visitor parking lot at Valley Hospital. What were we doing back here? Weren't we done with Valley Hospital, now and forever? Wasn't Bernie back to feeling tip-top? I studied his face. Yes, tip-top and then some, the healthiest man in the Valley.

"What's that look?" he said.

It was the look that says *turn the key and hit the gas, pronto.* It was not the look that says *open the door.* Which was what he did.

"How come you're not hopping out, Chet? You always hop out ahead of me."

I sat in the shotgun seat, made myself immovable.

"Tired?" Bernie said. "You can stay if you

want. Curl up. Grab some shut-eye." He got out of the car and started walking toward the entrance.

Shut-eye? Curling up? Sleepiness was not the problem! Bernie going back in the hospital? There's your problem.

There are two ways of stopping things that must be stopped: waiting for someone to do the stopping, or taking charge yourself. Taking charge is the Little Detective Agency way, as I bet you've already guessed.

And while you were guessing, I hopped out of the car, just as Bernie had wished, probably the hoppiest of any hop I'd ever hopped. I took off after him, caught up in a flash, and . . . now what?

He turned and saw me, smiled a big smile. "That's more like it!"

Meaning he got the point or not? He kept on walking toward the entrance. He did not get the point. Was he distracted? He did have a lot to think about, poor guy. This was not our easiest case. Myron Siegel was paying us, although for what? I was unclear on that. But when someone is distracted, you have to get their attention. One good way is to run around them in circles that get tighter and tighter and faster and faster.

Bernie laughed. "Whoa, there, big guy! A little unsure of your own mind today?"

Not sure of my own mind? I'd never been surer. My mind and I were on the same page, closer than we'd ever been, like peas in a pod. No time to get started on peas, because Bernie kept going, like he wasn't in the middle of a tighter and tighter and faster and faster circle. He took the last few steps to the door, reached for the handle. The very next second he was going to be back inside that hospital. What would you have done?

I, Chet, grabbed him by the pant leg.

TWENTY-FIVE

That was bad. I knew it right away, and if not right away, then the very next instant after right away. For one thing, Bernie was no perp. For another, I loved him.

And now? Now what we seemed to have was a situation outside the entrance to Valley Hospital with Bernie down on the ground and me sort of . . . standing on top of him? I had trouble believing that myself, but it was hard to deny.

He twisted around and looked up at me. His face — the most beautiful face on the planet — went through some changes. First came shock, an expression you often get on a perp face at moments just like this. But after that, when you usually see fear or anger or even rage, came puzzlement. And then, very slowly, a lovely smile spread across the lovely face. Whatever would have happened next remained a mystery, because people came running up: a couple of secu-

343

rity guards and . . . and someone we knew, namely Dr. Eliza Bethea in her white coat, formerly Doc but now Eliza to us.

"Bernie? Are you all right?"

Bernie scrambled up, dusted himself off. "I'm fine," he said.

"Did you faint?"

"Oh, no, nothing like that. Chet and I got tangled up, that's all."

The security guards backed away.

"Tangled up in what?" Eliza said. "There's no leash."

Bernie laughed. "Not a visible one," he said. "There's also the question of who's at which end."

Eliza's eyes narrowed. "Sure you feel all right? How about coming into triage and we'll take your vitals?"

Vitals? That sounded important. No way Valley Hospital or anybody else was making off with our vitals. They belonged to us, end of story. I planted myself in front of the door. Did some sort of backup start building on the other side? I'm good at ignoring things like that. Also aren't we the law, me and Bernie? That had always been my take.

"I feel great," Bernie said. "And . . . and I'm sorry our da— our lunch at Cleon's ended so abruptly."

"Work-related," Eliza said. "I understand,

believe me."

"Doc?" said one of the security guards. "Mind, um . . ." The security guard made a little shooing motion with her hands.

"How about coffee in the cafeteria?" Eliza said.

Bernie glanced at me. Now we had build-ups on both sides of the door. I was getting a bit edgy. Edginess is something that grows and grows until suddenly —

"Chet?" said Bernie. "Let's go for a little stroll." He took Eliza's arm — she looked surprised, but did nothing to take her arm back, if that's the expression — and moved away from the door, toward a bench.

A stroll? A stroll away from the hospital? What a great idea! I joined Bernie and Eliza, and pronto.

"Did you see the size of that dog?" said someone behind me.

"Keep it moving, folks," the security guard said.

"What's going on, Bernie?" Eliza said.

"The hospital seems to be verboten," he said.

Verboten? That was new. It sounded big and bad. That was Bernie, summing things up in his brilliant way. Meanwhile Eliza gave me a quick glance and then started laughing, that loud but very pleasant laugh of

345

hers. Was the hospital big, bad, and also funny? I didn't see the funny part, but maybe that was just me.

They sat on the bench. I sat on the ground at one end, namely the end between Bernie and the hospital entrance.

"You really do look good, Bernie," Eliza said.

"Uh, you, too."

"I meant in a medical sense," said Eliza.

Bernie's face reddened. Red always looks good on him, even if I can't be trusted when it comes to red.

"I, uh, didn't," he said.

Eliza smiled and laid her hand on his. "I'm sorry I was abrupt the other day."

"Oh, no. Not at all. I didn't explain very well and . . ."

She patted his hand. "But now here you are. How did you know I'd be in? In fact, I'm off today, just dropped in to clear some charts."

"Well, actually, this is work-related, too."

Eliza withdrew her hand. "So you didn't . . . ?"

"It's, uh, a bonus," Bernie said.

What was going on? Some human conversations, especially between men and women, are impossible to understand. Then came a stroke of luck, namely a Cheeto right under the bench. I squirmed my way over to it. On closer examination, not a Cheeto, but a Cheez-It. The smells are rather similar although the tastes are different. I prefer the Cheez-It taste but the Cheeto is crunchier, so in the end —

By the time I'd gotten that far in my thoughts, the Cheez-It was gone and Bernie was saying, ". . . name of Frederick Wellington, retired about twenty years ago."

"Before my time," said Eliza. "But I'll see what I can find out." She turned to me. "How about you guys wait out here?"

Bernie seemed to find that very funny. I myself didn't get it.

Eliza was gone for what seemed like a long time. Bernie was silent, kind of slouched and gazing up at the big blue sky. "It's like Pluto," he said after a while. "They couldn't see it but they knew it had to be out there on account of an unknown force acting on Neptune. In this case we're Neptune — that's the meaning of those potshots at Hector's grave. So now we try to get a fix on Pluto."

Whoa! Way too much information. I remembered those potshots, but Pluto? Neptune? There was Neptune's Seafood Shack, which I could smell all the way across the

Rio Vista bridge, but was now closed on account of some sort of stolen trout scam. The only Pluto I knew was a cartoon member of the nation within, who of course couldn't talk, although Goofy, another member of the nation within in the very same story, could. "How come, Dad?" Charlie had said. "It's just a cartoon," Bernie told him. Charlie got up and left the room. I went with him. We shared a snack or two in the kitchen until Bernie was done watching. But the point is I had no idea how Neptune and Pluto fit into our case. I sniffed the air for trout smells, came up with zip.

Eliza returned, accompanied by a woman in a white uniform and little white hat.

"Bernie," she said, "meet Tina Wellington, a nurse in our pediatric unit and the widow of Dr. Frederick Wellington. Tina, this is Bernie Little. And Chet."

Humans of different ages have different smells, maybe news to you. Tina Wellington smelled about the same age as Bernie's mom, although she didn't look at all like her. Bernie's mom is big and strong with a voice that penetrates walls, no problem; Tina Wellington was very small, with one of those soft voices that makes human listeners lean in close.

"Nice to meet you," she said, "but I don't know what this is about."

"Bernie?" Eliza said. "Tina's on lunch break. Maybe you could take her to Carmelita's." She pointed across the road. "Try the pulled-pork tacos."

Bernie smiled and gave Eliza the thumbs-up sign. You hardly ever saw the thumbs-up sign from Bernie. Something to think about.

But before any thoughts came, we were on the patio behind Carmelita's and pulled pork was in the air. Tina ordered the vegetarian taco, of no interest to me. Bernie had the pulled pork. I sat close to Bernie, my go-to move, but even more so in this case.

"Chet looks hungry," Tina said in her soft voice.

"Couldn't be," Bernie said. "He had a big bowl of kibble for breakfast."

Breakfast? I could barely remember it. Nobody makes sense every time, not even Bernie. I gazed at the pulled-pork taco in his hand, sending a message.

"I haven't had a dog in a long time," Tina said.

"How come?"

"Fred — my husband — was allergic."

"But he's been dead for some time."

"Sixteen years next month."

"Tell me about him."

Tina put down her taco. Her plate was near the table's edge, in easy reach. Why hadn't she ordered the pulled-pork? I was having a hard time understanding her.

"Can I ask why?" she said. "I think the world of Eliza — all the nurses do — and she speaks highly of you, but . . ."

"Did she mention I'm a private detective?"

"She said investigator."

Bernie smiled. "We're looking into an old case. Your deceased husband's name came up."

"In what way?"

"He signed a death certificate."

"Is that a problem? Because he was only a GP?"

"Any doctor can sign a death certificate in this state. I'm just trying to flesh out the details on everyone involved, no matter how peripherally."

Tina nodded, that slight sort of nod that goes with someone starting to budge. "When was this old case?"

"Almost fifty years ago."

"Goodness," said Tina. "I was just a little kid."

"There's still some of the kid on your

face," Bernie said.

Perhaps that was the kind of human speech called blurting. Tina shot Bernie a quick look, hard to describe. I just knew he now had her attention, and not in a bad way.

"What I meant," Bernie added quickly, "was that your impressions of him might help anyway."

Tina folded her hands on the table in a getting-down-to-business way. The Little Detective Agency is all about business, don't forget. I had a bad moment when I couldn't remember who, if anyone, was paying. And then it hit me: Myron Siegel! What great news! I waited for Bernie to say, "Champagne all around!" but he did not.

"To start with," Tina said, "there was the age gap between me and Fred. Plus it was a second marriage for me, fourth for him. But it worked."

"What attracted you to him?"

She gazed into her water glass. An ice cube made one of those cracking sounds ice cubes sometimes make, always a nice touch, although perhaps too quiet for the human ear. "It's not easy to sum up."

Bernie just sat there, looking like he had all day. This was called waiting patiently, one of our best techniques, especially Bernie's.

"Maybe this sounds foolish," Tina said at last. "But the heart of it was that he'd been through a lot of pain and come out the other side. It showed in his work — I'd never seen a doc who cared so much for his patients." She took her eyes off the water glass, turned to Bernie. "Eliza's a lot like that — in her case with so much technical brilliance added on."

"What was the cause of all Fred's pain?" Bernie said.

"A combination of things. The broken marriages, estrangement from his kids — they both took the side of the wives — nagging regrets."

"Such as?"

"The regrets? Fred didn't go into that very much. He was trying so hard to be positive. Which he kept up right to the end, through all the cancer. If there's redemption on this earth then he found it." Tina picked up her paper napkin, dabbed the corners of her eyes.

"Redemption from what?" Bernie sighed.

"Youthful mistakes," said Tina. "I don't know the details."

"Before your time."

"Exactly."

"Before my time, too. And Chet's." Bernie smiled at her. He has a number of smiles, all of which you'd love to have coming your way, except for this one.

Tina sat back. "What are you saying?"

"I understand about redemption," Bernie said. "But whatever the sin was, or the mistake, or whatever you want to call it — well, that often affects others, and stays with them, even passing down the generations. You can end up with people having no chance to understand their own lives."

Tina shook her head, a very vigorous kind of headshake, like Charlie when he really didn't want to eat his spinach. "You're blowing this out of proportion. Fred didn't kill anybody, or anything like that."

"You're sure?"

"What's going on?" Tina said. "Eliza told me you're a good person."

"Very nice of her," Bernie said. "Did your husband ever mention Tesabe?"

Tina's face lost all its color. "What do you know about Tesabe?"

"Not much. But I need the facts. It's the only way to help all the people who didn't get to be part of Fred's redemption."

"Eliza's wrong," Tina said. Her forehead bunched up in wrinkles. "You're mean."

Tina was way off base, but she seemed very upset so I cut her some slack. As for why she was upset, who knew? Did it have anything to do with her veggie taco? That was my only guess.

"Why do you say that?" Bernie said.

"Because you're attacking a good man who's not here to defend himself."

"Then you defend him."

There's a kind of rough-and-tumble that some folks just aren't cut out for, and I don't mean only in the human world — you see those types in the nation within from time to time. They just roll over on their backs! What's the fun in that? Tina did not roll over on her back, but she did start shaking.

Bernie took her water glass, held it out for her. She gripped it, but unsteadily, and water spilled out. Plus an ice cube — an ice cube that fell to the patio floor and was scarfed up by me. Meanwhile Bernie sort of wrapped his hand around hers and guided the glass toward her lips. She drank. In a few moments the shaking ramped down to nothing, and Tina lowered the glass by herself.

"He never called it Tesabe," Tina said. "It was always goddamn Tesabe. That's where his life went bad."

"How?" said Bernie.

"He . . . he never told me."

"Why not?"

"Maybe because he felt ashamed," Tina said. She looked down and her voice got even softer. "If you're familiar with the concept."

Bernie went still. I could feel him thinking very hard. He said nothing.

"Never felt ashamed?" said Tina. "Aren't you lucky?"

Bernie took a deep breath, and in the course of it happened to glance down and see me, now busy with a second ice cube I hadn't spotted right away. "I have been lucky," he said. He turned to Tina. "And maybe so have you."

"What do you mean?"

"Is it possible Fred kept the details to himself in order to protect you?"

Her heartbeat sped up. Pitterpat, pitterpat — a nice little heart now working very hard. "What is this? You know my life?"

"What was he protecting you from, Tina?"

She shook her head.

"Are you still in danger?"

"How could that be possible? After all these years?"

"It depends on what happened down in Tesabe. That's what I need to know."

Then came a surprise. Tina pounded her fist on the table. Maybe not pounded, her fist being so small and her arm so skinny.

"But I wasn't there," she said. "And I really don't know anything — not if you're looking for solid facts."

"Fred was dealing drugs," Bernie said. "Is that a solid fact?"

Tina didn't move, except for her hands, now below the tabletop, tearing strips off her napkin. She took a deep breath. "He wasn't dealing. Fred was a victim of drugs as much as anybody."

"So he was dealing just a little bit? To support his own habit?"

"I don't like the way you put things."

"But the answer is . . . ?"

"Yes," Tina said. "But you're a bully."

Whoa! How wrong could a person be! But if she really thought Bernie was a bully would her next move be popping him on the nose, which Bernie himself said was the way to deal with bullies? I edged closer to her. She showed no signs of gearing up to throw a punch, no sign of action of any kind, but I remained on high alert.

"Did Fred sell drugs in Tesabe?"

"He might . . ." She balled up the remains of her napkin, laid it on the table.

"Yes. Yes he did."

"To whom?"

"I don't know any names. You can badger me all you want."

Badgers were suddenly in the picture? What a nasty surprise! I'd had an unfortunate encounter with a badger out in the canyon back of our place, and learned never to go near them. Not long after that, I'd learned it even better. Maybe this case wasn't going as smoothly as I'd thought.

"Did he ever mention any of these names — Hector de Vargas? Flaco de Vargas? Rosita Flores?"

"None of them."

"What about Lotty Pilgrim?"

"The singer?"

"Yes."

"She was on the news," Tina said. "Something about killing her manager? Is that what all this is about?"

"Did Fred mention her?"

Tina's eyes got an inward look. "Once," she said. "A song of hers came on the radio. This was in the car. Fred hit the off button. I mean hit. Which wasn't him. There was no violence in Fred at all."

"Did you ask him why he reacted that way?"

Tina nodded. "He said he hated her. I was surprised and said something like I didn't realize he knew Lotty Pilgrim. Fred told me he didn't know her, hadn't even met her. But she was the cause of his moral failure."

357

" 'Moral failure'?"

"Those exact words. Fred had a quote 'episode of moral failure.' He also said the punishment came with it, part and parcel."

"The punishment was part and parcel of the failure?"

"Correct."

"What was the moral failure?"

"Fred never told me. It's not like we went over and over this subject. It came up in the beginning once or twice but . . . we lived our lives together, kind of in our own little universe. There's no getting away from the clock in a May-December relationship." Tina's back stiffened and she looked Bernie in the eye. "Do you know the word *mensch*?"

"Yes," Bernie said. I myself did not, and waited for an explanation. None came.

"Fred was a mensch." Tina checked her watch. "Is there anything else? I'm back on in five minutes."

"Just one thing," Bernie said. "What was the punishment?"

"He fell under the power of an evil person," said Tina. "Also a quote."

"Who was the evil person?"

"He wouldn't tell me — for my own protection, just as you guessed." Tina rose.

"An evil person or an evil man?"

"Person," Tina said. "Fred fell under the power of an evil person."

TWENTY-SIX

"We've never worked anything with a tail this long," Bernie said as we drove out of town. "The farther back in time you go the more unreliable everything gets." And he went on like that for a while, all about facts, memory, stuff like that, but I let it go by without even making an effort. Why? Because of the long tail. There was a long tail in this case? I searched my mind. The only tail I could come up with — besides my own, which had been a feature of all our cases — was Delilah's. I suppose her little mouse playmate also had a tail, although I hadn't noticed, but was the mouse still among us? Hard to say for sure. I tried to picture Delilah's tail. More slinky than long, and kind of annoying in its movements and also in its stillness. But there were no other tails in the case, unless . . . unless ponytails counted! And who had a ponytail? Rita! I'd thought my way into a tangle and then

360

thought my way right back out! Was that what being human was like? But just when I was feeling pretty good about myself, I remembered one more tail. Mingo's! Oh, no. What if Mingo was the key to the whole case? We'd never be rid of him!

"What's all that panting?"

I turned to Bernie. He was looking at me funny. Panting? I was unaware of any panting.

"Thirsty?"

Not at all. Actually yes. But no. Yes.

Out came my traveling bowl. I drank, making more slurping sounds than usual, just for fun.

"God in heaven," Bernie said.

Not long after that, we were on a dirt track that seemed familiar, rounding a long curve. And there in the shadows of the cottonwoods by the not-completely-dry dry wash — the best sort of dry wash in my experience — stood the RV. No yellow car.

"No yellow car," said Bernie.

Any remaining questions about why the Little Detective Agency is so successful, except for the finances part?

We parked in front of the RV. The RV door opened right away and Leticia came out. She wore big hoop earrings, silver and green, sparking off tiny rays of light. A happy sight, but Leticia wasn't a happy person. You get a feel for human moods when you're a member of the nation within.

"Are you alone out here?" Bernie said as we got out of the car. Too late, I realized I hadn't hopped out. Was something wrong with Chet the Jet? Had Leticia's mood somehow spread to me? I gave myself one of those shakes that mean business. Stray hairs and dust took flight, another happy sight, and so soon after the first one. We were in for a great day. There are signs in life. You just had to be on the lookout, and being on the lookout is what I do.

". . . they went back to Phantom Springs," Leticia was saying.

"But I —" Bernie began.

"I know what you wanted. This is better. Rita can take care of herself."

"And take care of Jordan, too?"

"Better than I can," Leticia said. "She's a crack shot."

"And what about you?"

"I'm a pretty fair shot myself."

"You're armed?"

Leticia reached behind her, into the waistband of her jeans, and pulled out a gun that looked a lot like ours. She kept it pointed at the ground. "I'm licensed," she said, "if that's where you're going next."

"It wasn't," Bernie said. "Next is Lotty. Is she a gun owner?"

"I'd be surprised, but I'm no expert on Lotty."

"Who is?"

"Can't help you there either," Leticia said.

Bernie tilted his head slightly, like he was seeing Leticia from a new angle. "Do you hate her?"

"Not anymore," Leticia said. "I've hardened to her inside, that's all."

Bernie took a step or two to one side and gazed down at the dry wash. A white bird sat on the water in the middle part, not much more than a puddle today. "I've seen Rosita's butterfly collection," he said.

"That's kind of amazing," Leticia said. "You went down to Tesabe?"

"We did," said Bernie. "Flaco de Vargas has it. Remember him?"

"I just remember him taking me on a horse when I was little. I think he and Rosita broke up not long after that. He went away, maybe to Colorado."

"Tell me about your dog."

"Patsy?" she said. "I loved her. She got me through my whole childhood."

Leticia glanced at me. I happened to be sort of sidling over toward the dry wash, with nothing definite in mind.

"I've been thinking about Patsy lately," she said, "probably on account of Chet here."

Patsy? Did I know a Patsy? I thought about that. Perhaps I'd think better if I got closer to the dry wash.

". . . just a little gal," Leticia went on, the sound of her voice fading a bit, but still very clear to me. "She wouldn't let anyone near me without raising a din — not even people she otherwise knew and liked."

"But wasn't she Lotty's dog?"

"Maybe at first. Lotty was a great one for leaving things behind."

The water in the middle of the dry wash felt pleasant on my paws. The desert was in one of its very quiet moods. The bird, not facing my way, ruffled its feathers. What a lovely sound, like tiny breezes! Who would want to do anything to disturb that? I took another backward glance, saw that Leticia had moved closer to Bernie. They both seemed to be looking my way. I looked their way, one paw raised above the water, just a quiet dude lazing away a lazy day.

"What do you know about your father?" Bernie said.

"Not his identity, if that's what you're after," said Leticia. "And how could it matter now?"

"Are you aware that Flaco de Vargas had an older brother? Hector was his name."

Leticia turned and faced Bernie. "I don't know about any brother. I hardly knew Flaco, as I already told you."

"Familiar with the Hanging Moon trail?"

She shook her head. "Is that one of those rides at the inn?"

"Yes."

"I didn't ride. Rich kids rode. That wasn't us."

"But you said Flaco took you on —"

Leticia's voice rose. The sound frightened my bird. It spread its wings, surprisingly large. Flap flap and my bird was in the air and gone. A watery splash or two landed on my head.

"I didn't ride," Leticia said. "Do you want it notarized? What's the point of all this? Doesn't she admit she killed Clint?"

"People confess to crimes they didn't commit."

"So I've seen on TV. But they always turn out to be dumb or addled or ignorant. Lotty's none of those things."

There's an expression you sometimes see on Bernie's face when he's talking to someone real smart — not as smart as him, of course. Goes without mentioning. There's another expression he gets when he's starting not to like somebody. Right now both those expressions were sharing his face, if that makes any sense.

"If she killed him I need to prove it to myself," Bernie said.

"Why should I get involved?"

"She's your mother."

"So what? Why did she have to come back here? We were doing just fine."

"Maybe I can help you get back to that," Bernie said. "Or even better. But first I have to know who your father was. Or is."

That surprised her. "He could still be alive?"

"Did Lotty ever say otherwise?"

Leticia was silent for what seemed like a very long time. Up above, my bird was drifting around in big circles.

"All she ever told me — this was the day she brought me back to Rosita for the last time — was that my father wasn't important. She'd made a bad mistake and gotten out of it — gotten us both out of it — as soon as she could."

"What sort of mistake?"

"She didn't say. But she's sure as hell mistake prone, bad ones her specialty."

Back in the car, Bernie said, "Was Hector the bad mistake? Hard to reconcile that with the way they worked together on 'How You Hung the Moon.' On the other hand . . ."

And he went on talking, only now just in his head, which I could feel but not hear. I curled up, got comfy, and fell into the rhythm of the road. Was this a good time for nodding off? I couldn't see why not, and was almost in dreamland — the sound of beating dream wings already on its way — when Bernie said, "One thing for sure — I don't like being hunted."

We were being hunted? That got my attention. It was so wrong. I'd waited and waited for a hunting trip, but not one where we were being hunted. I barked my angry bark, so scary it even frightens me.

"Damn right," Bernie said. "You could have been hurt."

Oh? When was this? I waited for more, but none came. Bernie reached over and gave me a pat, eyes still on the road. A shadow seemed to pass over his face, leaving behind a hard look.

Not long after that we stopped at one of those big box stores in the middle of nowhere. Bernie says those big box stores mean it won't be the middle of nowhere much longer, and he turns out to be right every time. But that's Bernie. We went inside and bought a spade and a shovel. Was gardening in the plans? Gardening usually happened between cases, but I was pretty sure we were in the middle of one. That was as far as I could take it.

Back in the parking lot, we got spade, shovel, me, and Bernie all nicely arranged in the Porsche, a fun time that was over way too soon, although I did notice that the sun was quite a bit lower in the sky when we were done. Bernie fired up the engine.

"How about we do some hunting of our own?" he said.

At last!

Nighttime on the Hanging Moon trail, the two of us walking side by side, Bernie with the spade and the shovel over his shoulder. So: a lot going for us already. Plus we had the moon above, and no Mingo. In short, a perfect night. The only question was what kind of hunting went with spades and shovels. After some hard thought, I gave up. Then, after no thought at all, it hit me: the hunting of underground creatures went with spades and shovels! Worms, for example. And also — uh-oh — badgers. Badgers again, and so soon?

We came to the eucalyptus grove, all shadowy except for the tombstone, shining silver in the moonlight, actually the same silvery color as the moon. Like . . . like it was a piece of the moon that had fallen down. Whoa! Scared — and by my very own mind. If pieces of the moon were going to start raining down, we were in big trouble.

Bernie placed his free hand on the stone. "Well, El Cantate," he said, "if it turns out that you're in some way seeing this, then apologies in advance. And if not, how can it matter?"

That was pretty baffling. Who was he talking to? What was he talking about? I had no answers. This time I didn't waste any effort in thought, just went straight to the no-effort method. Which I'm sure would have worked again, but before it could came something completely new: Bernie put down the spade and shovel, lowered his shoulder, pressed against the tombstone, and toppled it over!

Imagine my excitement! This was a first for the Little Detective Agency, and one of the most exciting firsts there'd ever been. When I'm excited I like to run — you're probably the same, meaning you too would have been racing round and round that toppled-over tombstone, ears straight back from your own wind, dirt flying up from your paws, tongue flopping and flapping all over the . . .

Maybe not.

"Chet!"

I came to a quick stop. Bernie put his finger crosswise over his lips, a signal I knew very well. I'm a pro, don't forget.

Bernie picked up the spade, drove the tip into the ground where the stone had stood. Did that mean the hunt had started? Worms, was it? Badgers? It didn't matter. If the hunt was on then I was part of it — a very large part, since digging was involved. I got myself right next to Bernie and started in.

"Chet? I don't . . ."

Something, something. Bernie has a special voice for when he doesn't really mean it, a voice he uses a lot with me and possibly never with anyone else. I dug and dug to my heart's content, digging alongside Bernie, the two of us turning out to be a primo digging team, dirt flying out of a hole that got deeper and fast.

Bernie, almost up to his waist, suddenly went still. He had a frown on his face, dark lines appearing on his moonlit forehead. I went still, too, just from the sight of him.

"This is way too easy," he said. "Like . . . like the earth's already been dug up. And not long ago."

He looked at me. I looked at him. How could too easy be a bad thing? That was my takeaway. But then: Why that frown? Humans — even the best of the best, meaning Bernie — can be hard to understand.

Bernie switched to the shovel. He got back to work, but slower now. I did the same, except at my usual pace. How do you dig slowly? I couldn't figure that out. Soon we came to a very hard layer of earth. Broken up boards, split and rotting, lay all over the place.

"It's like someone knew we'd be coming," Bernie said. He stooped and started sifting through the remains of those boards. Was he looking for something underneath? All I saw was that hard, dark earth. Much more interesting was a smell I picked up, wafting in from above.

I climbed out of the hole and followed that smell into the trees. There in the shadows stood one of those jeeps they use for desert tours — not a subject you want to raise when Bernie's around — the kind with the raised-up body and a hardtop roof. The passenger door was open and on the driver's seat lay what I'd been smelling, namely a thick and juicy steak. A raw steak, which is my preference. I also prefer rare, medium, and well-done. Digging is the kind of work that stirs up the appetite. I hopped into the jeep and —

And the passenger door closed behind me with a thunk, quiet but firm.

TWENTY-SEVEN

So much to take in all at once, and none of it good. The weirdest thing — not the worst, oh no, far from it — was that even though I knew the steak was right there beside me on the driver's seat I could no longer smell it. There was only one scent in the air: hair gel. That had to be important but I couldn't think why.

Had it really happened, the door thunking shut behind me and locking me inside this jeep? Or could it have been a bad dream? But how? I wasn't even sleepy.

I love riding in cars, but being locked up in one made it no different than a cage, and I hate being caged more than anything. I rose up and pawed at the passenger-door window, the driver's-side window, the windshield. And got nowhere. What about door handles? We'd done so much work on door handles, me and Bernie, although never car door handles. I tried the passenger door handle but it was impossible, flush with the door panel. That failure, after all the work we'd done, got me feeling kind of crazy, and I rose up again and pawed my very wildest at the passenger-side window, so crazy and so wild that I almost didn't notice the figure moving through the trees, a very large human figure, walking a man-type walk and carrying himself in a man-type way. As he stepped into the clearing, the moon shone on his face: the hair-gel dude. A huge man but he was moving in a silent and sneaky way that actually reminded me of a cat.

Meanwhile Bernie was standing in the hole, almost up to his shoulders, and busy with the shovel. And now for the very worst thing: Bernie had his back to the hair-gel dude and couldn't see him coming. The hair-gel dude reached the edge of the hole. The spade lay at his feet. He bent down, picked it up, hefted it in his hands.

Bernie! Bernie! Bernie! My own voice shouted at me inside. But only inside. What good would that do? *Chet! Get a grip!*

And then I barked, barked like I'd never barked before, a savage howling bark that scared even me. Two things happened at once. The hair-gel dude swung the spade at Bernie's head, swung it with terrible speed and force. And Bernie turned in my direction, not quickly at all.

He saw, so late, what there was to see. Moonlight shone in his eyes, brighter than the moon itself. Bernie ducked, the speediest duck I'd ever seen. Ducks themselves are far from speedy, so what they've got to do with ducking is a puzzler, definitely for some other time.

The spade flashed over Bernie's head — so close it ruffled his hair — and shot from the hair-gel dude's grip, flying off into the night. The hair-gel dude himself lost his balance, and in that moment Bernie grabbed one of his legs and yanked him down into the hole.

Into the hole and out of sight! What was going on in that hole? I threw myself against one door and then the other, barking and howling. The jeep rocked back and forth and side to side but didn't let me out. I needed to be free, and right away!

Bernie! Bernie!

A puff of dust rose out of the hole, turned silver in the moonlight. Then Bernie popped up, his shirt torn almost right off him, and started scrambling to the surface. Two enormous and powerful hands reached up and dragged him back down. I barked, I howled, I pawed. The shovel came flying from the hole, and then the hair-gel dude climbed out.

Except not quite. Bernie rose up, grabbed him by the back of his collar, pulled him down. But on the way down, the hair-gel dude snatched up the shovel, twisted around and jabbed the handle end into Bernie's chest, very hard. Bernie's mouth opened, round and black, and he sank from view. The hair-gel dude, his hair now plastered over his forehead and his face like a scary mask of all things bad, raised the shovel high, the blade pointed down, and thrust with tremendous power. At the same time he yelled something I couldn't make out, a yell suddenly cut off. He dropped out of sight, real fast, like the bottom part of him was no longer there.

Time passed. The night went quiet, except for me. Then I went quiet, too. The only sound was my heart, pounding and pounding.

Bernie! Bernie!

A hand appeared at the edge of the hole, a hand I knew and loved. Bernie stood up, shirtless now and with his nose bleeding. He climbed out slowly, in fact, almost not getting out at all. On level ground he glanced around and . . . and spotted me! He started walking in my direction, the first step or two maybe of the stumbling kind, but after that he moved like my Bernie, strong and steady. He gave the jeep a quick glance and opened the door. I leaped out and landed in his arms.

"Oof! Easy there, big guy, I'm not quite —"

Or something like that. I was too busy licking the blood off his face to really listen.

"Okay, that should do it." Bernie smiled. Wow! He still had all his teeth! What great news! "But how did . . . ?" He turned and looked into the jeep, spotted the steak. "Achilles' heel, huh, Chet?" Bernie said. "Come on — we've got work to do." He closed the door. I never wanted to be in that jeep again, of course, but how come the steak hadn't ended up on the outside?

We headed back toward the hole in the ground. Achilles? A new one on me, but he had to be a perp. I've got a feel for these things. Heads up, Senor Achilles. I hope you look good in orange.

We stood over the hole. A drop or two or maybe more of blood, black in the moonlight, dripped down and fell on the hair-gel dude. He lay faceup at the bottom of the hole, eyes open but not seeing. That's an expression you get to know in this business.

Whoever has it is gone and not coming back. The hair-gel dude actually didn't look too bad, not as bad as Bernie.

I pressed against his leg. He closed his eyes and sort of bowed his head. Whatever that was about, I felt glad when it was over.

"Stay here," he said. "Keep watch."

He climbed down into the hole. I sat at the edge, ears pointed straight up. That was what they wanted and I didn't object. The night was still, a big dark world with no one alive in it but us, me and Bernie. Had we solved the case? After solving cases comes a celebration, often involving steak.

Bernie crouched beside the hair-gel dude. He patted the hair-gel dude's pants pockets, fished out a set of keys. Then he reached around to one of the back pockets, slightly shifting the hair-gel dude. His head flopped sideways, a strange sort of movement that reminded me of the teddy bear Charlie had when he was real little, specifically after that one time I'd had it in my possession. I'm no fan of teddy bears. I dealt with a real bear once. That stays with you.

Bernie pulled a wallet out of the back pocket and looked through it. "Two fifties and a ten," he said, "but no license, no credit cards, nothing to ID him with." He laid the wallet on the hair-gel dude's chest and climbed out of the hole. "Let's take a look at the jeep."

What a great idea, even if a little long in coming! We left the clearing, passed a few trees, walked slowly around the jeep, me because Bernie was doing it, Bernie for reasons of his own.

"No plate," he said.

He popped the hood.

"No VIN."

He opened the passenger door and then the glove box: empty. He checked the side compartments and under the seat.

"No registration. No papers of any kind."

And only after all that did his gaze fall on the steak, by far the most interesting thing about this jeep. He picked it up and . . . and sniffed it. That was unusual, and even more unusual was what happened next, Bernie holding the steak under my nose and saying, "Smell anything?"

What a stunner? Where to even begin? This was steak we were talking about, thick and juicy and meaty. Meaty: that was the whole point. Steak was as meaty as it gets. Was it possible Bernie didn't know that? I looked at him. He looked at me.

"Anything bad, I mean," he said.

Anything bad? How could that be possible? This was steak, possibly even rib eye or strip, the meati—

At that moment, I picked up one single non-steaky scent coming from the steak, not unpleasant. It reminded me of almonds. In my many — although not nearly enough — dealings with steak, this was a first. Interesting, although not important in the big picture. The big picture was all about that steak and me. My mouth opened nice and wide and —

And Bernie pulled back the steak, out of reach. How awful! Especially since Bernie himself had very strict rules about never ever teasing members of the nation within. My tail drooped right down to the ground.

"Sorry, Chet. It may not be safe."

Steak not safe? That made no sense to me. What kind of a world would that be, if steak wasn't safe?

"Tell you what. We'll take this in for testing and then we'll chow down on those steak tips at the Dry Gulch."

My tail rose up, but didn't start wagging. It was somewhat pleased.

Bernie wrapped the steak in one of the floor mats and we walked around to the back of the jeep. He swung open the door. Inside stood a giant-size cooler, the kind for big picnics. Bernie leaned in, raised the lid, peered inside. For a moment he went still.

Then he wedged the wrapped-up steak beside the spare tire, lifted out the cooler, and set it on the ground.

Bernie took the lid off the cooler. We stood side by side, gazing in. The sight of a human skull wasn't new to me. Don't forget I've had a long career in the desert, solving crimes and exploring abandoned mines, sometimes both at once. This particular skull, yellowish in the moonlight, had a hole in the top, over to one side. I was familiar, too, with skulls that had holes in them, and also with dried bones, of which we had plenty in the cooler.

"He dug up Hector's remains," Bernie said. "He — or they — knew we'd be coming to do the same thing. The question, big guy, is what didn't they want us to see."

Wow! The "he" had to be the hair-gel dude, but the rest of it? That was Bernie at his best. The moonlight dimmed slightly, maybe from one of those gauzy clouds passing over, and I thought I caught an expression on the face of the skull, a look that said, *You're so right about Bernie.*

Bernie crouched down and began sifting through the bones. They clicked against one another, not a loud sound but very clear in the night. "I wonder . . . ." Bernie said, and then his hand, way down under the bones,

stopped moving. It closed around something, emerged from the pile, slowly opened.

There on Bernie's hand lay part of a rusty
knife blade, broken off at one end and
pointed at the other. Bernie took it by the
broken end and gently stuck the point into
the hole in the skull.

"The drug overdose was a crock, big guy.
Hector was stabbed to death. Dr. Wellington
signed a false death certificate." I could feel
Bernie thinking, heavy thoughts that seemed
to move like slow birds over my head.
"Stabbed to death with a knife," he said.
"Just like Clint." He moved the knife around
in the hole, trying it this way and that.
"Notice the entry point is on the left, and
from the angle I'd say Hector was stabbed
from in front. I'm no expert, but if it's true,
then . . ."

Then what? I waited for more, but no
more came. And just when I'd been following along pretty well! The only puzzling
thing had been the no-expert part, totally
wrong. Maybe Bernie was getting tired. I
studied his face. He didn't look tired, in
fact looked good, except for the blood. And
what was with his nose? Did it seem . . .
somehow better than before?

"What are you staring at?"

Nothing. Not me. Someone else. Nobody.

I lifted my leg and marked one of the back wheels of the jeep, my only thought, but never a wrong move in my opinion.

Meanwhile Bernie was on the phone. "Nixon? I know it's late but I need a favor."

Even though he wasn't on speaker, I could hear Nixon on the other end. "Anything," he said. "I owe you till the end of time."

"I'll pay, of course."

"Goes without saying," Nixon said.

We stood by the hole, gazing down at the hair-gel guy. His head was still turned that bad way, like no human head I'd ever seen. Bernie picked up the shovel. "We walked into a trap, big guy," he said. "What happens if we set the exact same trap ourselves?"

Sounded like a good idea to me, whatever it was. Bernie scooped up a shovelful of earth from the pile he'd just dug out and . . . and then hesitated. "Chet? Go do something. Play."

Play? I didn't get that at all. Weren't we on the job? Didn't play come after? Or before? But maybe I was wrong. Maybe Bernie was about to lay down the shovel and produce a ball or a Frisbee, or some new toy I didn't even know about.

None of that happened. No ball, no Fris-

383

bee, no new toy. Instead Bernie took a deep breath and tossed the shovelful of earth back into the hole. The earth landed right on the face of the hair-gel dude, covering it completely except for one silvery open eye. I decided to wander off for a bit, in no particular direction, for no particular reason.

I sat by a eucalyptus tree, safe in the shelter of its smell. After a while I lay down and watched Bernie at work in the moonlight, filling in holes, not being nearly as interesting as digging them. When he was done, Bernie raised the tombstone, shifted it back into place, and dusted off his hands. Dusting off hands is a nice human thing, a bit like giving yourself a good shake. I got up and did exactly that, and felt much better, even though I hadn't been feeling the slightest bit bad to start with, certainly not very bad.

Bernie came over and scratched between my ears, a lovely, long scratch and just right. "Okay, big guy," he said. "Let's get started."

Started? Weren't we finished? Was it possible we had to dig up the hole again? And refill it? Over and over? What a scary idea! I tried to forget it and failed. Then I didn't try and succeeded.

■ ■ ■ ■

We put the cooler in the hair-gel dude's jeep, plus the shovel and the spade, and drove slowly away from the eucalyptus grove. Soon we came to a rough track which took us to the old Yuma Road, and finally the parking lot at Rancho de la Luna, an unlit parking lot where the Porsche waited in the darkest corner. Also waiting was Nixon, at the wheel of his wrecker.

"What happened to your nose?" Nixon said.

"Still bleeding?" said Bernie.

"I don't mean that," Nixon said. "It's straight."

"It is?" Bernie felt his nose, looked surprised.

He set the spade, shovel, and cooler down beside the Porsche.

"Whose jeep?" Nixon said.

"Good question," said Bernie. "It needs to be under wraps. Literally — throw a tarp over it or something."

"Oh, I can do better than that," Nixon said. "I've got a whole garage over in South Pedroia for just this kind of thing."

Bernie gave him a look. "You think I'm suddenly into car theft?"

"No way," said Nixon. "More like a lost and found situation."

"That's what your garage is? A lost and found?"

Nixon laughed. "Maybe I'll write off the mortgage payments as a charitable deduction."

He hooked up the jeep and drove away. Bernie opened the glove box of the Porsche and took out the .38 Special. "I know what you're thinking," he said. "Closing the barn door after the horses are gone."

Oh, no. I hadn't been thinking anything of the sort. But what a nightmare! I listened for galloping hooves, heard none. I sniffed the air: plenty of horse scent around, including Mingo's, but none of it recent. That was as far as I could take it on my own.

Soon after that, we hit the road — me, Bernie, shovel, spade, and that big cooler with the skull and bones inside, all jammed in together. We followed Nixon's exhaust trail all the way to the highway. He was out of sight but I thought I heard him, still laughing. The moon slid behind the crest of a black mountain and vanished.

Twenty-Eight

"Suppose," Bernie said, "that Person X knew Dr. Wellington was dealing drugs. That puts Dr. Wellington in Person X's power. So that's the leverage, Chet. Now we just need to find Person X."

I opened my eyes. The first sliver of sun popped up at the edge of the sky, a beautiful sight. The air smelled fresh and . . . and so did I! Have I mentioned my smell yet? There's something peppery about it, unusual in the nation within, and highly desirable in the minds of certain she-barkers I've run across. But no time for that now. I had to concentrate on what Bernie had just said. I'd been hearing about Dr. Wellington, but had we met him yet? I wasn't sure about that. As for Person X, I recalled no one by that name. Was this case going well? Not well? We'd started with a dead body, namely Clint, and now we had a cooler containing a skull and a bunch of bones. If they'd killed each other, then we were done and on our way to pick up the check from Myron Siegel. We seemed to be entering South Pedroia. Did Myron Siegel live in South Pedroia? I didn't think so.

"Was Person X a dealer, too? Is it all about drugs? I just —" Bernie fell silent as we passed our self-storage. Inside was an entire shipment of Hawaiian pants, and another entire shipment on top of that, all those Hawaiian pants made special just for us. I still remember the day, riding in the car just like this, when Bernie had snapped his fingers and shouted, "Hawaiian pants!" Exactly what the whole wide world was waiting for! We'd been so excited! I'd practically peed right there in the shotgun seat — an absolute no-no — and possibly Bernie had come close to doing the same. But that finger snap had ended up cratering our finances, the tin futures play that came later just non-icing on the non-cake, as Bernie had put it, a brilliant analysis and far beyond my understanding.

We turned a corner, the self-storage disappearing from my side mirror. Bernie let out his breath. "Music and drugs — wouldn't be the first time. Wouldn't be the millionth. But for that very reason I'm not buying that this is about drugs, not fundamentally. Call me a contrarian if you like."

Never. That was totally off the table.

We stopped in front of a very small stucco house with a tiny yard and no trees out front. There are blocks and blocks of houses like that in South Pedroia but this was the one where Medic lived. Medic was an old Army buddy of Bernie's, kind of in the same business as us, except he only worked cold cases, meaning pretty hopeless ones, if I was understanding right, and only those cold cases that could be solved from his computer.

Bernie carried the cooler up to the front door and knocked. A woman in a hospital-type outfit opened up. Her eyes got wide and she put her hand to her chest, like . . . like she was scared at the mere sight of us. How was that possible? We were harmless, me and Bernie, sometimes for days and days at a time.

"Who's there?" called a man from inside the house, a man whose deep voice I recognized. Medic had the very deepest voice I'd ever heard.

"A man," the woman said. "With a cooler. And a very large dog."

"Is there beer in that cooler?" Medic called again.

"Tell him no," Bernie said.

Why wasn't Bernie raising his voice to tell him himself? That was one of those human mysteries. They cropped up a lot when Bernie's Army buddies were around.

"He says no," called the woman.

"Let him in anyway."

The woman opened the door wide and backed away.

"He won't bite, I hope?" she said.

"Chet? Never," Bernie said.

For some reason that was the moment my mouth decided to open way up.

"Oh, dear." The woman pressed herself into the wall.

"No worries," Bernie said. "That's just his sense of humor."

"I didn't know dogs had a sense of humor."

"A dominant trait in some of them."

We headed down a narrow hall toward the kitchen, me in the lead. Medic was at the table. He closed his laptop and came wheeling over. Bernie put the cooler on the floor and leaned down to him. They hugged and pounded each other's backs. For a few moments it sounded like we had drummers on the scene.

"You son of a bitch," Medic said. "I heard you almost checked out."

"I'm here," Bernie said.

"Sure as hell better be. Try any premature bullshit and I'll beat the crap out of you when we meet again."

Here's maybe a good spot to mention again about human mysteries and Army buddies.

Meanwhile Medic had turned to the woman. "Consuelo's my visiting nurse. Meet Bernie. You wouldn't be here today except for him."

"Excuse me?" said Consuelo.

"I woulda been a goner is why. Bastard saved my life."

"Nice to meet you, Bernie," Consuelo said. "Were you a medic, too?"

"Why would he be the medic?" Medic said. "I was the medic. That's why they call me Medic."

This was not easy to follow. Maybe Consuelo was also having the same problem.

Her hand was over her chest again.

"But don't they usually call medics Doc?" she said.

"If I'd wanted them to call me Doc, they'd have called me Doc." His voice rose. I felt it through the floorboards. "Ever heard of human rights?" His eyes shifted, as though he were listening to something. A strange silence descended on the kitchen, not comfortable. Medic spoke again, but much

391

more quietly. "Are we about done for the day?"

"There's just the stretching exercises left," Consuelo told him.

"I hate the goddamn stretching exercises," Medic said, still softly.

"Then maybe tomorrow?"

Medic nodded.

Consuelo happened to look my way, catching me in mid-yawn — not sleepy, not bored, just simply yawning. Soon after that — in fact, right then — she left the house, possibly in a bit of a hurry.

Medic wheeled closer to the cooler, gestured at it with his chin. His voice got stronger. "If not beer, then what?"

"Open it," Bernie said.

Weren't we going to give Medic a chance to pat me before we got down to business? I went over to him.

"Look at the size of this guy." Medic rubbed my neck. He had real strong hands and at the same time a soft touch — the kind of combo you dream about. "What's he weigh?"

"Chet's a hundred-plus pounder," Bernie said. "Nailing down the exact number means getting him on the scale."

Medic laughed, a loud, rolling laugh, like he was back to his normal self. "Any chance he's hungry?"

There was every chance! I sidled my way toward the fridge. Medic laughed again — why, I wasn't sure. Didn't food come out of the fridge? Actually not in this case. Moments later I was in the corner, enjoying a Slim Jim. In fact, we were all enjoying Slim Jims. The world shrank down to this little kitchen and us dudes chowing down. Life is full of nice moments. You just have to be there.

Medic opened the cooler. He gazed inside, not saying anything. Bernie also said nothing. He gazed at Medic. I gazed at the cupboard where the Slim Jims were stored and considered various possibilities.

Medic cleared space on the table and began unpacking the cooler, piece by piece. The skull ended up leaning against the fruit bowl, the broken knife lying on the butter dish, not quite touching the butter. Medic went into gazing mode all over again. Bernie sat down, crossed one leg over the other. Soon his hand would pat his chest pocket, meaning the hand was thinking about cigarettes, of which there were none on Bernie, cigarette smell unmissable. I sat down myself, found a tiny scrap of Slim Jim way back in my mouth and tried to make it last.

Bernie's hand was just reaching up to pat his chest pocket when Medic sat back. He rubbed his face, sort of smoothing it out — a human move I always like to see — and said, "Did you show all this to the ME?"

"Nope," Bernie said.

"How come?"

"You're better."

"Did the fact of her being an official play into it?"

"There is that," Bernie said.

Medic waved his hand at the stuff on the table. "What do you want to know?"

"Everything."

Medic nodded. "One thing's for sure — you didn't kill him. You weren't even born."

"Dodged a bullet," Bernie said.

Medic's eyes got an inward look. "What is it about guys like you and me, Bernie?"

"How do you mean?"

"Do you ever get the feeling that the world is racing by the other way?"

"Yup."

"What are you going to do about it?"

"I'm willing to listen to suggestions."

"Came to the wrong place," Medic said.

I rose. If we were in the wrong place, shouldn't we hit the road?

Medic reached for the skull, placed it on his leg, the one that ended just above the knee, the other leg not as long. I sat back down.

"A Caucasian gentleman," he said, "with some Mesoamerican ancestry, in his early twenties. Probably about five feet eleven when fully assembled, strongly built, no sign of childhood injuries, malnutrition, or serious diseases. He was stabbed in the head — very convenient to have a partial murder weapon, Bernie. You do good work. That's the cause of death, practically instantaneous." Medic gave the skull a little pat. I got a strange feeling on the top of my own head, not pleasant. "Way too young to die, as we say."

He turned to Bernie. They exchanged a look. I knew it meant something, but that was as far as I got.

"Anything else?" Bernie said.

"Aside from the fact that the killer was right-handed and almost certainly a man, based on the force required? Not that I can think of," said Medic. "What's with your nose, by the way?"

Sometimes on a case like this, Bernie likes to swing by home for a quick shower and a change of clothes. I myself have only been in the shower once, and very briefly — although I took the shower with me, as Ber-

nie always says when he's telling the story
— and for clothing I usually stick to my
gator-skin collar, the black leather one being for dress-up.

"What's this?" Bernie said, as we drove
up Mesquite Road.

A long black car was parked in front of
our place. Old man Heydrich was standing
beside it, talking to the driver through the
rolled-down window. Have I mentioned old
man Heydrich already? For neighbors, we
have the Parsons and Iggy on one side and
old man Heydrich on the other. He has a
thick and grassy green lawn that he waters
morning, evening, and in between; is not
fond of me and my kind; and collects Nazi
memorabilia, whatever that is, exactly. Other
than that, we don't know much about him.

We parked in the driveway and got out of
the car. Bernie looked at old man Heydrich.
He didn't stare or glare, just looked. Old
man Heydrich caught the look, lowered his
own gaze, said, "Pleasure meeting you," to
the driver, and headed toward his house.
His sprinklers started up the moment he
went inside.

The driver opened the door of the long
black car and stepped out: a big suntanned
man with a big strong chin, big strong nose,
and a full head of white hair. I recognized

him right away, meaning I was on my game, so on my game that I knew for certain his name would come to me sooner or later.

"Mr. Riggs?" Bernie said.

"Boomer, please. Don't make me tell you again."

Right! Boomer Riggs! The name had come to me already. What a day I was having! Slim Jims and now this!

"Or what, Boomer?" Bernie said.

Boomer laughed a big laugh, possibly the kind called booming. I came very close to making a connection. "Glad I caught you," he said. "Been away?"

Bernie shrugged. "Coming and going."

"Not according to your neighbor's log," Boomer said. "He says you've been gone for two days."

Bernie glanced over at old man Heydrich's house. "The son of a bitch keeps a log on us?"

"Not just on you — the whole block," said Boomer. "Mr. Heydrich has a spreadsheet on his iPad. He was just about to show me when you drove up."

"God almighty," Bernie said.

Boomer laughed again, came forward, shook Bernie's hand. "Have a nice trip?"

"Not bad," Bernie said.

I caught a whiff of something in the air

and was suddenly very glad to see old Boomer.

"Work or play?" he was saying.

"Why do you ask?" said Bernie.

"No reason." Boomer reached into his pocket. "Almost forgot — can Chet have one of these?" He held up — yes! — a white truffle–infused Kobe beef jerky treat!

Bernie . . . sniffed the air? How strange! Then, even stranger, he said, "Nice of you — but he just had his treat for the day. I can keep it for him if you like."

"That's all right," Boomer said, repocketing the treat, which smelled just like the last one. "If this works out, there'll be other treats from me in his future."

"If what works out?" said Bernie.

"You made it clear you wouldn't join Western Solutions as an employee, but we didn't discuss contract work. I've got a three-month job starting in a day or two, pays sixty K plus expenses."

Bernie shook his head. "We're busy."

"Doing what?"

"Working a case."

"Mind telling me what case?"

"I do," Bernie said.

"Totally understood," Boomer said. "I like how you work, Bernie. You remind me of myself when I was young. But if it's still the

Lotty Pilgrim matter, word is she's pleading guilty tomorrow morning. Meaning your case is over."

"But the arraignment's not till next week," Bernie said.

"They moved it up to tomorrow."

"How do you know?"

"I happened to be having drinks with the judge," Boomer said. "Pure coincidence." He took out an envelope. "Here's our standard three-month contract with all the details of the case, plus an on-signing check for thirty grand."

"I'm really not —"

"At least look it over." Boomer's eyes got a little twinkly as though he was smiling inside. "The case just came up — urgent and right up your alley, which is why I'm here."

"Right up my alley?"

"It's about a dog fighting ring operating in a number of southeastern states."

Bernie took the envelope.

They said goodbye, Boomer heading toward his car and Bernie toward the house. I was kind of trailing Bernie, still keeping an eye on Boomer in case some private arrangement with the white truffle–infused Kobe beef jerky treat was in the cards. It turned out not to be, but I did catch one of those human double-takes: Boomer noticing the spade and shovel sticking out of the Porsche, and then re-noticing them for a little longer. As for why I didn't get my treat, I had no clue. I'd already had my treat for the day? When was that, if I may ask?

TWENTY-NINE

The phone was ringing in the house. Bernie picked up. A voice I knew — male, old but not weak — came over the speaker.

"Bernie? Myron Siegel here. Anything to report? I'm getting anxious."

"Nothing to be anxious about," Bernie said. "I don't normally report until there's a final result."

Myron's voice rose, at the same time sounding thinner and less powerful. "There's plenty to be anxious about. I'm missing Oksana."

Oksana? I remembered how she'd raised her beer mug: *Here's to this beautiful creature.* Am I the type who forgets my fans?

"I don't understand," Bernie said.

"I'm missing her because she's not here," said Myron. "I sent her away for her own safety."

"Have you been threatened?"

"That's what I'm trying to tell you! Speed

401

up a little, Bernie."

"We'll be there in twenty minutes," Bernie said.

Myron wasn't poolside at his condo, but indoors with the curtains closed and a few lights on. That's something that makes me uneasy in the daytime.

Myron led us into the living room. He opened a tiny gap in the curtains and peeked out. Golden dust specks buzzed around in the narrow gap. "Are you armed?" he said.

"Yes," said Bernie. "And you?"

"Too old to take up gunslinging." Myron closed the curtains and the dust specks vanished in mid-buzz. "And don't ask where she is. Somewhere safe — that's all I'm telling you or anybody."

"Fine with me as long as you're sure she's safe," Bernie said. "What happened, Myron?"

Myron raised his voice, again sounding older. He also looked older, his face all shadowy in the dim light. "What happened? Two nights ago a thug broke in here — well, he got in somehow. There was actually no damage. But the point is he waved a gun in our faces — we were in our bed! — and threatened our lives unless we quote 'dropped the Lotty Pilgrim matter.' "

"What did you do?"

Myron shook his head. "I made a stupid reply, the first thing that came to mind."

"Which was?"

" 'Fuck you.' I forgot that my inner self is pretty much disconnected from my outer self these days — something Oksana likes about me, for what it's worth."

"And then?" Bernie said.

"He walked up to Oksana's side of the bed and stuck the gun in her mouth. I could have killed him." Myron hung his head. "Except I couldn't, of course. Instead I told him I'd do as he asked. He warned me not to call the cops — he said if I did he'd know right away — and then he left. I got Oksana out of here within the hour."

"Did you call the police?"

"No," Myron said. "I believed him on that."

"But why didn't you call me?"

"Because I had no intention of dropping the case," Myron said. "I don't like getting pushed around."

"Have you switched out the locks?"

Myron nodded. "Plus I put in deadbolts."

"What did this guy look like?" Bernie said.

"Huge," said Myron. "NFL-lineman size. Well-spoken, obviously educated, wore a suit. When I call him a thug, I mean morally."

A big guy in a suit? I hadn't been listening my very closest, but that little detail slipped into my mind. It bumped into another little detail that was just waiting there, namely the image of the hair-gel dude. What a pleasant bump, if very tiny.

"You don't have to worry about him anymore," Bernie said.

"Why not?" said Myron.

"The details don't matter," Bernie said. "Right now I need you to think back to high school in Fort Kidder. What kind of offense did the football team run when Lotty was there?"

"Is that some kind of joke?" Myron said.

"Far from it," Bernie said. "If it was a single wing — which a lot of high schools in the state were still running back then — then I need to talk to the fullback. If it was modern pro-style, then it's the center."

"What's going on?" Myron said.

"Depending on the system, those would be the players most likely to have a close relationship with the quarterback."

Myron gave Bernie a careful look. "I'll see what I can do," he said, sounding more like his normal self. "Okay to bring Oksana back home?"

"Not yet," Bernie said.

We were on our way out when Myron started opening the curtains. Daylight poured in and followed us through the doorway.

In the car, Bernie got on the phone and called Rick Torres.

"Is Chet there?" Rick said.

"Yup."

"Awake?"

"Extremely."

"Meet at Donut Heaven? I'm off in an hour."

"Can't," Bernie said. "But I need a favor."

And Bernie went on to describe some favor, possibly about a jail. I wasn't really listening because . . . because we'd just turned down a chance to drop by Donut Heaven? *Tackle the most important task first.* Wasn't that something Bernie said all the time? Or at least once? Plus I was starving.

Bernie hung up. The phone rang again.

"Bernie? Myron. I checked all police reports, Valley, suburbs, and three counties. No hits."

"What are you talking about?"

"The intruder. No one matching his description has been arrested, injured enough to require EMTs, or otherwise incapacitated in the past thirty-six hours."

"Myron, for god's sake — there's a reason for that."

"A reason that would still my worries?"

"To the stillest," Bernie said. "And aren't you supposed to be working the football question?"

"That was easy," Myron said. "Got a pen?"

"What are we going to do if Charlie wants to play football?" Bernie said.

Buy him a football: that was my only idea. I was thinking about the big problem with football — namely the unwieldiness of the ball, which you need to deflate a bit to get it properly in your mouth — when we pulled into one of the playing field complexes we have in the Valley, not the fancy kind with the unreal grass and shady trees, but the other kind with mostly no grass and no trees. Out on the fields, kids — some little, some not quite as little — were practicing football. Practicing means the coaches are out on the field yelling things. In games, the coaches yell from the sidelines.

"Any chance you'd prefer to stay in the car?" Bernie said. "Maybe grab a few z's?"

What was that? Something about the car?

I was already some distance away and had missed most of it.

"Okay, then," Bernie said. "Best behavior."

But of course! What other kind was there? We walked around a couple of fields, stopped at the sideline of the next one. A guy in sweats, maybe Bernie's age, was writing on a clipboard. He glanced up at Bernie.

"We're looking for the Lions," Bernie said.

Uh-oh. This was a bad development. I'd had an experience with a mountain lion, felt no desire for another one anytime soon, or ever. A trace of lion scent still lived in my brain, would maybe be there forever. I tried sniffing the air. No lions. So maybe we were looking for lions but had come to the wrong place? I was fine with that.

The guy checked his watch. "We got twenty more minutes."

"We don't want the field," Bernie said. "Just a few minutes with the coach, Ernie Flowers, I believe. Is that you?"

The guy frowned. "I'm the head coach," he said. "Assistant Coach Flowers handles the linemen." He pointed to two rows of little kids in football gear lined up and facing each other, hands and feet on the ground. Hands and feet on the ground — what a great game! A big round dude with a

407

stogie sticking out the side of his mouth was pacing back and forth between the two lines and yelling, "Hands and butts, hands and butts — how many times I gotta tell you potato heads?"

"A coach from the old school," Bernie said.

"As old as it gets. Go on out there if you want. He likes company."

We walked onto the field, mostly dirt with tufts of grass here and there. Coach Flowers had moved out from between the two rows of players, now stood to the side. We stopped nearby. Coach Flowers put the whistle in his mouth, sort of nudging the stogie to one side, and talked around them.

"On the whistle, potato heads. Not before, not after. All set?"

He blew the whistle, a sound I hate, but at least I'd known it was coming. The two rows charged each other, thumping together with lots of grunts and shouts, none of the shouts actual words, more like the kind of noise you hear on Animal Planet. The kids finished knocking each other around, picked themselves up, dusted themselves off.

"What the heck?" said Coach Flowers. Or something like that — he wasn't easy to understand with the whistle and stogie in his mouth. "Call that hitting? Don't look like hitting to me. Looked like hugging your sister."

One of the kids said, "I'm a sister, Coach."

Coach Flowers turned to her. "Did I ask for your opinion, Taneeka?"

"Not yet, Coach."

"Take a lap."

Taneeka jogged away, her face all dusty and sweaty.

"Down," said Coach Flowers.

The rest of the kids scrambled back to their rows, got down in hands and feet position.

"Butt is the engine," said Coach Flowers.

"Butt is the engine!" the kids yelled.

"Hands is the tools."

"Hands is the tools!"

"On the whistle, potato heads. All set?" He blew the whistle. Then came the charging, thumping, grunting, shouting, falling, after which Coach Flowers told them that was still hugging their sister, not hitting. They did the whole thing over a few more times. Over on the sidelines, the coach with the clipboard blew his whistle and yelled, "Time!"

"Already?" said Coach Flowers. "How the heck are we gonna beat the Eagles on Sattiday?"

"Hit 'em hard and often," said Taneeka.

Coach Flowers gave her a look. "Scram," he said, taking the whistle out of his mouth. "Alla yus."

"Go Lions," the kids shouted, and ran off the field.

Coach Flowers turned, seemed to notice us for the first time.

"Fifty-two looks real good," Bernie said.

Coach Flowers squinted at him. "The fat one with the glasses?"

"Footwork, timing, balance. But the best thing is he's humming a little tune the whole time."

The coach nodded. "I noticed that. You with the league?"

"Just a spectator," Bernie said. He held out his hand. "Bernie Little."

"Ernie Flowers." They shook hands.

"And this is Chet," Bernie said.

"What's he doing with that ball?"

"Chet!"

I dropped the ball, no problem. Funny how it didn't bounce, instead sort of flopped down like an old shoe. The coach picked it up, peered at what might have been an insignificant hole or two. "It's ruint," he said.

"I'll pay for a new one." Bernie reached for his wallet.

The coach waved it away. "That's all right. Pup dint know what he was doin'."

I glanced around, saw no pups, no members of the nation within at all. Perhaps I'd misheard on account of the stogie in his mouth — a very thick stogie, frayed and sort of slobbery. I was starting to like Coach Flowers a lot.

"You musta played," he said.

"Some," said Bernie. "How about you?"

"High school," said Coach Flowers.

"Where was this?"

"Coronado High down in Fort Kidder."

"The Renegades," Bernie said.

"That's right. How'd you know that?"

"I was based in Fort Kidder some time back, took in a game or two."

"Program went to shit after the move. We made state finals one year when I was there."

"What was your position?"

"Center."

"Who was the quarterback?"

"His name, you mean?"

"Yeah."

"Boomer Riggs."

"Tell me about him."

"Huh?"

"No one knows the quarterback like the center."

"True enough," said the coach. "But Boomer never went on to the pros or nothin' like that."

"Have you kept up with him?"

"Nope."

"How come?"

"No interest in it."

"Sounds like maybe you didn't like him much," Bernie said.

Coach Flowers shrugged. "Long time past."

"Yes and no," Bernie said.

The coach squinted at him again, normally not a good look on humans, especially small-eyed ones like Coach Flowers, but it sort of suited him. "What's goin' on?"

"Do you remember Lotty Pilgrim?"

" 'Course. Prettiest gal in the state back then. And real talented, too. She in trouble? My wife mentioned something."

Bernie handed the coach our card. "We're trying to help Lotty."

"That's nice," said the coach. "But what's it got to do with high school football way back when?"

"That's where you come in," Bernie said. "Tell me about Lotty's relationship with Boomer Riggs."

"Like in what way?"

"Anything that comes to mind."

"Well," said Coach Flowers, "it was kind of upside down."

"How do you mean?"

"Boomer being the QB and all, big man on campus, well-off family, especially for down there in those days. He coulda just played the field, had any girl he wanted — which he did, before things got going with Lotty. He kind of surprised me after that."

"How?"

"Boomer got real serious. Talked about wanting to marry her, go away to college together. Getting married young wasn't so unusual then."

"What was Lotty's reaction?"

"That's the upside-down part. She was way more casual than him — not wanting to . . . what's the word?"

"Commit?"

"Yeah," Boomer said. "Then when she met that Mexican or whatever he was down in Tesabe and dropped out to be with him, Boomer just went ape."

"Oh," said Bernie, his head going back just a little. I love that move! It makes him look even better, almost an impossibility, you might think.

"Boomer got drunk and beat the shit out of Jose Riaz," the coach said. "Night before our last Thanksgiving game — meaning the seniors. Knocked Jose right out of the game. Boomer shoulda been suspended, of course, but the coach didn't have the balls." Coach Flowers gazed across the field. "We lost."

"I'm a little confused," Bernie said. "Was Jose Riaz the Mexican Lotty got involved with?"

"Naw," said the coach. "Jose was just a Mexican — a handy nearby Mexican for Boomer to take out his rage on. And Jose actually wasn't a Mexican, came from an old-time Arizona family going back hundreds of years. American as you or me, is what I'm tryna say, if you get my meaning."

"I think I do," Bernie said.

I myself did not get the meaning. But if apes were in the picture things had taken a bad turn.

THIRTY

"Go in and take a seat," Rick said, opening a door for us. "You're on camera but there are no mics."

"Sure about that?" Bernie said.

Rick laughed. "Beware the unknown unknowns, huh, old buddy?" He handed Bernie a bottle of water as we went inside, and closed the door behind us.

This was the kind of room where you don't want to spend much time: cement floor, cinder-block walls, one plastic table, two plastic chairs, no windows, a heavy metal door on the far side of the room. Bernie glanced around and sat down. "He's right about the unknown unknowns. But what's the funny part?"

I couldn't help Bernie on that. Instead, I sat down beside him, nice and close. Human tears leave a smell in the air, a bit like the ocean, but way tinier. I was picking up that smell in this room. It reminded me of our trip to San Diego. We'd surfed, me and Bernie! At first on the same board and later we each had one. I preferred sharing a board, but there'd been issues, possibly involving who stood where. When you're in front you get that ocean spray full in the face. I was thinking about how much I love ocean spray full in the face when the door on the far side of the room opened, and Lotty Pilgrim came in, wearing an orange jumpsuit. The door closed with a solid clang. She saw us and stopped.

"It's you?" she said. "That's not what they told me." Lotty backed toward the door.

Bernie rose. "Sorry for the subterfuge," he said. "But not using it would have been a greater sin."

"Why is that?"

"I'll explain." Bernie walked around the table, pulled out the other plastic chair.

Lotty didn't move. "Why should I trust you? Not that it matters in the big picture, but you set me up."

"The sheriff planted a GPS tracker under my car," Bernie said. "I'm ashamed of myself for being careless, but I didn't set you up."

Bernie ashamed? I must have heard wrong. I licked his foot, always more interesting when he wore flip-flops, like now.

For a moment or two, Lotty stayed put. Then, very slowly, like her legs had gotten real heavy, she came forward. She looked small in the orange jumpsuit, even though I knew she wasn't a small woman. Also her silvery blond hair had lost its pouf, hung straight down, sort of limp, and had gone pure white at the roots. Bernie angled the chair for her and helped her closer to the table, like a gentleman at the Ritz, where I had actually once been myself, if very briefly.

Lotty turned her head to look up at him. "Do all private detectives talk in terms of sin and shame?" she said.

"None of them, including me," Bernie said. "That was a first."

Lotty rested her hands on the table, strong, square, nice-looking hands, even if kind of oldish. "You seem like a good man," she said, "and the way you and Chet get along proves it, but I don't know what you hope to achieve. I'm pleading guilty in the morning."

"Guilty to what?" Bernie said.

"Murder."

"Whose murder?"

Lotty sat back. "Clint's, of course."

"Okay, let's start there," Bernie said. "Take me through it."

"We've already done this."

"No," Bernie said. "We've done your avoidance of it. What happened that night at the ranch?"

"I killed Clint. That's the bottom line."

"How?"

Lotty closed her eyes. Her eyelids trembled for a moment, then opened. "I can't talk about it."

Bernie leaned forward, laid his hand on one of hers. "You sense things, Lotty — more powerfully than most people. You must be sensing that this is your last chance — maybe the only chance you ever had — to straighten things out."

"What things?" Lotty said.

"Your whole life."

Lotty's head twisted to the side, almost like she'd been hit.

"How did you kill Clint?" Bernie's voice was quiet, but not at all soft.

Lotty tried to slide her hand out from under his, but Bernie didn't let her. It wasn't like he pressed real hard or anything like that. He did it more with his eyes, if that makes any sense, and I'm pretty sure it doesn't.

Her eyes shifted as though she was hearing some faraway sound. "With a knife," she said.

"What knife?" said Bernie.

"It . . . it must've —" she began and then stopped herself. "A kitchen knife," she said. "I took one of the knives from the kitchen."

"Which one?"

"I don't remember. I just went and grabbed it."

"Think back," Bernie said. "What were you doing before you grabbed the knife?"

"Why are you humiliating me like this?" Lotty withdrew her hand. Bernie didn't stop her.

"I don't see what's humiliating about it."

"No? An old bag drunk out of her mind? In bed with her cheating boyfriend and acting like a whore even though she knew he was cheating? And finding he was all tuckered out from a previous engagement?" Tears rose in Lotty's eyes but didn't overflow. "Humiliating enough for you? Want more?"

Bernie just sat there. A silent time went by. Often in those silent times I feel Bernie's thoughts, but not now. Was he just letting a silent time go by? At last he spoke.

"At what point did you go to the kitchen for the knife?"

Lotty's mouth opened. Bernie had surprised her in some way, surprised her bigtime. Her tears dried up. "You're so god-

419

damn dogged," she said.

That again? Hadn't it already come up with Leticia? Like mother, like daughter — wasn't that a human expression? How nice the two of them had realized Bernie and I were alike in some ways, both of us dogged, of course, but was it possible I was kind of whatever dogged would be going the other way, toward human, if you see what I mean? I myself did not see what I meant and abandoned the whole thing at once.

"Was Clint still awake?" Bernie said.

"I don't know," said Lotty. "I was drunk. Blacked-out drunk. Ever been blacked-out drunk?"

Bernie nodded.

Whoa! I'd never seen him like that, or anything close. Had it happened in that time before we got together, me and Bernie? Some times are more important than others. That one didn't really count.

"Then you know what it's like," Lotty was saying. "In the morning you re-create the goings-on from the mess left over."

"What sort of mess?"

"Do I have to spell it out? I woke up with Clint's body beside me, our legs intertwined." Her voice rose. "There's a nice detail for you. Our legs intertwined, him with a bloody hole in his chest and me with a bloody knife in the palm of my hand."

"But you don't remember getting the knife."

Lotty rose. "I've had enough."

"We're not nearly done," Bernie said. "We haven't even come to Hector yet."

Lotty sat down hard, like her legs had given out.

"Let's go over the death of Hector," Bernie said. "The late Dr. Fred Wellington signed his death certificate — officially a drug overdose. Did you know Dr. Wellington, Lotty?"

She nodded. Her eyes were locked on Bernie's now. It's a look you see in my world, for example — what with Delilah so fresh in my mind — when a mouse suddenly notices that there's a cat in the room.

"Did Hector buy drugs from him?"

She nodded again.

"Do you find it strange that the drug dealer signed the death certificate? Wouldn't he want to distance himself from any customer ODs?"

"I don't know how his mind worked," Lotty said.

"Sounds like you didn't like him much," said Bernie.

"He wasn't important to me."

"No? That death certificate was very

important to you. Still is."

"What do you mean?"

"You know the answer to that."

"I most certainly do not." Lotty's legs tensed like she was going to rise again, but she stayed where she was. I'd seen that before at some of our interviews, perps stuck to their chairs. Was Lotty a perp? Or not? Was it possible that this was a case with no perp? What a horrible thought! A bit like tin futures, although I couldn't have explained why.

"What didn't you like about Dr. Wellington?" Bernie said. "Did he have some sort of influence over Hector?"

"His drugs," Lotty said. "I didn't like his drugs." She got a distant look in her eyes. Bernie sat very still. So did I. "I liked Hector's drugs," she went on at last. "They were part of a ritual, had meaning. Wellington's drugs meant nothing but enslavement."

"Did they enslave Hector?"

"Yes."

"And kill him in the end?"

Lotty was quiet for a long time. It went on and on. Bernie never interrupts these silences. I'd seen that a jillion times, the biggest number out there, according to Charlie. But this time Bernie spoke.

"I've seen Hector's body," he said. "Some-one dug it up."

Lotty turned white. Not white, exactly. It was more like the skin of her face went dead. She started to topple over.

Bernie caught her before she fell. He can be very quick, as I'm sure you know already. Not long after that, he had her sitting up straight and was helping her hold the water bottle. Lotty drank and began looking more like her normal self. She was one of those tough cookies we ran into from time to time. A strange idea: no cookie I've tried came close to being tough, my teeth making quick work of each and every one. Maybe it's all about the big difference between my teeth and yours, no offense.

Lotty put down the bottle, took a deep breath. "Who . . . who . . . ?"

"Who dug him up?" Bernie said.

She nodded.

"We haven't been able to identify him. A big guy, forty to forty-five, educated, self-confident. Any of that familiar?"

Lotty shook her head.

"Did Clint know someone like that?"

"No. What are you saying?"

"Just excluding possibilities, remote in this case."

They looked at each other. I was reminded

423

of some of the old boxing matches we'd watched, in the days after Leda and Charlie left. A crazy thought. Bernie punching a woman was out of the question. Also he liked Lotty a whole lot. But still, wasn't she getting hurt?

"Flaco has a tape of you and Hector working on 'How You Hung the Moon,' " Bernie said.

"My god," said Lotty.

"Pretty goddamn wonderful," Bernie said. "I just can't fit it together with what came out of that grave."

Lotty clasped her hands and squeezed them tight.

"The death certificate was false," Bernie said. "Did you know that?"

Lotty nodded, the slightest little movement.

"Do you know the true cause of death?"

And now, with no warning, came the tears. Lotty sobbed and shook. She covered her face with her hands but tears and even some snot leaked out between her fingers. The sound, the sight, the smells: all terrible.

"I killed him, too," she cried. "I kill what I love. I'm a monster."

I knew monsters from movies that Bernie and I were too scared to watch. Lotty didn't look or sound like any of those monsters. I changed positions and pressed against her leg, not hard, just barely touching. The shaking in her leg — in her whole body, in fact, ramped down a bit.

"What knife did you use on Hector?" Bernie said, his voice calm, like we were discussing something interesting but not particularly important.

Lotty ran her hands slowly down her face, somehow changing it into a simple face, like a kid's. It didn't get any younger, just simpler — and kind of beautiful. "Hector's own knife. He always carried a knife."

Bernie nodded, a nod that said, *Got it.* "And that just leaves the question of why you did it, and then we're about done."

"I already told you," said Lotty. "I'm a monster."

"That doesn't answer the question of why Hector specifically. Did he hurt you? Threaten you? Was there an argument about the writing credit for 'How You Hung the Moon'?"

"None of those things," Lotty said. "Hector loved me. He built me up. He showed me what I had inside."

"Did he think a monster was there?"

Lotty's eyes shifted. She thought for what seemed like a long time. "No," she said.

"Maybe he was right."

"Obviously not," Lotty said.

"What about the song credit? Why is it in your name only?"

"That . . . that was just how it played out."

"But the publishing rights are owned by QB Inc. Is that you?"

Lotty shook her head.

"Who is it?"

"These things get bought and sold. Michael Jackson bought the Beatles catalog."

"Should I be looking into Michael Jackson?"

Then came a surprise. Lotty laughed, just a short laugh, a sort of bark. The combination of that bark and her teary face made me press a little harder on her leg. Some humans are capable of a convincing sort of bark and Lotty was clearly one of them. As for Michael Jackson — a new one on me. A perp, perhaps? If so I hoped he looked good in orange. Most humans didn't, but maybe he was one of the lucky ones that way.

After the barking episode, things got quiet in this unpleasant room. Their eyes met. Bernie's still had that detached expression. Lotty looked like she was steeling herself for one more round.

"What led up to Hector's death?" Bernie said.

"I stabbed him. Isn't that enough?"

"When did you stab him?"

"Sometime in the night. When I woke up in the morning he was dead beside me."

"Just like Clint."

"I haven't missed that point," Lotty said.

"And just like with Clint, you have no memory of the actual stabbing?" Bernie said. "Were you drunk that night, too?"

Lotty shook her head. "Hector loathed alcohol. Much too crude for what he had in mind."

"Which was?"

"Luring out the inner song — that's how he put it. Peyote was one of the tools, and toward the end mixed with some of Wellington's drugs as well." I felt her body sag. "What got lured out of me should have stayed inside."

"I'm not convinced," Bernie said. "How did you get Wellington to falsify the death certificate?"

"Who cares now?" Lotty said. "Are you going to tell the DA about Hector or should I?"

"Neither of us," Bernie said. "It would be bearing false witness. Also don't plead guilty tomorrow, no matter what."

Lotty shook her head. "I want my punishment."

"Your punishment, no problem," Bernie

said. "But not the punishment due to others."

Lotty blinked. "Others like who?"

"I can't answer that," Bernie said. "That's why I need time. And your help."

"Help with what?"

"Facts." Bernie leaned forward, all that detachment popping away like a bubble. "Who was Leticia's father?"

I felt Lotty's hand in the fur of my neck, gripping it hard. That was fine with me, didn't hurt at all.

"How can that possibly matter?"

"I'm sure it matters to Leticia," Bernie said.

Lotty started crying again, but soundlessly this time, tears wetting her face.

"Was it Hector?" Bernie said.

"That would have been nice," Lotty said quietly, almost like she'd fallen into a quick dream.

"Was it Boomer Riggs?"

Lotty didn't answer. She lowered her head. A tear or two fell on my muzzle. I raised my own head and licked the rest of her tears off Lotty's face.

A guard opened the far door. "Time," she said.

■ ■ ■ ■

We were barely back in the car before Nixon called.

"Did you check the left rear wheel well?" he said.

"What are you talking about?"

"Come on, Bernie — you're supposed to be sharp. You told me there was no VIN on that jeep. Did you check the left rear wheel well? The days of VINs only on engine blocks and dashes are over. They hide them all over the place these days."

"I didn't know that."

"Luckily you got me in your corner. And I sure hope it's . . . what's the word?"

"Reciprocal."

"Bingo," Nixon said. "The jeep's registered to some outfit called Western Solutions. I'm guessing you still want me to keep it under wraps? Literally and . . . what's the other one?"

"Figuratively," Bernie said.

"You're a smart guy, Bernie." Nixon laughed and hung up. Bernie was a smart guy, of course, so no surprise Nixon knew that. But his laugh sounded a bit like the mocking kind. Maybe he had some perpiness left inside. That was as far as I could take it on my own.

THIRTY-ONE

Nighttime. A moon, but smaller than the night before. What was with the moon? Bernie knew. There he was, walking the Hanging Moon trail beside me. Maybe he'd turn and explain about the moon, maybe not. It didn't matter. I could feel him, full of life, strong — and dangerous, if he needed to be. He was all the way back to being the real Bernie. Or even more so! More Bernie than ever — can you imagine? This was living.

And when you're really living you don't ask a lot of questions. Like, what were we actually doing out here? How come we'd left the Porsche parked behind some bushes just outside the gate to Rancho de la Luna? Was this work or play, either one fine by me? Although play paid nothing, and our finances were a bit of a mess, so maybe work would be the best choice. What was a third mortgage? I remembered a hard-to-follow discussion about that while Bernie was still in the hospital, Suzie saying, "When should we tell him?" and Ms. Pernick, our accountant, saying, "There's no good time."

The one-armed saguaro rose up ahead of us. Even though I can see much better in the darkness than you, no offense, the night can do strange things. In the daytime, this would have been just one more saguaro — all of them oddballs if you look closely — but at night it was something else: a cop with his hand raised in the stop sign, for example.

Bernie glanced at it. "Only the moon hanging in the sky, or a nice moon for a hanging?" he said.

We kept going. I got the feeling that we were on the same page, as humans often say. As for hanging, I hoped nothing like that was in the cards. It reminded me of the broom closet case, how we'd gotten there too late, and what had happened after that. We've solved every missing kid case we ever took, except that one. The little girl's name was Gail. Later that night, we'd been the law, me and Bernie. "Lock it in a deep dark place, throw away the key, and never think about it again," he'd told me. I'd had some success with that, but why was it cropping up now?

Not long past the one-armed saguaro, Flaco's casita appeared at the top of a slope, no lights showing but separating itself from the night by being squarish. Bernie gave me the quiet sign, finger crosswise over his lips, but of course I was already quiet, certainly more quiet than him. Did he think I was about to let loose with a round of barking or something crazy like that? A round of barking at a time like this would never have occurred to me . . . but now that it actually sort of had occurred to me, was there any reason why a bark or two wouldn't —

Bernie laid his hand on my neck, just the gentlest touch. We moved soundlessly on, across a pebbly wash and slanting up a ridge. When I looked back, there was nothing squarish to see.

Some time later — it felt longish but maybe not — I smelled the kind of tea Bernie's mom likes to pour her bourbon into. I'm no expert on time, bringing other things to the table, but on a night like this, just me and Bernie on the move — and the .38 Special, better get that in here while I have the chance — I become even more of a non-expert on time. What if the whole world was only this — me, Bernie, .38 Special? Ah.

But back to that tea smell. With it came something lemony and woody. We headed down a gentle slope and into the eucalyptus grove. A peaceful spot, especially since we had it to ourselves, no other beings around, especially not Mingo. The gravestone stood nice and straight, just the way we'd left it. Who was buried under it at the moment? Almost right away, I remembered. Was I on top of this case or what?

Bernie gazed across the clearing, over at the eucalyptus trees on the other side. Somewhere beyond them ran the dirt track that led to two-lane blacktop and another sort of world. Nothing moved out there, and the only sound was Bernie's breathing, slow and even. We made our way between two trees and up a short rise. A fat barrel cactus grew at the top.

"Let's look like cactuses," Bernie said, very softly.

Wow! That was a first. I had no idea where to even start.

"Sit," Bernie said.

I sat beside the barrel cactus, close but not too close — I'd had an experience with a barrel cactus, and later with an even nastier one. Bernie sat beside me.

He smiled, his teeth the color of the moon. "Now we hunt," he said.

Now? Just when we'd taken a seat? I got ready for Bernie to rise, but he did not. We stayed where we were. Would whatever we were hunting come to us? That had to be it. Just when you think Bernie's done amazing you, he amazes you again.

The moon drifted across the sky. The stars, too, were on the move. Other than that, the night was still, except once when Bernie's head lowered itself to his chest. His sleep breathing rhythm started up, like music to me. We'd done this kind of thing before. It's called keeping watch, and never gets old.

Have you noticed how the mind can wander while the body stays still? That was happening to me while I kept watch by the barrel cactus overlooking the eucalyptus grove. When my mind wanders, it often tends to revisit a certain night down Mexico way, featuring some interesting she-barking behind a little cantina, and the events that followed. The mind part of me was kind of lost in all that when from somewhere above I heard HOO HOO. Not somewhere above in Mexico, but somewhere above right here, near the gravestone. I knew that HOO HOO, of course — the call of an owl. Once on a night not too different from this one, I'd seen an owl glide down, snare a snake in its talons, and fly off into the night. Not a big snake, but still. Since that night, although I'm no fan of birds in general, I've made an exception for owls.

And there was this particular owl, not swooping down, but soaring high above, silvery in the moonlight and then suddenly turning black as it crossed the face of the actual moon. No snakes around tonight, my owly friend? I was sniffing the air — and picking up a slight snaky aroma, not recent — when a faint sound reached my ears, a human sound, specifically the thrum thrum of a car on the move. The thrum thrum grew louder, and not long after that, headlights shone behind the trees on the far side of the grove, over where the hair-gel dude had parked his jeep. I glanced at Bernie, deep in dreamland, and barked my low rumbly bark, a bark so quiet you have to be almost next to me to hear it.

Bernie's eyes opened. His head jerked up, and fast. Bernie can change from sleep to full go in no time flat. He saw what there was to see and drew the .38 Special from his pocket. Moonlight gleamed on the barrel, a lovely sight. Were we going to shoot somebody? I wondered who.

The headlight glow came closer and closer, quickly getting through what I remembered as being rough ground, and entering the grove itself: not a car, but a very big ATV. We're not fans of ATVs in the desert, me and Bernie, although we'd never shot any of the drivers.

The big ATV stopped at the inner edge of the trees. The engine kept running and the headlights stayed on. A door opened and thumped closed. The glare of the headlights blocked my view of what was going on, but I heard the crunch crunch of hard shoes on the desert floor. Then the silhouette of a man appeared in the beams, a man entering the clearing. He changed direction slightly and I saw he was carrying a spade and a shovel over his shoulder. Hey! Just like us. In fact, he appeared to resemble Bernie, just as tall and broad-shouldered, and also somewhat wider — not the soft kind of wider you see on a lot of dudes, but the hard type that means strength. His head suddenly turned in our direction. We weren't in the headlights — which I was pretty sure meant he couldn't see us — but I got a real good look at him. He had a full head of white hair and a deeply tanned face, a face of the powerful type, and not kindly. It was Boomer Riggs.

Boomer Riggs crossed the clearing and approached the gravestone. He walked slowly around it, toeing at the ground here and there. Then he came closer, reached out and tapped the gravestone with his hand . . . the way a human checks to see if something is real. That was strange, but there was no time to get to the bottom of it, especially since I had the feeling it would remain bottomless to me no matter what.

Boomer laid down the spade and shovel and just as Bernie had done, put his shoulder to the stone and toppled it over. He had to be much older than Bernie, but toppling the stone had been no harder for him. Boomer dusted off his hands, picked up the spade and started digging. Dust and dirt swirled in the headlight beams. It got sort of intense in the eucalyptus grove, partly from the way Boomer worked, and partly from the way we watched him.

After not very long, Boomer switched to the shovel. He seemed to be working quickly now, down to knee-level in the hole. Holes are easier to dig if they've been dug before — as I knew very well — and Bernie had already dug this one. And had someone else also dug it, before Bernie? I had a feeling the answer was yes. This was an unusual hole.

Boomer dug, down and down. He grunted from time to time and huffed and puffed a bit. Sweat gleamed on his face. Flying dirt caught in that full head of snowy hair. Earth piled up around the hole. The moon still hung high above, but it seemed to have lost its brightness. That made me uneasy.

Now Boomer was almost down to shoulder level, where Bernie had found the scraps of wood. Were the scraps of wood still there? I thought so, but now they had something else down there with them. Boomer tossed out a shovelful of earth, and another, and then stopped all at once and peered down. He took a flashlight from his pocket, switched it on, peered again, and then cried out, a harsh and terrible cry that filled the night. Boomer dropped the shovel, scrambled out of the hole, looked around wildly, a big, frightened, dirty creature.

Bernie rose, and so did I. "Freeze," he said, not loudly. "You move, you die."

Boomer whipped around in our direction, but after that he froze as ordered. Good enough? Or was Bernie going to pull the trigger? He held the .38 Special, but pointed at the ground, so we were letting Boomer get away with one. Bernie's perfect, as you must know by now, but sometimes he's a little too nice.

We walked down from our spot by the barrel cactus and entered the clearing. Their eyes met, Bernie's and Boomer's. Boomer's were full of hate. Bernie's had that detached look we'd been seeing recently. It was growing on me, but I'd never want it aimed my way.

"You murdering bastard," Boomer said. "You killed Ronny."

"I never got his name," said Bernie. "Hands up."

Boomer raised his hands. Bernie had the gun pointed at him now. He stepped forward and patted Boomer down. I moved around Boomer and stood right behind him, which is how we handle this situation.

"What's in that pocket?" Bernie said.

"Just my wallet and keys."

"Turn it out."

Boomer turned out one of his front pockets. A wallet and a keychain fell out, a keychain with a few keys and one of those fobby things on it.

"Start with Tesabe," Bernie said.

"What about it?"

"The part where you stabbed Hector de Vargas in the head," said Bernie.

Boomer gave Bernie an ugly sort of smile, possibly called a sneer. "You're way off base," he said.

Bernie shook his head. "Hector was a much better lover than you, at least in Lotty's eyes. He took her places that Mr.

High School Quarterback couldn't go. You couldn't stand that."

Then came something amazing. Even with a .38 Special aimed right at him, Boomer took a huge swing at Bernie. Maybe a bit on the slow side. Bernie just tilted his head a bit and Boomer's fist whizzed on by. This was a good moment for pulling the trigger, but instead Bernie punched Boomer in the gut with his free hand. Just one punch, and not Bernie's hardest, although hard enough to bring some pleasure to Bernie's eyes. Boomer fell, so fast his calf twisted clear out from between my teeth, even though they seemed to have gone ahead and locked that calf in a strongish and somewhat bloody grip. I shouldn't leave out the sounds Boomer made, an "Oof," an "Aiiee," and another "Oof."

"Sit up," Bernie said.

Boomer groaned once or twice, but got himself in sitting position.

"Look at me," Bernie said.

Boomer looked up at him. If eyes could kill — was that a human expression? If so, I now understood it.

"The sickest part," Bernie said, "was making Lotty think she'd killed Hector. Getting her to pay for the cover-up of her supposed crime with the earnings of her whole career

440

comes second."

Boomer said nothing.

Bernie prodded him in the side with his foot, not hard, just a touch.

"What made you think of that?" he said.

"Drug fiends are the sick ones, not me," Boomer said. "And that's bullshit about her whole career — I never touched her appearance money."

Bernie prodded him again, perhaps more than a touch this time. "What about Wellington? Was the blackmail a one-time event or did you keep bleeding him, too?"

Boomer said nothing. Didn't he see Bernie was getting angry? That hardly ever happens, but when it does you can't miss it even though nothing changes except his eyes.

"Answer the question," Bernie said, his voice not rising even the slightest bit.

"I have the right to remain silent," said Boomer.

"Not out here you don't." And Bernie prodded him again.

Boomer opened his mouth like he was about to answer, but out came a sort of gurgle. Then Boomer clutched his chest and slumped sideways, gurgling and gasping. Bernie leaned over him.

"Nitro pills," Boomer groaned, or something like that. All the gasping and gurgling

441

made him hard to understand. "Glove box."

"Why should I?" Bernie said.

Their faces were close. Their gazes met. Boomer gasped and gurgled. His eyes closed.

Bernie rose. "Watch him, Chet." He rose and ran toward the ATV.

I stood over Boomer. His eyes opened. He no longer gasped or gurgled, in fact, looked much better. I was wondering what I should do about that, if anything, when I caught a whiff of a very important scent coming across the clearing, a scent I knew well from K-9 school. Yes, I'd flunked out, but not because of missing this particular scent. I hadn't missed it once. I took off after Bernie. And then stopped. Wasn't I supposed to stay with Boomer? I glanced back at him. He had the keychain in his hand and was doing something with the fobby thing. I looked the other way, at Bernie. He was running into the thick of the scent. Bernie! My Bernie!

I raced after him, hit top speed, and hurled myself at his back. He fell like he'd been hit by some impossibly mighty thing and I landed on top of him. And then: KA-BOOM! A tremendous KA-BOOM and the ATV blew sky high, rising on a fireball and blasting itself into bits that flamed all around us. One even singed my tail, a scary moment.

We picked ourselves up. "You all right?" Bernie said. He patted my sides. I was fine, even better than fine. Who doesn't like a bit of excitement?

Little fires were burning here and there along the edges of the clearing. In the clearing itself, Boomer was on his feet, no longer suffering from that gurgling and gasping problem. He saw us, turned real fast, and started running. We took off after him. He swerved toward the Hanging Moon trail, but I cut him off, forcing him back into the clearing. I closed in. Boomer picked up speed, not a bad runner at all, especially for an old guy, but he was in big trouble because now I was angry, just like Bernie.

Maybe Boomer sensed that. He glanced back at me, maybe why he lost his balance and went flying. Boomer cried out in midair, a sharp cry but sharply cut off by another sound, this one horrible. Smack went Boomer, headfirst into a corner of the toppled-over gravestone. It happened fast and slow at the same time, and that horrible sound of head against gravestone had something liquid to it, like the inside of Boomer's head was made of fruit. The stone was just stone, through and through.

We stood together, me and Bernie, looking down at him. The flames didn't spread, maybe because there was no wind, but died away, dimming to nothing. Up above, the moon was back at its usual strength.

"You're a good, good boy," Bernie said.

"Steak tested positive for cyanide," Rick said.

Bernie got a dark look in his eyes.

"Plus," Rick went on, "we got Ronny DNA off that kitchen knife at Lotty's ranch."

Bernie nodded. "Ronny had a nasty skill set you don't usually see — that business with the earring was a nice touch — but in the end he was just an employee. Clint made the mistake of looking into things Boomer didn't want looked into. Ronny's job was to put a stop to Clint or anyone else headed down that road."

"Did Clint think he was on his way to some sort of jackpot?"

Bernie nodded. "But he was clumsy and word got back to Boomer. Boomer replayed the first murder, with variations."

"As we say in the music world," said Rick.

They turned to the little stage in the corner, where Lotty was just setting up. This was on the patio at the Dry Gulch Steakhouse and Saloon. We'd taken over the whole place and there was one monster party going down. No actual monsters were in attendance, but just about everyone else showed up. Even Iggy had put in an appearance, although not for long.

I trotted over to the stage. Lotty was pulling a stool toward the mic stand. She peered down at me.

"Stick around, podner," she said. "I've got a surprise just for you."

Lotty looked way better than she had the day we delivered the news, Bernie doing the actual delivering and me standing beside him, later sitting, followed by lying, and finally dozing. It was a long story, not so easy to follow even for me, familiar with all the people in it: Hector de Vargas — although I was actually only familiar with his bones and skull; Ronny, the hair-gel dude who worked for Boomer; Boomer himself, who never knew he was Leticia's father, according to Lotty; and a whole lot of others moving in and out of the picture, like they were trying to confuse me. What I remembered best were Lotty's eyes as she began to understand what Bernie was telling her. Human eyes are often like doors to keep you out, but sometimes like windows to let you in. Lotty's eyes had turned into windows, and I'd glimpsed something violent inside, like a terrible wreck. After that, her face had reddened, the red rising from her neck to her forehead. Sometimes humans get red when they're embarrassed. In the nation within our tails droop, not a pleasant sight, but not as bad as the red face, in my opinion. And Lotty's had been very red, as though she'd gone somewhere far beyond embarrassment.

But now was different. She had a smile on her face and her skin was glowing. Nixon came over.

"How's the Caddy?"

"Driving beautifully, thanks to you," said Lotty.

Meanwhile music was playing over the speakers and lots of dancing was going on. Myron Siegel — who'd handed Bernie a check the moment he arrived, a check that had Bernie saying, "This is too much," and me thinking, *Oh, Bernie* — seemed to be the most energetic dancer in the house. First he'd danced with Rita, but now he was with Nixon's sister Mindy Jo, who once or twice threw her ripped and tattooed arms around him, picked him right up, and whirled across the floor. Jordan was dancing with Ms. Pernick, our accountant. He seemed a little awkward, but she was the best dancer out there, if I properly understood the importance of shaking that thing in dancing.

Bernie was at our table with Eliza, Rick, Flaco, some lawyer buddy of Myron's — who was going to handle Lotty's lawsuit against Western Solutions, if I'd heard that part right — and Oksana. Eliza got up to go to the bathroom. Oksana slid closer to Bernie.

"I have younger sister in Russia," she said.

"Oh?" said Bernie.

"She is good-looking one in family."

"Well, I wouldn't —"

"Also free thinker."

"Free thinker?" Bernie said.

"Not so inhibited like me." Oksana adjusted her halter top, a simple garment and not at all big, but she seemed to have trouble keeping it in place. "You will love her. Perhaps a trial visit? Maybe next week?"

Eliza returned, gave Oksana a funny look. Oksana slid over a tiny bit and Eliza squeezed in next to Bernie, put her arm over his shoulder. At that moment, someone cut off the music and Lotty stepped up to the mic. She wore tight blue jeans, red cowboy boots, a white shirt with red fringe. In short, a lovely sight.

"I'm going to sing a song I wrote this

morning," she said. "My daughter will help me out. Come on up here, Leticia."

Leticia walked onto the little stage. Applause. Lotty hugged her. Leticia hugged Lotty back, if only a little bit. Lotty picked up a guitar and handed it to Leticia.

"We haven't had much time to rehearse but Leticia's a very talented musician, something folks may not know."

"Where she get that from?" called out somebody at the back, possibly Shermie Shouldice.

There was laughter. Lotty let it die down. She pulled the mic stand closer. Leticia began to play something I liked right from the get-go.

"This is called 'Song for Chet,' " Lotty said. And then she sang.

Well, you're the kind that runs around
Can't stop to think until the ship has
    sailed
Till the milk is spilled, till the safe is blown
Till the day is done and we're all alone.
If they were all like you, would there be
    darkness?
If they were all like you, would there be
    pain?
If they were all like you, would there be
    teardrops?

448

If they were all like you.
When I come undone, you are the one
Who gives me hope, who brings the sun
Your big brown eyes say this each day
I'll always love you, any way.
If they were all like you, then those tears
    don't flow
And though the pain may come, it will
    always go
If they were all like you.
And I'm the kind that loves you back
From here and now, oh down the track
To sunset, where the birds are flown
And the day is done and we're all alone.

After that came a moment or two of silence. Then clapping started up, the sound rising and rising, and folks were on their feet, hootin' and hollerin'. I myself seemed to be prancing around. I hadn't even realized I was doing it, but prancing around seemed exactly right. Sometimes you just stumble into perfection. What a life!

It was while all that prancing — to say nothing of the hootin' and hollerin' — was going on that I happened to glance over at the patio doorway. There was Suzie, watching with tears in her eyes.

ACKNOWLEDGMENTS

Many thanks to Kristin Sevick for her very smart and very supportive editing of this book.

ABOUT THE AUTHOR

Spencer Quinn is the *New York Times* bestselling author of the Chet and Bernie mystery series, as well as the bestselling Bowser and Birdie series and the Queenie and Arthur series for middle-grade readers. He lives on Cape Cod with his wife, Diana — and dogs, Audrey and Pearl.

spencequinn.com
chetthedog.com
Facebook.com/ChetTheDog
@ChetTheDog